Paramourtal™
volume two

More tales of undying love and loving the undead.

Edited by

Kevin Hosey and K. Stoddard Hayes

cliffhanger
BOOKS.COM

Dallas, Texas

Published by:
Cliffhanger Books, Dallas, Texas
www.cliffhangerbooks.com

First Cliffhanger Books trade paperback edition (March 2013)

Cover and book design by Kevin Hosey
Interior illustrations by Mark Offutt

Published in the United States of America

Tales

For everyone who ever loved and dreamed.

K. Stoddard Hayes
and Kevin Hosey

Bump in the Night

Nicole Dethmers

AS MAGGIE HEYWOOD lay in the half-darkness listening to the chomping coming from underneath her bed, several thoughts floated through her sleep-addled brain: 1. She should probably stop eating pistachios while reading before turning out the lights; 2. She didn't have any pets, she lived alone, and the landlord had *guaranteed* her no pest problems existed, so if she looked down there and came face-to-face with a rat the size of her toaster, she was going to be *livid*; and 3. Really, no more eating in bed. That was how her mother had added on those stubborn five pounds after her divorce, and God knew she and Maggie shared the same metabolism.

From the shadows clinging to the walls, and the artificial yellow-white light suffusing through the blinds, she could tell night still held sway over the city, and the streetlight outside her window was doing its best impression of a navy searchlight. Chicago was never dark enough, a fact that had kept her up for weeks after she moved to her one-room apartment in Lakeview. Nor was it ever quiet enough. Sirens seemed to go off somewhere every half hour on the hour; and two different neighbors liked to have lengthy shouting matches with their respective TVs every night between the hours of 11 pm and midnight. When Maggie *was* able to fall asleep, she had trouble staying asleep, so she wasn't surprised the *crack-crunch-crunch* had woken her.

Unfortunately, after the sleep drained away, all that was left was the creeping sense of nameless terror that always accompanied unexpected sounds in the night.

Maggie propped herself on her elbows, careful to make as little noise as possible. A quick glance around the room showed no intruders. Just the lone dresser with its broken drawer sitting crookedly in its frame, a firmly closed closet door, and a half-full plastic tote Maggie had been

5

using for dirty laundry. The nightlight in the hallway glowed softly in the crack underneath the door.

The pop of pistachio shells being pried apart and the crunching of the nuts continued unabated. Reaching out, Maggie grasped the flashlight she kept on her bed stand and lifted it. The sounds of mastication ceased, only to be replaced with a quiet, distracted hum of "Danny Boy."

She laughed. She couldn't help herself; the situation was just too absurd. An invisible intruder humming an Irish ballad? Catching herself, she let go of the flashlight to slap her hand over her mouth, but whatever was under the bed had obviously heard her because all sound ceased.

Breathe, Maggie told herself. *In, out, in, out, not too loud, it's all right….*

"WOOOoooOOO," came a deep, quavering voice from the darkness. A chill descended in the room.

Maggie reached out for the flashlight again, hefting it in her hand to test its weight. She had bought the heaviest she could find at the hardware store, thinking of self-defense, but she had certainly never thought she'd use it to defend herself against something under her bed that went "woo."

"Woooo?" The voice seemed a bit uncertain, as if not expecting her lack of a reaction.

"Oh, come off it," Maggie said, exasperated. "You're not a ghost."

Silence. Then: "Why not?" It was a nice, smooth voice, kind of like melted caramel, but marred by an inflection of irritation.

"Because they don't exist. Who are you and what are you doing in my bedroom? I'm going to call the cops, I have my cell phone right here—" And of course she didn't, she realized suddenly with a sinking feeling. She had left it plugged in, out in the living room where she had organized her desk and workspace.

"So what are you afraid of?"

"Like I'd tell you!" Maggie squeezed her eyes shut. *I can't believe I'm arguing with someone hiding under my bed. I must be still asleep!*

"No, no, of course not. It's my job to figure that out." A sigh. "You're just very hard to read."

Maggie blinked. *My job?* "What the hell do you mean by that?"

"Ghosts are out," the voice said, ignoring her. "So that probably means other spiritual beings won't work, either…."

"Who *are* you?"

"What about spiders? Are you afraid of those?"

Somehow, the anger at being ignored was suddenly stronger than every other feeling coursing through Maggie's body. She switched on the flashlight, hung over the bed side, and prepared to blind someone in the eye. But no one was there. A lone sock curled up around one of the feet of the bed, and a few dust bunnies whirled around in a frenzy from her exhalation of surprise, but that was it.

"What the hell—?"

"How about mice?" The voice seemed to come from nowhere and everywhere at the same time, and quite as suddenly, the space under the bed was filled with wriggling white mice.

Maggie barely flinched, too shocked to pull herself up.

"No," she heard herself reply lamely, "I think they're cute."

The mice vanished.

"Festering molds?"

Heaps of rotting food appeared, white, green, and black fuzzy spots creeping over bread and bananas.

"Disgusting, but not scary."

"Sharp instruments?"

Syringes, scissors, and razors took the place of the food.

Maggie cringed but said, "They're just laying about not doing anything." She shook her head. "This is insane. I must be hallucinating with all this blood rushing to my head." She grasped the edge of the mattress to ease herself into an upright position.

"Wait a minute! Give me a break here. I'm new at scaring adults. Kids have such easy, tangible fears. Clowns, you know. Bears. Vacuum cleaners."

"Vacuums? Really?" Maggie stayed hanging over the side of the bed, peering into the gloom, hoping to get a glimpse of something.

"A boy in Detroit. Apparently, earlier in the day, his sister chased him around the house saying it wanted to suck his toes off. That was an easy job; a couple 'vrooms' and he flew screaming from the room."

Maggie exhaled noisily. This really was ridiculous. She was conversing with a disembodied voice, and instruments of supposed terror were appearing underneath her bed. But no doubt about it, she was awake and fully in possession of her wits. So whatever was happening, it was real.

"Okay. I'm going to ask one more time, and I'd really appreciate it if you'd answer me in the clearest possible way: Who are you, and what are you doing here?"

A long-suffering sigh was the response, followed by a moment of silence, then: "I'm a bogeyman, here to scare the bejesus out of you."

"You're the Bogeyman?" Maggie laughed. The faintest stirring of darkness caught her eye and she trained the flashlight in that direction, but nothing appeared.

"Not 'the,' just 'a' bogeyman. With over six billion people in the world, you think only one of us can do the job?"

"I thought you were just...you know. Imaginary, for one. And a terrorizer of kids, for another."

"The economy is shit right now, so everyone's pulling double or triple duty. I've got a friend who's trying out the market in scaring dogs and cats. Apparently it's paying off, but a bogeyman's got to have standards. So...." Another swirl in the darkness, and the voice became inviting. "What do you say, can you help me out here? Give me a few hints at least?"

Maggie considered. Even supposing for a minute that the bogeyman was telling the truth, did she really want to be scared to death in the middle of the night? Did she even have to *ask* that question? The answer was a resounding "Hell, no!" but a thought occurred to her, and she decided to go for it.

"Yeah, okay," she said, hiding her grin behind her hand. "Ready?"

"Yes."

"I'm terrified of men."

Silence.

"Seriously?"

"Oh, yeah! Especially really hot ones. The sexier they are, the more they make my skin crawl." Maggie wondered if bogeymen could recognize double-entendres.

"Huh."

"Yep. So, there you go. Give it a shot."

And, quite suddenly, a dark-haired man with glittering green eyes lay on his side under the bed, draped in liquid-like black fabric. His exposed bronze skin gleamed in the beam of the flashlight. An aquiline nose pointed toward the hardwood floor as those mesmerizing eyes looked up through thick, charcoal lashes.

"Wow," Maggie breathed, her skin definitely crawling but in entirely all the right ways.

The bogeyman's eyes narrowed.

"What do you mean, 'wow'? I thought you said this would scare you."

"I meant, 'wow, I can't believe how frightening you are.' Honestly." Maggie swallowed hard, unable to tear her eyes away. Another thought occurred to her. Did she dare? "Uh...you know what would be even worse? If you were naked."

And POOF! Not a stitch of clothing remained.

Holy hell, Maggie thought, pushing herself away from the edge of the bed. The blood coursing through her burned like oil lit on fire. She leaned back into her pillow, biting the heel of her hand to keep down the giggles. "Are you terrified now?" came the eager voice from below.

"Scared stiff," she replied without thinking, and then couldn't hold back the peals of laughter.

A thump from underneath the bed suggested the bogeyman had punched the underside of the mattress. "Hey! Did you lie to me?"

"I wouldn't dream of it!"

"God, I hate adults. They're all such smartass jack-holes."

"Hey, hey, Bogeyman. How do you feel about yoga? Because I think it's one of the scariest things a hot, naked man can do. Seriously."

"That's it, we're done here. Enjoy your fright-free night, Mood-Killer."

An audible POP followed the bogeyman's words, and when Maggie checked, the nude phantasm was gone.

"Hello?"

No response.

Oh well, Maggie thought, turning over onto her side and snuggling into her blankets. *This was definitely the best night I've had since moving to Chicago!*

In the morning light streaming through the kitchen window, Maggie mulled over everything that had happened the night before and tried to dismiss all of it. She poured a bowl of cereal, added milk, and crunched her way through a logical explanation.

God knew she'd been stressed to hell and back for a month now. Moving to such a fast-paced city from her quiet hometown, starting a new job at a big database content analysis company, breaking up with her boyfriend of five years: Maggie certainly had her fair share of major life events. And stress has been known to cause sleeping problems. Maybe hallucinations that felt incredibly real were another, less talked-about side effect.

Maggie sighed. Nope, she was pretty sure what happened last night had been real. Bogeymen were real. Smoking hot, charmingly insecure bogeymen were as real as the fire engine siren wailing in the distance and the puddle of spilled milk on her table.

I wonder if he'll show up again, she thought as she set her dishes in the sink. *Probably not. He didn't seem too happy with me when he left.…*And I can't tell if that's a good thing or a bad thing.

She kept thinking about him even as she got dressed for work, applied her makeup, and quickly checked her email before heading out the door.

Sure, the novelty of a bogeyman appearing under her bed was enough to keep her mind active for a while. But, if Maggie were to be completely truthful, it was the image of his naked human form that her mind kept returning to. Even if he never showed up again, at least she'd have that.

Outside, the fresh air seemed to clear her head a little. As she stepped onto the sidewalk, Maggie tucked her purse in tight against her side and made her way to the train station. Every time she crossed an open alleyway, she tensed. Every runner who flew past her, appearing in the corner of her vision as if by magic, gave her a mini-heart attack. Every unmarked white van that pulled up to the curb started up in her head a movie starring herself, a trio of hooded criminals, and an abduction scene rivaling anything she'd seen come out of Hollywood.

Thinking about the bogeyman made her think of all the things she really was afraid of. Granted, most of her fears of the city had come from her mother, who had decided it necessary to give Maggie all the statistics of muggings and sexual assaults and shootings in Chicago before Maggie had moved there. If she hadn't been paranoid before, she certainly was after that.

When the train carrying her toward the Loop stopped halfway between platforms and the lights flickered, her stomach seemed to drop to her knees. She felt certain there had been a hijacking or murder. Even the voice-over of the conductor saying there was a technical difficulty did little to ease her mind until she'd disembarked at her stop, clattered down the stairs to the street, and entered the building where she worked.

Thousands of people go out into the city and come back home alive at the end of the day, she told herself in the elevator. *You can be one of them. Just be vigilant. And don't do anything stupid.*

The elevator arrived at her floor, but the doors didn't open right away, and she swallowed a nervous gasp. She took a deep breath, pushed the "Doors Open" button, and exhaled slowly when they finally did.

And don't get psyched out by the little things.

Somehow, bantering with the bogeyman under her bed seemed infinitely preferable to facing the real world.

When he made his second appearance, Maggie was just drifting off to sleep. The copy of *Great Expectations* propped up on her chest started to list backward, her hands sliding down the sides until the weight of the book toppled it out of her grasp. Roused just enough to remember the light was still on, she reached out and fumbled for the switch of the lamp.

"Nuclear fallout," said the now familiar voice from beneath her bed.
Maggie paused, blinking the sleep out of her eyes.

"Scary, yes," she admitted. "But how on earth are you going to fit that down there?"

Silence, then: "Financial ruin."

"Really? That's the best you've got?"

"The NRA."

Maggie threw aside the covers, got up, and knelt beside the bed. She glanced around at the various dust bunnies, but nothing else manifested.

"I'd really like to see how you'd pull that one off," she said.

A very quiet "Damn it" emanated out from the darkness, followed by a POP! and the sense of being alone once more.

Maggie got back into bed, unable to wipe the giant grin from her face.

She wasn't sure if she was more annoyed or amused with the bogeyman's nightly visits. On one hand, he stole precious time that could be used for sleeping, but on the other hand, if he wasn't the one doing it, it'd be her TV-watching neighbors, or the wind whistling through the cracked molding around the windows, or the dogs from 2A barking their heads off at shadows. And trying to trump the bogeyman had started to feel like a game, and so far, she felt like she was winning.

Also, his human form was extremely nice to look at, whenever she could catch a glimpse of it.

On the corner of State and Monroe, Maggie experienced her first real Chicago fright, and it came not from a supernatural creature but an aggressive panhandler.

"C'mon, you look like you can spare some change," the greasy-haired man said, shuffling closer to Maggie as she backed away from him toward the road. A bicyclist whizzed past, missing her by a hair's breadth, and she propelled herself back onto the sidewalk.

"Um...." She hesitated, not sure what to do. Her mother had told her never to give money to strangers in the street, but the guy clearly looked like he could do with some good food and a hot shower. Maggie's knuckles turned white from grasping the strap of her purse.

"Just a dollar, lady!" His fingers brushed her arm. Panicking, Maggie jerked backwards and took off running. A block away, she slowed down, her feet aching from her high heels. People shot her strange looks, and she could feel her face burning. Maybe none of *them* would be freaked out by a random beggar on the street, but she wasn't like them.

Feeling a little ashamed, Maggie ducked into a coffee shop and stared at the wall of pre-ground coffee beans, waiting for her heart to resume a normal pace. Would that man have tried to actually take her purse? Maybe. Maybe not. Did she overreact? Taking a few deep breaths, she conceded that she might have. All she needed to have done was give a firm "no" and move on.

When a barista asked if Maggie was ready to order, she murmured a negative and left the shop. Coffee was the last thing she needed if she ever hoped to sleep again. Nerves, neighbors, and a visiting bogeyman? No need to add caffeine to the list of things keeping her up all night.

It was one thing to explain away scary stuff beneath her bed that couldn't really be there. It was another thing entirely to be frightened by a real situation in the light of day.

The next night, a deep, reverberant growling woke her shortly after midnight. A soft plash of saliva hitting the floor brought an image to Maggie's suddenly very active mind: a squared canine muzzle, lips curled back, teeth bared and trembling with the urge to bite, frothy slaver running down a dark, brindled throat, red eyes glaring from the darkness under her bed.

The sound, the image, the idea were truly frightening, and Maggie lay paralyzed in bed. But it's just him, she tried to reason, clutching the bed sheets. *The stupid bogeyman playing tricks. It's not a real dog. It's not a real anything. Shadows and suggestions and...and....*

"I like dogs," she whispered. Catching the tremor in her voice, she tried again, louder: "I love dogs, even...even those with bad reputations."

The growling subsided.

"They're not bad dogs," she added. "They just have bad owners."

The eerie, witchlike yowl of a cat, spitting and hissing, rose from the vicinity of the floor directly below her. Maggie sat up, hair raised, arms full of goose pimples. A memory of a vicious cat scratch from her youth streaked through her mind.

"Look, I know it's you, so it's not going to work," she shouted. "Kids think all sorts of things are out there in the dark, but I KNOW these animals can't be in my room. I didn't let them in. They can't get in. It's called REASON. It's called LOGIC."

"It's called not having a good imagination," the bogeyman said.

Maggie flopped over the side of the mattress to address the darkness but, to her surprise, met the bogeyman eye to upside-down eye. He was in human form and, unfortunately, clothed. She hadn't expected him to be visible. Or so close, for that matter.

"I have a perfectly good imagination," she replied, heart fluttering. He was so close she could see the tiny Cupid's bow of his upper lip, just visible in the streetlight illumination. The orange light caressed the curve of jaw and cheek, the edge of his shoulder, and the length of his arm that propped up his head as he stared moodily at her. The rest lay in shadows.

"Give me your hand," he said.

"Why?"

"Just do it."

Maggie dropped her hand but pulled back at the last second.

"What are you going to do to it?"

Without responding, the bogeyman reached out with his free hand, wrapping his long fingers around hers, his thumb pressing lightly on her palm. Maggie shivered at the touch, yet she wasn't cold. His hand was actually warm, quite warm, and more solid than she would have thought.

"Yeah. Thought so," he said. "This line here, see? Proof that you lack creativity and have no appreciation for the fantastic."

"I…I do, too!" she protested. She snatched her hand back and flexed it in front of her face. She could barely make out any lines. "What kind of bogeyman reads palms?"

The bogeyman shrugged. It was an elegantly indifferent move. His skin rippled in the light.

"I guess I shouldn't be surprised you can see in the dark," she added.

With the fluidity of large cat he rolled onto his back and inclined his head toward her.

"There's a lot I can do that you don't know about."

Maggie bit her tongue, afraid of the flirtatious words that had been about to fall out of her mouth. Get a grip, she thought. *He may look gorgeous but he's not human.*

"Why don't you get a job helping people sleep instead of waking them up and annoying them?"

The bogeyman's eyes narrowed.

"Most people I don't annoy, I terrify. This usually isn't an issue. Besides, sleep is not my territory. And I wouldn't want to work for the guy in charge of it, anyway. For the last couple hundred years he's been peculiar as hell. Something about an increase in caffeine consumption, I think. Or maybe it was a woman. I'm not sure."

"Jeez, how old are you?!"

"A true gentlebogey does not disclose his age."

13

Maggie stared at the bogeyman, hard, trying to read what little she could see of his face. He looked human, and his mannerisms were human too. It took all of her concentration to remind herself he wasn't…normal.

"I always thought great white sharks were quite terrifying," the bogeyman continued, looking thoughtful. "If I were mortal, that's probably what would keep me up at night."

"But sharks don't just…." Maggie sighed. "A shark can't hide under a bed. It's impossible. The size is wrong, and it's a sea creature—"

And suddenly Maggie's nose was touching the great, rubbery hump of a great white shark's scarred snout. Its rotten pink gums were bared, rows of serrated teeth lunging for her face. She flung herself backward, pulling all her blankets and sheets up to her chest. Her heart hammered away so hard and painfully she thought it would knock itself right out of her chest. *Not possible, no way, not possible*, she thought, the words blurring together in mental panic. *It can't be a shark, can't be a shark, not a shark; oh my god, those teeth—*

"The thing about being supernatural," the bogeyman's voice drawled, indicating his return to a human, or at the very least a non-corporeal, form, "is that normal rules don't apply." His voice turned smug. "So, you're scared of sharks. That's good to know."

Maggie closed her eyes, breathed in deeply, and exhaled "It's still not real. Only an illusion. And I wasn't scared, just startled."

Her declaration was met only with an exasperated sigh and the by now familiar pop signaling the bogeyman's departure.

He was tenacious, Maggie had to admit, though he didn't show up every night. The first time she slept through the night with no interruption, she felt an odd mixture of relief and disappointment when she woke the next morning. She received a certain satisfaction from foiling the bogeyman's business. Whenever she got the upper hand with him, she always felt like she was more ready to deal with whatever the real world threw at her the next day.

Then he had come the following night, bearing the gifts of a grizzly bear, a Burmese python, and a swarm of bees. Two nights later, he tried the shark again, but Maggie, having taking a page from Hemingway's *The Old Man and the Sea*, punched the giant fish in the gills. The bogeyman instantly reverted back to human form, coughing, with his elegant hands clutching his throat.

After that, he paid tribute to horror movies for a while, which were hit-

or-miss for Maggie—knowing who was behind all the masks took the terror out of some of them—but the horde of decomposing zombies was pretty convincing.

Bird-eating spiders. Alligators. Porcelain dolls. Sad-faced clowns. Glowing red lights with no discernible source. A wriggling, writhing mass of worms. Bulbous-headed aliens. Mummies. Swamp creatures. Curiously, the things that scared Maggie the most during the day never came up with the bogeyman at night. What if he turned into a drug-crazed kid with a knife looking to do her serious harm? Not wanting to ask but unable to stop wondering, she posed the question to him one night.

"That's not my style," he said with a dismissive wave of his hand. "I work for the scares, not the psychological torment." He looked thoughtful for a minute, and then, with an expression bordering on confusion, added, "You...are a different kind of challenge for me."

"Challenge? Different how?"

Now he looked downright embarrassed. "I don't know. I can't explain. It's like I can read you but not understand you."

That didn't make any sense at all to Maggie, and she said so.

He coughed. "Look, I'm drawn to you. Partly because of my job. Partly because...something else. I can't put it into words."

Feeling a pleasant warmth grow in her chest, Maggie accepted this answer and didn't push it any further. His admission made the nights all that much easier to tolerate. She even—dare she say it?—looked forward to his visits. Whenever she spurned his horror shows, he had the cutest pout.

So he continued to come back, trying new things, sometimes revisiting old scares that had worked, but never really committing to any. Instead, he'd revert back to his human shape, Maggie would sit on the floor, and they'd have a conversation about the job market or the evolutionary origins of fear or why the Loch Ness Monster always appears blurry in photographs (camera-shy and low self-esteem, apparently).

"Why do you always go back to human?" she asked him one night as she picked a stray thread from the hem of her pajama pants. The bogeyman was stretched out on the floor beneath the bed, head on his hands as he looked at her.

"I don't know." He shrugged. "It's comfortable. And it fits in all the right places."

"Don't you have your own form? What does a bogeyman look like?"

"We don't have unique tangible forms. I guess you could say we're more a collection of thoughts and ideas."

15

"But somehow it feels right to be human?"

The bogeyman's sharp gaze, which had strayed to Maggie's hands at her feet, snapped back to her face. He seemed to study her for a long time, and under his scrutiny Maggie blushed.

"Yes. More than I would've thought. This experience has been…enjoyable, and I can't say I get a lot of opportunities to feel joy."

Maggie felt a thrill run through her. There was something in his eyes, in the way he looked at her….

"Successfully scaring someone doesn't bring you joy?" she asked.

"Satisfaction of a job well done is about as close as it gets." The bogeyman smiled then, a heart palpitation-inducing smile. "So thanks for toughing it out."

Maggie grinned in return, wondering, not for the first time, if his supernatural status gave him enhanced hearing, and if he could hear her pulse quickening.

"Anytime," she said.

"I'll hold you to that," he replied with a wink, and just as suddenly he was gone.

He can hold me anytime he wants, Maggie thought, and then chuckled at her own cheekiness. She climbed back into bed. *Falling in love with a bogeyman is bizarre. Extremely, definitely, irrevocably bizarre. And to think my mother thought my last relationship was messed up….*

On her way to work in the morning, she passed a homeless man stretched out on a bench, his back to the street and a pile of newspapers under his head for a pillow. She wondered if the bench constituted a bed and if a bogeyman could appear under it. The mental image of her naked bogeyman crouching underneath the bench made Maggie burst out laughing. A few people around her turned to give her a strange look. Still grinning, even if a little embarrassed, she hurried on.

A different panhandler was at the corner of State and Monroe. As Maggie drew close, she felt her back and neck muscles tense. *Nothing to worry about*, she thought. *You can't be afraid of everything in the whole world.*

"Spare a quarter?" the man asked, holding out a dirty plastic cup.

"No," she said firmly and walked on.

Instead of grabbing her or spitting epithets at her, the man turned away with a gentle nod and quiet, "Thank you."

Maggie hesitated. She turned her head to take another look at the man. He had returned to his bench, on top of which he'd placed his stained, worn-out backpack. It was probably packed with his entire worldly possessions, and like an arrow through the heart it struck Maggie that this man had probably had a family, a job, a home at some point in his life. He wasn't a nameless terror lurking in the alley or just a statistic. He was a real, living and breathing person.

"I don't have any quarters," she said, rummaging around in her purse and drawing out three dollar bills, "but here's a couple bucks."

A smile lit up the man's face as he took the proffered money. "Thank you, thank you," he said. "God bless."

Sure, she thought as she continued on her way, a smile on her own face. *Maybe I have been blessed. In a strange, roundabout, supernatural way. Who'd believe it was a bogeyman that helped me get over my paranoia of the city?*

When Maggie woke up late one night to find the bogeyman, human but clothed in his dark, silky material, leaning over her bed and outlined by a brilliant orange light, she thought she was dreaming.

"Not now," she murmured. "I have to work in the morning…."

"You need to get up," the bogeyman said, and the unusual urgency in his voice pierced through Maggie's foggy brain.

"What? Why?" She blinked up at him.

"This building is on fire."

"WHAT?!" Maggie shot upright, head swinging toward the bedroom door. Smoke curled along the ceiling, and although she couldn't see any flames, she could feel heat and hear a distant crackling.

"You have to go," the bogeyman said. "Now!"

"But what…how did it happen? I didn't leave the stove on or something, did I?" Maggie babbled as the bogeyman guided her to the floor and to the hallway.

"The fire started in the next apartment over. I popped in under the couch your neighbor was using for a bed and the place was ablaze. I don't know enough to tell what started it, but that's not important right now."

Maggie crawled into the hallway. Her living room seemed to flicker and wave in her vision, the smoke and heat and flames playing tricks with her eyes. *Oh my god. My computer. My books. All my photos…*Thinking for one wild moment she could just pop in there and save her belongings, she turned as if to go in after them, but the bogeyman pulled her back toward the kitchen.

"Thanks," she gasped, followed by a bout of coughing. Her eyes watered and stung.

"Don't talk. Keep moving."

Together they made it to the kitchen and the door to the back porch and emergency exit. Forgetting herself, Maggie reached up and grabbed the doorknob, which burned her hand "Shit!"

"I've got it." The bogeyman stood up, disengaged the locks, and opened the door. Maggie pushed against the screen door, suddenly thankful for its broken catch, and dragged herself onto the porch.

Gulping down fresh air, Maggie got to her feet.

"You saved my life—" she started to say, but noticed she was suddenly alone. "Wh-where did you go?" She peered into her apartment and saw the bogeyman on the floor, slumped against the kitchen table. Had she pushed herself right past him to get outside? Had she forced him aside?

Getting to her knees and holding her pajama sleeve over her mouth and nose, she opened the screen door, crawled in, and reached out to pull on the bogeyman's leg. The material of his clothes seemed hardly real; it felt like steam under her fingers.

"Come on!" she yelled, voice muffled.

The bogeyman coughed. "I'm still not quite used to a human body," he said. "I inhaled a lot of smoke—"

"Shut up and come ON!"

"It's no use." The bogeyman pushed away Maggie's questing hands. "I can't exist so far from a place of rest. I can't go with you."

"Oh, for god's sake!" Maggie grabbed a foot and tried to drag him, but he was surprisingly, realistically heavy.

"Stop." He grabbed her wrists and held them down. He peered into her eyes, which were brimming with tears; of anger or from the smoke, Maggie couldn't tell. "I will cease to exist if I follow you out there; I can only leave through the space beneath your bed. But you're safe, and that's what matters. If anything had happened to you…I don't think I could bear it. Funny," he laughed, "all that time I spent trying to figure out what scares you, and instead I've found what scares me."

He leaned in even close, took her face in his hands, and kissed her. Everything had seemed to be moving at warp speed, but this moment stopped the clock.

Maggie pulled away.

"Get back to the bedroom then, if you can," she whispered.

He grinned. "In another time, another life, maybe, I would've loved hearing those words from your mouth."

He pushed her away gently, and Maggie scrambled back outside. She took one last look over her shoulder to see the bogeyman disappear down the hallway, but the heat was now so intense she couldn't spare a moment more. She took the stairs to the ground floor and joined the other building inhabitants a safe distance away. Some crying, some stony-faced, the former apartment dwellers watched as their building went up in flames. Maggie wiped her eyes and looked away, cradling her burned hand.

Months passed before Maggie stopped having frequent nightmares about dying in a fire. She had moved in with some cousins on the other side of the city while she saved up money to get a place of her own. She liked her family well enough, but not enough to live with them for any extended period of time. It didn't help that her bed was now a lumpy couch in their study, and her cousin Carl was up half the night, every night, playing an online game as a wizard raiding virtual caves.

"Ten more minutes, Mags," he would say, and then continue to play for another hour. He seemed so passionate about his game, she didn't have the heart to tell him to get the hell out.

It's not like I could sleep, anyway, she thought one evening as she sat up with a cup of tea and watched Carl destroy a battalion of armored dragons. *I don't think I'll ever get a decent night's sleep again.*

Eventually she found a small, one-room apartment in Roscoe Village, not so very far from her last place. Barren and somewhat depressing, since Maggie hadn't a chance to replace all her belongings yet, the apartment constantly reminded her of all she had lost. Particularly the bedroom.

She bought a close-to-new frame and headboard from a used furniture store and ordered a brand new, super deluxe mattress, hoping its orthopedic wonders would help her sleep better.

It didn't.

Maggie slept uneasily, both from the recurring nightmares and from lying awake at night wondering what had happened to the bogeyman—no, her bogeyman. If he was gone, truly gone, it was partly her fault: he had stuck around to help her escape. He could've left her and saved himself. But he didn't. Could a bogeyman even die? Was his human form helpful to him in the situation, or was it a hindrance that cost him his life? He had supernatural powers; maybe he was invincible. Or was fire his one weakness? Could he still be out there, somewhere?

She didn't know, and that ate at her.

Maggie flopped over on her side and stared at the blank wall past the TV tray she was using as a bedside table. Her body was drained from a long day at work but the never-ending litany of unanswerable questions in her mind refused to let her sleep.

"I can't believe I miss a jerk who spent most of his time trying to scare me," she muttered.

She suddenly felt a small, almost imperceptible change in the air pressure, and her heartbeat seemed to trip over itself.

"Well, I can't believe said jerk fell in love with the Mood-Killer he was trying to scare," said a very familiar voice.

Maggie dropped her head over the side of the bed, heart in her throat.

"Is that so?" she asked, gaze immediately seeking out the bogeyman's handsome human face.

"Nearly got fired for it," he said, grinning. "Pun entirely intended. But I put in a request for a permanent human form; apparently there's a lot of untapped potential in your government for fostering fear. I'll be working for the city any day now."

Maggie reached down and grasped the hand she could see.

"You're really here."

"Well, in a fashion. It won't be permanent for a few days yet. But I had to come see you; it's been far too long. I would've come sooner, but I've had a ridiculous amount of paperwork to fill out. 'Sign here. Initial there.' Bureaucracy is a bitch."

Maggie laughed, trying to imagine the bogeyman at a place like the DMV. "You have paperwork where you're from?"

"Sort of. The metaphysical equivalent of it, anyway."

"So does this mean you'll stop riling me up at night?"

The bogeyman slid out from under the bed and sat up. His jaw grazed her cheek as he leaned in, lips next to her ear, sending shivers down her spine. "Depends," he said quietly, "on how you define 'riled up'."

"I can think of a few ways," Maggie replied.

And that, she later had to amend, was the best night since moving to Chicago.

Split Apart

Nicky Peacock

CONTORTED IN SHAPES of death, the bodies of Genevieve's family lie sprawled across the room. Their blood, soaking the carpet beneath her bare feet, creeps between her toes.

Her anger erupts with a swift adrenaline that rushes her body. She screams until she is hoarse. Her small twelve-year-old frame breaking beneath the strain, she falls to the floor.

Gen awoke with a jolt.

She realized she'd only been dreaming; it was all just a sickly memory wrapped in a nightmare

Suddenly a shadow leaned over her. Her hand flailed for the light nearest the bed.

"It's all right, dear," the shadow said.

She stopped fumbling for the switch.

"Bloody hell! What are you doing?"

The shadow settled on the edge of the bed. "I heard you screaming and came to wake you from your nightmare."

"Nitch, you scared me!" Gen leaped off the bed.

Nitch gently nodded. "Yeah, probably would have got myself fried if you hadn't woken yourself."

Taking a deep breath, she fell back onto the bed, reached up and hugged her Imp friend. "You could have withstood it. You taught me how to control it."

Nitch hugged her back. "I still wouldn't want to test that theory, Gen."

Imps looked human, and to anyone else Nitch would appear like a normal thirty-something man: average height, average build, average looks. None of it was by accident either. The last thing an Imp would want was to be recognized.

21

He kissed the top of her head then got up to leave the room, "Good-night, dear."

Gen pulled her legs to her chin and wondered, not for the first time, where she would have ended up if Nitch hadn't taken her in. With her family murdered and Huntsmen on her trail, without being taught to use her powers, she would have, all too soon, been one dead Dark Fae.

Sleep eluded her for most of the night, so eventually she picked up an old romance novel and after a few minutes of reading found herself think-ing, "Life is never really like a romance novel; a tragedy maybe, but not a romance." Then she realized, "That's why we need them."

The spotlight was bright, and the people sitting in the surrounding dark-ness were quiet and unknown. The smell of fresh sawdust and sugar laced the air. Gen smiled as the dazzling white light gently eased onto her.

"Ladies and gentlemen, welcome to the Dark Wing Circus!"

The crowd yelled and clapped as she bowed, taking off her black satin top hat and allowing her long golden blonde hair to flood her low-backed purple leather corset.

"Tonight, for your amusement, we will perform death defying feats of" —she pushed fire through her hands and lit the nearby tiki torches lin-ing the stage— "pure magic!"

The crowd reacted in united surprise. Gen smiled.

"We will shock you," –she fluttered the fires again, making them grow higher— "amaze you," —the fires began to spurt in patterns— "and even," —the fires grew small and intimate— "seduce you."

She adopted a flirty pose and winked. The crowd giggled, and cat-calls came from the back of the tent.

"But above all, my darlings, we are here to entertain you!" The fires roared back to life, lighting up the whole crowd.

With a sweeping motion Gen pointed to a nearby sign and read it aloud. "Please remain seated until the show end. Please turn off your mo-bile phones."

There was a ripple of bleeps through the crowd as they all obeyed.

Scanning their faces, Gen basked in the limelight, until her eyes fell on one face in the front row. A man about her age – about twenty-five, dark hair and eyes, a lopsided smile, a poorly concealed weapon bulging in his jacket and an intense look she'd seen before; he was a Huntsman, she felt it deep down in her supernatural bones.

Her high heeled boots suddenly felt unsteady. The sawdust beneath her feet began to smolder and blacken. With more effort than normal, Gen reached into her gut and pulled her fire back inside her.

The music started and she put her top hat back on. "Enjoy the show!" One more final sweeping bow and she quickly strode off backstage.

"What happened, Gen?" Brenda, the clown, intercepted her, grabbing her arm with an oversized novelty hand.

"There's a Huntsman in the audience. They know we're here."

Brenda's eyes widened, "They're cowards, they hunt in packs. Maybe he's just a random punter?"

"Well if he was, he's not anymore. He just saw me manipulate fire. He knows, and that means the rest of his anti-Fae, gotta-kill-em-all buddies are gonna know, too."

Brenda looked thoughtful, but then smiled. "Maybe we should get him before he gets back to his buddies? I'd certainly like to get my hands on a Huntsman."

"That sounds like a good idea." Nitch slipped effortlessly into form beside them, making Gen wonder how long he'd been there. Imps had a habit of using their invisibility to eavesdrop.

"How long have you been listening?"

"Long enough. Now let's keep an eye on the Huntsman. After the show we'll grab him and you can exact a little fiery revenge." He grinned then disappeared again.

"What the hell did that mean?"

Brenda shrugged. "You've never killed before. I think maybe Nitch wants you to pop your cherry. I mean what are you, like twenty-seven already, and you've not killed anyone?"

"Shut up!" Gen knew all too well that to live as a Dark Fae, you had to do a little killing. Reputation was everything in the Fae world and the Dark ones had the very real reputation of being the Fae you didn't piss off. The Dark Fae Queen Karheritte encouraged her subjects to enforce this belief whenever possible–but without killing innocents. Their usual prey was other supernatural creatures who were stepping out of line.

Of course there were also Huntsmen, humans who had taken it upon themselves to kill outside their natural jurisdiction. Gen was never quite sure how the Huntsmen managed this. They had no real powers and seemed to be equipped with almost pre-historic weapons. Yet still they hunted and successfully killed her kind, her family being just one example of their effectiveness.

"Right, wish me luck." Brenda put on her nose then bounced out to a roar of claps and laughter.

"Kill him quick." Nitch appeared again by her side.

She jumped, a small flame firing from her fingernails and rocketing to the floor. She stomped it out and rolled her eyes. "Nitch, I've warned you about sneaking up on me."

"Sorry, dear, just checking in. The show will end within the hour. As the people leave, I'll be-spell his seat to hold him. When everyone's gone, simply walk up to him and burn him where he sits." Nitch quickly hugged her and was gone.

Peeking through the curtains again, she saw her victim laughing and clapping at Brenda's antics. She smiled at his dimples and twinkling hazel eyes, but inside her belly was rolling around an old, sharp, jagged memory.

At the end of the show Gen swept back into Center Ring. She did her speech: thanks for coming, stay safe, visit us again soon. Then, for her finale, she produced rings of twisted cord soaked in whiskey which she lit and hula-hooped with, juggled then levitated in the air. It was obvious magic, the kind that only silly Fae use when they want to draw attention to themselves, but she did it anyway.

Throughout her performance she kept catching the Huntsman's eye. Not on purpose, but she couldn't help but look at him. Unlike his amusement with Brenda, he wasn't smiling now. His eyes were narrow and his hand was resting on what looked like a knife strapped to his belt. Even though Gen knew she was tipping her hand, she felt her eyes wander to him. Like she was looking at a car accident on the highway—you slow down to see the carnage rather than to help.

When she finished, the applause was deafening. She felt the adoration swarm around her like a heady perfume. All the while his stare was still firmly placed upon her. Although she swore that sometimes it faltered and fell to her breasts, or further down to her shapely legs covered in fishnet pantyhose. To him, maybe she was a car wreck too.

The audience stayed longer than usual, and Gen found herself talking to them. She flirted with random punters and chucked children under their chins. Strangely, the Huntsman was still seated. If Nitch had magically secured the Huntsman to his seat, he must not have noticed, or he'd have been wriggling like a fish on a hook.

All too soon, the only two left were her and him.

"You should leave," Gen said.

He struggled to get up.

She knew he was sticky with Imp magic.

"What the..?" He reached inside his jacket for his cell phone.

Gen flexed a flame through it, sizzling the SIM card inside.

He dropped the now useless plastic lump. "Great! I had a seven-month plan on that!"

Her lips twitched with a smile. Humor was the last reaction she'd expected. "I think that's the least of your problems right now." Taking off her top hat, she threw it into the air to be caught by Nitch, who suddenly materialized in the Ring.

"Shit!" The Huntsman struggled in his seat.

"Do it!" Nitch grinned at Gen then disappeared.

"Do what?" asked the Huntsman. "Kill me? I'm not your type."

A flash of pain swept across his eyes, the type of pain that Gen recognized immediately. It was from the loss of someone you loved.

Gen raised an eyebrow. "What do you mean, 'type?'"

"I'm not a teenage girl."

Gen leaped onto the seat in front of him and straddled it. "No, you're not a teenage girl, you're a Huntsman. You kill *my* kind."

"You bet your ass I do."

Gen bent her head and raised her eyes to him. He stopped struggling.

A full minute went by with them looking at one another. All the while Gen wondered if she could actually bring herself to kill him. Something didn't feel quite right. He had a swoon-worthy face set in a stern expression—he thought he was in the right. A tug from something in her chest was telling her not to stoop to his level.

Maybe she could talk to him? Broker a truce?

"What's your name, Huntsman?"

"Michael Lakes."

"I'm Gen Black."

"Gen."

She watched his lips curl and purse round her name; she then shook off the stray thoughts.

"My kind are not killers," she said. "We certainly don't kill the young. We protect them. Humans are the sick ones. You kill and maim one another. You wage wars without end."

"So you *protected* all those missing teenagers?"

"What missing teenagers? What the hell are you talking about?"

"The ones that have disappeared since the Dark Wing Circus came to town. It's why I'm here. I put the pattern together."

"Of course, blame the Dark Fae! It couldn't be anything else, could it? No, because we're supernatural creatures, which makes us the killers."

"Let me go."

"Not my magic keeping you here."

"No, you're a fire-bug, right?"

Gen squinted at him, taking in his broad shoulders and tanned skin. She theorized he must work out in the sun, run or something, maybe swim in the wild lakes in the open air…His tall strong body moving the water about him like a….

"Kill him already!" Nitch yelled from behind her.

Gen glanced at him, then looked back at Michael.

"Yeah, go on, kill me," said Michael. "Prove me right."

"Shut it, you!" Gen felt her fire tingling, tip-toeing up her spine and caressing her neck. It ached to get out, but when she looked into Michael's dark hazel eyes, she didn't see a malevolent killer. Then something else started burning a little deeper.

"What the hell?" Nitch barked. "Gen! Kill him!"

Michael looked up at her, and she put her hand squarely on his chest. She could feel his heart thumping through his thin white shirt. Defiance danced in his eyes. She realized he would gladly die for his cause. He'd prove the Huntsmen right. Michael the martyr.

"No," she whispered.

"Kill him!"

"No!" She turned and screamed to Nitch, who promptly disappeared.

Nitch's spell was beginning to falter, allowing Michael to get up, keeping Gen's hand on his chest as he stood. He was taller than her, so even in heels she had to look up at him.

"I'll be seeing you." He flashed a lopsided smile and then jogged out of the tent.

Gen slumped back onto the seat.

Was that a threat or a promise?

She looked around at the now empty Three Ring. Sparkling dust danced on the breeze and the smell of cotton candy laced her every breath: edible air. Even without the Fae magic, it was magical. Once again, she silently thanked her luck that the circus had been in town the night her family had been slaughtered in their sleep by Huntsmen.

"I know their address." Nitch's sudden re-appearance at her side broke her thoughts.

She took a moment to breathe out some sugar-coated air, turned to her Imp friend and raised an eyebrow. "I don't want to lower myself to their level, Nitch." She finished her sentence with a sigh.

"Level? Gen there's no level here. It's kill or *be* killed!" Nitch was so angry he suddenly went bright red. Sweat started to drip down his face and wet his clothes. "I didn't raise you to just lie down and die. You need to fight back!"

"You think it's the same Huntsmen that killed my family?"

"There's no way of really knowing, but it doesn't matter. The same or not, they'll finish the job and kill the whole circus, given half a chance. Think on it, Gen." With that, Nitch disappeared again.

Gen took another deep breath. She couldn't taste the sugar anymore, just the acrid smell of wet wood chips and Nitch's sweat.

It wasn't that she couldn't muster the anger for vengeance, or even the fear of an attack on her new family. It was that killing Michael just didn't feel right. Sure, he was a Huntsman; he'd probably murdered hundreds of Fae, but the look in those eyes when they fell upon her, his lips when he spoke her name, and the feeling that stirred deep in her chest when she had had him at her mercy—she'd never felt anything like it. It radiated through her bones like hot shivers dancing on her skin, pushing her fleshly boundaries.

The tiki torch nearest to her suddenly burst into flames. Not just the top, but even the staff thrust into the floor. Gen moved away and shook her head in an attempt to rid her mind of Michael. She tried to pull the fire back, but couldn't.

A clown from backstage, in oversized shoes and a wild red wig, pushed Gen out of the way and squirted soda water onto the fierce flames. They spluttered and reluctantly died, leaving a very black tiki torch with a funnel of smoke that spiraled and climbed into the air.

She couldn't sleep that night. Her caravan felt too small. Every time she closed her eyes she saw Michael sitting on that chair, helpless and dangerous all at once. She imagined straddling his lap and running her lips down the soft yielding skin of his throat, making him whisper for more, and yearn to be free to hold her.

Shaking the thoughts from her head, she got up, her long black silk night gown a creature in its own right slinking behind her. The moon outside called to her. The night was her natural time; it reached out and pulled her toward the caravan door, down the steps, past the silent and still carousel, and into the empty Three Ring.

The feel of fresh sawdust beneath her feet and the scent of candy apples eased her tension. She had used the Dark Wing Circus, first as a crook to lean on while in despair of the loss of her family, then as a soft and warm childhood home. Now it was also her work place where she performed watched by thousands of sparkling eyes, like stars in the darkness. Only each time the constellations were different.

Closing her eyes, she breathed deep. "Dark Mother, guide me," she whispered into the light breeze that seeped beneath the edges of the tent and played with her long unbound hair.

The Dark Mother, Queen of her Court, controls air and darkness. She hears all spoken into both. Queen Karheritte, seven foot tall, willowy and pale, sharp teeth and hair a mixture of black feathers and grey silken strands. Only the Dark Fae dare speak with her, only they get a reply.

A sudden wind whipped about Gen, enveloping her in a warm soft hug. She eased into it and saw a flash of black feathers out of the corner of her eye.

"Follow your heart," the breeze whispered. "Love is never wrong."

***

Gen drove to the local police station with the intention of finding the person, or persons, responsible for the missing teenagers. Sitting around and doing nothing wasn't her style, and finding the killers might just get the Huntsmen off the Circus' back.

A bit of flirting with local law enforcement and she knew all about the girls: all in their late teens, all last seen in the circus. The worst part though, was that one body had already turned up, a girl named Sara Swan.

Gen hesitated over taking her investigation forward. She'd learnt enough to know that it wasn't her people who'd committed the crimes. But whoever it was, they were using her territory to commit them. They had to be stopped. The Huntsmen were looking in the wrong place and weren't exactly known for their forgiving nature.

She headed down to the morgue. She needed to pick up a trail, a smell, anything that could point her, and her fiery temper, in the direction of the real killer.

The morgue's front desk was manned by a thin nerd in a crisp grey shirt. He was reading and didn't look up until Gen leaned on the desk and lightly coughed. His eyes widened when he saw her, and, with an uncoordinated jerky movement, dropped his book, which Gen swiftly caught and gave back to him.

He grinned and pushed his glasses further up his nose. "Can I help you, ma'am?"

"Hi, I'm here to see the girl who was brought in yesterday."

"Ummm, yes, which girl?"

"Sara Swan."

The clerk fumbled with his book. "Why are you here?"

"I'm an investigator." The moment the words left her mouth, she knew she couldn't back them up. If he asked for credentials she'd be sunk.

"Okay, the police are in there at the moment. I'm sure they won't mind if you take a look with them."

Suddenly, finding the exits seemed really important. Gen scanned the corridors and rooms as the clerk led her through them, all the while formulating an exit strategy.

The walk seemed to take forever until the clerk, with more flourish than necessary, opened a set of double doors at the end of a tight clean corridor. Gen had a second to regret taking it this far, before she walked straight into Michael.

The clerk addressed Michael. "Detective Lakes, this is—" He suddenly hesitated as his face turned ashen. He glanced at Gen. "Oh my, what did you say your name was?"

"Genevieve Black." She quickly recovered from her initial surprise and extended her hand, along with a healthy dose of malice.

Michael took it. The moment their flesh touched she felt a warm tingle start to work its way down her spine. Looking up at him, she saw a similar blush kiss his cheeks.

"Nice to meet you." Michael coughed and let her hand go.

Gen couldn't help her eyes scanning Michael. Gone was the leather jacket and jeans, replaced with crisp white shirt and dress pants, his gun pride of place on his belt along with a fake badge.

"She's here investigating the deaths," the clerk managed to push out.

The other 'policeman' standing with Michael pushed forward and examined Gen like she was a piece of gum stuck to his shoe. The look of disgust in his eyes betrayed him. Another Huntsman. He was so close she could smell his breath. He had had too much bad coffee that morning, and smoked at least two packs of cigarettes. He was about mid forties and had a belly that hung over his belt like an apron.

He also looked strangely familiar, but she had no idea where she would have seen him before.

Raising an eyebrow and setting her lips in a firm line got him to move back out of her personal space. Dark Fae don't start fights, but they don't back down from them either.

"Can we get on with this please?" Gen asked. She was trying to look like a cool, confident private detective, but deep down her nerves jangled like pixie boots.

"So how did you know the victim?" The other 'policeman' flipped open a spiral notepad and began to scribble.

"I know her family," Gen replied. "I actually went through all this in the station with Detective James. You can call him, if you like." She punctuated her sentence with a slight grin. They all had something to hide, but the Huntsmen's deception was a bit more illegal than hers.

"That's okay, I believe you." He spat the words and turned his nose up.

"May I speak to you outside, Ms. Black?" Michael motioned for her to follow him out the door and into the narrow hallway.

She nodded, and they left the clerk and the other Huntsman to talk.

The smell of disinfectant and old blood hung in the air. Gen felt a dull ache in her chest; she missed the circus.

She and Michael looked at each other longer than necessary.

"Nice suit," Gen said.

Michael fidgeted.

"We didn't do this." Gen stared up at him, hoping her eyes would plead her case. The one thing she'd always clung to about Huntsmen was that they were human. Surely as such, he'd recognize her innocence.

His eyes rolled. "*I'm innocent!* Isn't that what all killers say?"

"Probably, only some actually are. Anyway, when we pitch up, none of us leave the safety of the circus. We couldn't have dumped a body. We can't be in two places at once, you know!"

"I bet some of you can."

"We're not monsters. What do I have to do to make you understand?"

With a huff of obvious annoyance, Michael's fellow fake policeman came out of the morgue.

Michael motioned at his partner. "Kellar here says it's a Dark Fae kill."

"*Kellar* has it wrong!" Gen stomped her foot and felt her fire bubble.

"I didn't have it wrong when the Dark Fae killed your family did I, Michael?" Kellar moved to put a firm hand on Michael's shoulder.

"What?" Gen felt her eyes widen. Memories of her own family's abrupt death sentence tumbled from her subconscious.

"Yeah, that's right, you're not *all* monsters," said Michael. "Well, only the ones still breathing." And with that he flung himself at Gen, toppling her back. The force broke the door open behind them and they both stumbled into another examining room. It was dark, and Gen could make out Kellar's silhouette blocking the door. Michael grabbed her torso and pulled her high into the air then slammed her onto a static metal trolley. Holding her down with an elbow over her collarbone, he climbed on top of her and pinned her with his thighs. He then reached into his jacket and pulled out a knife. Gen knew it was made of Iron, the only metal that could kill a Fae.

She could have used her powers, burnt him to cinders, but what would that prove? That she was the monster he thought she was. Instead, she relaxed her clenched jaw and looked into his eyes. She got past his initial anger and found that behind all that pain was a man with eyes like hot chocolate on a cold day.

His arm faltered.

"Kill her now!" Kellar yelled.

Michael held the blade high. Gen pushed a tingle of warmth from her skin. The magic caught on her sweet citrus perfume and she watched as Michael softened. She knew it was a cheap trick, but her life was in danger and although all her senses screamed to kill him, she found herself coming up with every excuse not to.

She could now see in his eyes an undercurrent of soft yearning beneath his river of murderous rage.

The dagger sagged in his grip.

Gen eased her leg from under him. But instead of gaining the advantage and pushing him off, she caressed it up the side of his body, contracting it on his hip and pushing their bodies into a gentle collusion.

Michael dropped the dagger and relaxed his body onto hers.

Everything felt so right, apart from the fact they were on a mortician's trolley being yelled at, but Kellar had been tuned out. In their world he didn't exist. There was only each other in that moment; them and the clerk finally bursting past Kellar through the door.

"I thought I heard a crash." His eyes found them on the trolley. "Oh my, what happened?"

"Oh, Ms. Black fainted. My partner was just laying her down, um... putting her in the recovery position." Kellar rolled his eyes.

"I see." The clerk went to Gen's side.

Michael hesitated then slid off her.

"I'm fine, really." With the poise of a veteran actress, Gen swept a hand to her forehead.

"Are you sure? You look kinda flushed." The clerk put his clammy hand to her cheek.

She recoiled at the touch. It felt like a snake slithering over her grave.

"Just dandy, thanks!" She jumped off the trolley and strode into the morgue. She still had to see the body to make sure it wasn't a Fae kill.

Flicking the sheet back, she looked at the pale form beneath. It had cuts so deep she could see bone. The wounds were definitely made by a blade, so the culprit had to be human. Dark Fae would use magic and their bare hands.

So why had Kellar and Michael been so convinced it was a Fae who'd committed the crime? They had seen the body too.

Gen replaced the sheet and felt an unexpected tear dribble down her cheek. Then she said, "Well, I need to get back." She turned to see Michael staring opened-mouthed after her. "Thank you for your help."

Kellar was sneering for all he was worth, and the clerk grinned at her.

She deliberately sauntered slowly past them out of the morgue. Once she left the building, Gen put her back to the building's wall, slid down, curled up and cried.

***

Back at the circus, surrounded by her people, Gen rolled the days' events about in her mind.

At times like this, she had always turned to Nitch to talk things through. So with a sigh on her lips and a question in her heart, Gen walked into his make-shift office.

"Nitch?"

No answer. Gen checked around the tent but found nothing, apart from a paper left on his desk. It was a page from a yellowing book with scrawled handwritten notes over it. The page, from what she could make out, talked about Plato and his "Split Apart" theory. The Ancient Greek believed that people are all half of a whole, split by divine intervention, always searching for our other half, our true love.

The handwritten notes were somewhat less romantic and erring on the creepier side. They spoke of eternal damnation for both the Fae and Humans if a Split Apart were to kill its other half. It was the true suicide that the Bible had spoke of: your Split Apart was your gift from God; rejecting it would mean that he would turn his back on Earth and all who chose to dwell on it.

Gen turned the paper over, wondering where it had come from.

Nitch appeared to her side, his eyes focused on the stray page in her hands. "Gen?"

"What's this, Nitch?"

"Oh." He took it from her. "It's nothing, just a theory really that myself and another Imp have. It's nothing important, dear."

"What other Imp?" She'd never met another like Nitch.

"Oh, he's quite the theologian, and also quite the fantasist, too." He put his arms around her, their mutual warmth a familiar sensation that reminded her of being a young girl again.

"You know," she whispered, "Michael says that his famly was killed by Dark Fae."

Nitch held her at arm's length. "Michael? You are on a first name basis with that killer?"

Gen shuffled her feet and cast her eyes to the dusty floor. "Dark Fae wouldn't do that. He's wrong, isn't he?"

"Of course he's wrong!" Nitch waved his arms in the air with almost Muppet-like abandon. "He's a Huntsman, they're always wrong! It's one of their most predictable traits!"

"I know there's someone else abducting the teenagers in this town."

"You do?"

"Yes, I investigated."

"You know I don't like you putting yourself in harm's way like that. I'd have done it if you'd have asked."

"I know you've always kept me safe," said Gen, "maybe a little too sheltered at times."

"So who is it? Huntsmen?"

"No. The girl was human. I saw the body. She was cut up. No Fae would do that, which only leaves—"

"—a human as the killer." Screwing up his face, Nitch whined sarcastically, "Humans are never evil, only supernatural creatures kill! *Humph*. Like Hitler wasn't human!" He started to turn red, sweat beads forming on his forehead.

Gen had seen his "noble Huntsman" impression before. She smiled and patted his back. "Huntsmen will learn."

"Yes, but how many more Fae will die before they do? You have to kill him, Gen. Kill him before he kills you. Do you hear me? He'll kill you! And I won't be able to stand it!"

A claret tear rolled down his face just before he disappeared, the torn page still in his hand.

That night the circus was filled with laughter and sticky hands. Gen loved these nights the most, the magic on the kid's faces, and the beginnings of magic in the adult's eyes—a much harder response to elicit, yet so much more prized among the Fae folk.

Brenda was getting ready for her performance. Since Gen was already dressed, she settled next to her in the tent. They spoke of the warm weather, the state of the carousel, and Brenda even mentioned how nervous Nitch was about the appearance of the Huntsmen.

As Gen got up to leave, she noticed the red wig of the unidentified clown from the other night sitting on a chair nearby. "Brenda, is this yours?" She picked it up, held it and suddenly got the aroma of bad coffee and cigarettes.

"No, not mine. I thought one of the other clowns left it here!"

Gen sniffed again. It was Kellar she could smell. *He'd* been the unknown clown who'd put out the flames in the tent the other night. That was why he seemed familiar at the morgue.

What was he doing at the circus anyway? Keeping an eye on Michael? If so, why hadn't he helped him?

Things were getting more and more complicated. Stranger still, the one she wanted talk to about it was Michael.

Gen strode out of the make-up tent and into the thrum of the crowd of customers on the fairway. She always did laps before a show. She helped some children onto the Haunted Hayride and watched their older sister abandon them in favor of chatting with a boy. No, a man; a skinny man in a grey shirt with glasses he pushed up his nose in a familiar tick.

It was the morgue clerk.

"Hi, don't I know you?" Gen moved between the clerk and the teenage girl. The girl used the distraction to catch a ride with her siblings.

"What?"

"Gen, from the morgue."

"Yes, I remember. How are you feeling?"

"I'm getting there. I'd like to get my hands on the killer, though." She reached up and placed her hands lightly on his shoulders. He was even creepier now than when he was surrounded by dead bodies.

She smiled at him and he grinned back. Gen watched as he slid his arm to his back and casually touched the exposed hilt of a surgical knife. The type of blade that makes long thick slashes on young skin.

Several short thoughts sprinted through Gen's mind.

"You should get your hands off me or I'll make sure you end up on my table too!" He spat the words like a bad taste in his mouth.

Gen accidentally flexed heat through her hands and the killer's eyes momentarily dilated. She pulled her hands away and looked round to see if anyone had noticed.

They had. Michael stood a meter away with disappointment all over his face. A moment passed between them, long enough for the clerk to start moving with a forceful walk toward the circus' grounds exit.

Gen cursed her dumb luck. If she let him go, he'd kill again. But if she went after him and killed him, she'd justify every bad rumor about the Dark Fae in Michael's eyes.

She chose to go after the killer, hoping Michael would let her explain before one of them killed the other.

Pushing her way through the mobs, Gen kept her eyes on that grey shirt bobbing in out of the crowd; it looked like a dorsal fin against multi-colored waves. Daring to look behind her, she found Michael gaining.

Behind the carousel, Gen spotted the killer bending over trying to catch his breath. She moved to block his exit.

"What the hell are you?" he yelled at her.

"I'm the ringmaster of this circus. You took those girls. You're the one who killed Sara."

The man rolled his cold eyes. "What about the others? You don't want them to come to harm, do you?"

The other abductees were still alive? Gen sighed. What should have been easy was suddenly becoming very hard.

Then Michael arrived.

"Wait, I need to explain," she told him.

"Explain what?" he said. "That you're the actual Dark Fae killing teenagers? That you put on that act of investigating it to throw me off your trail?"

"What? No! Why would you even think that?"

"Kellar told me everything."

"No! He's the killer!" Gen pointed at geeky clerk, who threw his hands up. "You saw the body, Michael, do Dark Fae use weapons?"

Michael's expression slowly turned from anger to relief. "Yeah, I saw the body."

"Then why the hell have you been after me?" Gen yelled.

Eyes wide, Michael put his hands up. "Kellar was so sure."

Suddenly the knife was out of the killer's belt and in his hand. "Okay, you want to play, then?"

"Whatever." Gen pushed a flame at the knife. The metal conducted the heat, burning the killer's hand. He dropped his weapon as the color drained from his face.

"Remember the other girls," he warned. "If you kill me, they'll never be found."

Michael stepped forward, threw the clerk into the carousel's steel struts, and patted him down. He found his wallet and read out his driver license address, "Twenty Campfire Gardens."

The killer's expression turned slack.

"Yep, I'd say that's where they are," Gen said, leaning closer.

Before Gen knew what was happening, the killer pushed her down and rolled on top of her.

"You bitch!" he screamed into her face as stray gobs of salvia showered down onto her skin.

She could have encircled him in a flame-filled hug—God knew he'd have deserved it—but she couldn't do it. Instead, she wriggled beneath him and watched as he reached for his fallen knife.

Michael got to him first. He swiftly grabbed his own knife and put it to the killer's chin.

Gen looked up at Michael for help and he hesitated.

The killer stiffened, and the madness that had seemed to overtake him dissipated. He reverted into a wide-eyed geeky guy. He put his hands up in surrender and took his weight from Gen's body.

Just as she breathed a sigh of relief, she saw the knife glisten in the killer's hand as he shoved it toward Michael. Still on the ground, stumbling forward, she pulled her arms about the killer to hold him, but her powers had other ideas. Catching him in a fiery embrace, they burned him up so quickly he didn't even scream.

But inside, Gen did. Horrified, Gen tried to speak. "I didn't mean to...I just." She slumped toward the floor, but Michael caught her.

"It doesn't put me off giving you a hug," he whispered as she relaxed into his arms.

"So do you believe me now, that not all Dark Fae are killers?"

"You did just kill someone in front of me," he said through a grin.

"Yeah, but I really didn't mean to. He forced my hand."

"You probably saved lives, Gen. It's not like we could have turned him over to the authorities. We had no evidence, and what we did have was obtained illegally."

"Yeah, and he did deserve it right?" She looked up at him.

"My family didn't deserve it."

"Well, neither did mine." Gen pulled away.

"What?"

"Huntsmen killed my whole family. That's why I'm here. Nitch found me and raised me."

"My family weren't Huntsmen. I only became one because Kellar adopted me."

"Dark Fae wouldn't kill innocents. We have rules. The Queen would know and punish us. There would be no point to it."

"You're called *Dark* Fae, so of course you kill. How dumb do you think I am?"

"Dark is just the name of our Court. We were named that well before *dark* became something sinister in your language. How narrow-minded are you, Michael?" Gen backed away from him.

"Kellar was there," Michael said. "He said he saw the Dark Fae slit my parent's throats!"

"Kellar was there?"

"Yeah, he saved me. Came out of nowhere, and scooped me up."

"Was he your neighbor? Why was he there?"

Michael threw his hands in the air. "I don't know. I'm just glad he was or I'd have ended up dead like my parents."

"Why was he there, Michael?"

Memories of Nitch's sudden and dramatic appearances reared in Gen's mind. It was an Imp trait; no other supernatural creature had that ability and certainly no human. It would explain how Kellar had gotten in and out of the circus the night she'd met Michael.

"Kellar's an Imp," she whispered.

"Kellar's human. He's been a Huntsman for years. He's not an Imp."

"Does he often quote conversations he was never in?"

"What does that mean?"

"That he was there, only invisible. Imps love to eavesdrop."

Michael looked thoughtful. "Yeah, he does."

Gen rolled this new information around in her mind. Imps were rare and Nitch had mentioned a friend. One he'd never spoken of before. All these years, and suddenly another Imp turned up helping Huntsmen. It was more than just a coincidence. It had to be.

Michael must have thought the same. His legs buckled and he sprawled on the grass, running his hands through his thick brown hair.

Gen lowered herself down beside him, sitting so their bodies touched. "I trust Nitch, but Imps are generally troublemakers. They're demons with a tentative truce with the Dark Fae." She swallowed and took a deep breath. "We share such similar childhood tragedies, Michael, and I've never seen Nitch so intent on me killing someone."

"Kellar's been the same. But he can't be an Imp if they have a truce with the Dark Court. Why would he target you?"

"I don't know. Could it have been Kellar who killed your family?"

Michael shook his head.

"You said it yourself, Michael, he was there." She reached for his chin and gently pulled his head up so their eyes could meet. "I don't want to kill you. I never did."

"Me neither. I can think of a lot of other things I want to do with you, but a battle to the death isn't one."

He grinned and pulled her to him. Their lips hovered on each other, a light soft touch, neither committing to a full kiss, but both happy to be so near the other. Michael put his hand on her face and stroked her cheek. Gen lightly rested her hand on his chest; the now familiar thumping of his steady heartbeat making her smile.

"Gen," Brenda yelled as she ran up behind them. "You're meant to be in the ring!"

She pulled Gen to her feet, squinted at Michael then dragged her reluctant ringmaster toward the Three Ring.

Her powers flowed and the fire danced around the ring. She felt strangely at ease, even though a thousand questions kept popping into her head; questions that could only be answered by Nitch.

Thunderous applause burst from the tent as Gen ended the show; her powers almost spent and her body heaving with exhaustion.

"Thank you one and all for visiting us tonight. May your journey home be safe," —she bowed low enough to expose her cleavage— "and your dreams be sweet."

Another round of applause and the crowd began to disperse. As she turned to leave, Gen spotted five men working their way from their seats to the centre of the Ring. There were Kellar and Michael, and three strangers, all burly and with tell-tale lumps in their jackets.

Brenda and the clowns leapt back into the ring, tumbling and flip-flopping into action.

"Michael?" Gen looked at him, but his face was stern.

"We need to kill them all!" Kellar rallied the other Huntsmen, who all reached into their jackets for their iron knives.

"Wait!" Nitch appeared between them. "She's just performed, her powers are weak. It's not a fair fight!"

"Fair? Who said anything about it being fair?" Kellar cocked his head with an evil grin.

Michael moved forward toward Gen.

Both sides tensed for a fight.

Nitch looked at Gen with a shameful expression then closed his eyes.

Michael and Gen circled one another. She watched his arms, the arms she'd just been in, tense as he clenched his fists. The anger in his eyes burned stronger than the passion she'd seen before. Her powers spluttered and spat like a dying engine in her belly. She blinked, and he had his knife in his hand. Gen looked around and saw her circus family wide eyed, paler than their make-up and stiller than she'd ever seen them.

Suddenly she was a child again, the corpses of her family with black hole eyes littered around her like dead tiki torches. The thought of killing Michael was as if the knife had already pierced her heart, leaking deadly iron poison into her veins; her limbs heavy and useless. The smell of blood caught her by surprise. She blinked then searched for its source.

Michael had pulled his knife's blade up into his own grip and his fresh blood was now dripping from his palm onto the sawdust below. The look on his face was painfully set, but his weapon was now sheathed in his fist rather than pointed at Gen.

She took a deep breath and rushed toward Michael. When they collided, both wrapped their arms about one another and finally their lips met. Their kiss was long, soft and all the things a first kiss should be.

Gen felt her powers flex, so she pulled away from Michael's embrace. Suddenly the almost dead tiki torches around the Three Ring fluttered to life. They burned so bright that the battle-itching armies were no longer shadowed in darkness. They were now staring at each other in full light.

"Great! Where does that leave us and our bet?" Kellar yelled with his hands on his hips.

The other Huntsmen began to murmur and back away from him.

Nitch grinned. "I guess the urge was too strong. We were wrong to do this, Kellar."

Kellar screamed like a banshee then lunged at Gen. "I don't care! No rules now!" He lifted his hand to strike her, but was caught by Nitch.

"No more, Kellar. It's over. We both lost the bet. They are Split Aparts. We'll never get one to kill the other, no matter what stories we tell."

Gen stepped back and nestled in Michael's easy embrace. Then she glared at Nitch.

"I'm sorry dear, truly. I was different before I knew you, before I loved you." Nitch took her hand and knelt on the floor before her. "Can you ever forgive an Imp who's been led so far astray? I lied. Huntsmen didn't kill your family. Kellar did. He killed yours too, Michael."

Michael closed his eyes and buried his head in Gen's hair. The warmth of his breath crept from the top of her head to her toes.

Nitch had brought Gen up. He had been her mother, father, trainer and friend. He'd never claimed to be anything other than an Imp, and by their nature they cause trouble. He'd been there when she'd needed him. As much as an Imp could love, he'd loved her and she just hoped he still did.

"Nitch, you declared your allegiance to the Dark Court and have betrayed us." Gen kept her eyes on him. "If you wish to surrender yourself, you will be judged by our Queen and punished accordingly."

She expected him to disappear there and then, but he didn't.

"Believe me when I tell you the only thing I do not regret is raising you." Nitch closed his eyes. "Let the Queen punish me."

Gen breathed a sigh. "Tell me why you did it."

"We're immortal!" Kellar ranted, pushing Nitch out of the way. "We get bored!" He manically waved his arms around his head. "We found out about the Split Apart theory. We decided to see if we could manipulate one into killing the other. Then we made a bet as to who would be the killer and who would get slaughtered."

"Why us?" Michael asked.

"You were perfect, opposite sides of a war; one Huntsman and one Dark Fae. We could damn both races with one kill."

"You're a monster," Michael whispered, his eyes narrowed and fixed on Kellar.

"Don't be so dramatic." Kellar turned and kicked Nitch as he tried to get up. "You fragile humans die all the time!"

And with that declaration, he launched himself at Michael.

Gen threw herself between them, tensing to take a blow that didn't come. Instead Kellar's eyes lost their mad gleam and his body fell limp onto her. As she caught him, she saw Nitch had materialized behind her attacker. Kellar's spine dangled from his bloody hand, freshly ripped out of his back.

Gen felt her knees give way, and she fell into Michael's waiting arms.

"You okay?" he asked.

She looked from him to Nitch. "I am now."

Gen laid her hand on his cheek then drew him to her for another kiss. She knew they would never be split apart again.

The Fourth Wish

Tarl Kudrick

MELANIE'S NEWEST MOM, Candace, and the new nurse, Gwen, had finished cleaning Melanie's face, tray, and wheelchair after Melanie had sort of accidentally spilled her oatmeal. And of course once Melanie was clean and didn't need anything else, Candace and Gwen left the room. Melanie had just wanted to try eating without a spoon, like cats did. Cats put their whole face in the bowl and smacked their mouths when they ate and everyone liked them. They purred when they were happy, too. Melanie had tried purring once. The noise made Candace run to get the nurse.

The only time Melanie didn't feel lonely was when the little green man visited her.

Melanie nudged the stick by her left hand, spinning her chair to face the Mickey Mouse clock. Both of Mickey's hands pointed straight up. Time for TV, unless the green man visited. Candace came in and gave her a baby cup with a straw, plus a TV remote with five buttons. Melanie turned the TV on by slapping the big red button. Candace left. A shimmering light appeared next to Melanie and she slapped the TV button again to turn it off.

He'd come back.

He was green and shiny like a lizard and he had pointy ears and he was big around the middle just like she was. He made funny faces at her and she stuck her tongue out or made her jaw drop or shook her head until she got dizzy, and he laughed. The green man wasn't in the room with her; he was looking through a window that just happened to be in the middle of Melanie's bedroom. He'd first visited a few days ago, with two other green men, and the other two had looked bored and made excuses to leave, like a lot of people did when they saw her.

But the round green man had said, "Hi," and when she said, "Hi," back he looked so surprised! He'd said, "You can hear me?" and Melanie

42

said, "Yes," and the green man said, "You're amazing," and just like that, Melanie liked him so much that when he left, she felt warm and excited and embarrassed, and she wanted him to come back right away.

Candace didn't know about the green man. Melanie was scared she'd find out.

Far from the human world, Skragg, the world's last wish-granting genie, bristled at himself, the universe, and his human master, Candace. Candace was no ordinary master who believed in the "three wishes" propaganda and all the other lies genies had spread thousands of years ago. Candace knew the right way to put gold dust on a cloth before rubbing his lamp; she knew how genies could distort wishes to turn dreams into nightmares; and worst of all, she knew that the bond between genie and master was for life. She'd get one wish every ten years, for as long as she lived, as long as she didn't abuse her wishes. Which she hadn't.

At least not yet.

If he couldn't solve what he thought of as his "Candace problem," maybe he could do something about the imps. They were creatures of pure chaos he unfortunately shared his magical dimension with. Lately they'd been crazier than usual, which meant something big was going on.

They were charging at him right now, leaping like puppies across the dry red dirt of Skragg's homeland. One was short, and came up to Skragg's knees. Another was tall (for an imp), coming up to Skragg's waist. The third was fat, and that imp's height was halfway between the short one and the tall one. If they had names, Skragg didn't know them. He called them Shrimp, Wimp, and Blimp. While Shrimp and Wimp resembled wingless gargoyles, Blimp's body was shaped like a scaly watermelon. Skragg was nine feet tall and looked like a scarecrow stuffed with barbed wire, yet even with his leather jacket, blue jeans, sunglasses, and Mohawk hairdo, he couldn't intimidate the imps. Not even his always-fiery hands and feet bothered them. They said his flames tickled.

The imps landed at his feet. "Hi, Skragg!"

The tall one, Wimp, came forward. "Today, on Imp Theater, we present a dramatic tale that'll shock you!"

"I know what your play's about," Skragg said.

Wimp fluttered his ears in surprise. "Really?"

"It'll start as a travesty of some human play, then change its plot every five seconds because you idiots have the attention span of a manic gnat."

Shrimp stepped up. "We make human plays *better.*"

"*Fiddler on the Roof* doesn't start with a huge crowd shouting 'Jump! Jump!'" Skragg said.

Blimp burst into the conversation. "Enough talk! It's time to play dominoes!" The three imps waved their hands, and a piñata appeared. As it floated in circles, the imps whacked it with hockey sticks, then tried to convince it to run for Congress.

Skragg's choices were simple: watch the imps make the piñata wrestle a second piñata they'd just summoned; open a portal to the human world to see what the universe's *second* most irritating life forms were doing; or stare at his home's cracked red plains in silence until his head burst from boredom.

He chose the plains.

"Hey, Skragg," Blimp said. "Won't Candace summon you soon?"

"Probably."

Shrimp said, "Can we go with you?"

Blimp leaped up and down. "I can see my friend!"

Skragg briefly wondered what "friend" Blimp was referring to. The imps spent so much time watching the human world, it could have been anybody. "No. First, all you cause is trouble."

"Woo-hoo!" The imps high-fived each other.

"Second, haven't you noticed you never get the reaction you're looking for? Your own magic keeps humans from noticing you. No matter what you do, they see it as ordinary."

"This time we'll train their pets to sing opera!"

Skragg said, "And they'll act like that happens every day."

Shrimp, who came the closest of any of them to being smart, said, "Then why not let us go?"

"Because imps cause real problems for that world, whether humans notice or not."

"Nonsense!"

"Abstract painting was supposed to be a joke. When you two barfed on that canvas, imp magic made them take it seriously."

"It was Projectile Vomit Day!" Blimp said.

Skragg went back to his usual tactic: threats. "You enter the human world again and I'll make your lives so miserable—"

A prickly sensation flowed through Skragg, cutting off his ultimatum. A wavering, round doorway to the human world formed next to them.

"She's getting good at that!" Shrimp said. All three imps moved in front of the portal, blocking Skragg's path and making it clear Skragg wasn't going without them.

Skragg knew when he was beat. "Now listen, meatheads. We're going to see Candace, she'll abuse my power—"

"She never has," Wimp said.

"She will this time. I can feel it. So we'll teach her a lesson about greed, then I'll be free of her forever. Got it?"

The imps, who were unable to hold a serious conversation for more than a few moments, replied with their usual non-sequiturs.

"Steak and eggs, captain!" Wimp said.

"Is it okay to call a scared turkey a chicken?" Shrimp said.

Blimp created a lemon meringue pie and ate it in one huge chomp.

The human world pulled harder at Skragg. The imps waited by the portal as patiently as they could, which meant poking each other and arguing whether a yo-yo would work in zero gravity if you attached a rocket to it. Skragg tried to think of something that might prevent the upcoming calamity, then gave up and entered the human world.

In her room, Melanie felt the air sizzle and heard the green man say, "Here I come!" But when she spun her chair around, he wasn't there.

Skragg and the imps appeared in a living room Skragg had never seen before. His genie senses told him it was part of a three-bedroom single-family home. The tasteful but not expensive sofa, television, tables, and other decorations reminded him that Candace had still not let the power of a genie go to her head. But today....

Wimp and Shrimp ran off to explore the house and probably knock half of it over. Blimp went a different direction, saying more random nonsense ("Melanie Melanie Melanie") so softly only Skragg could hear him. Skragg looked for Candace, and found her behind him, on a small chair next to the sofa.

She was in her late thirties, which was well into adulthood by pathetic human standards. She was wearing thin, black-framed eyeglasses that humans would say made her look intelligent. Skragg's lamp rested next to her like a pet. What seemed out of place was the bottle of whisky. She was almost sliding out of her chair and her face was bleak with drunkenness.

With a struggle, she sat up straight. "You brought imps."

Something in her manner kept his bitterness at bay. "I couldn't stop them." From the direction Shrimp and Wimp had gone he heard a crash, followed by "Whoops," followed by "This'll fix it," followed by "That's much better!"

Candace's unhappiness thickened the air in the room. "I wish the imps hadn't come along."

Skragg hoped that wasn't her real wish. He'd never get his freedom back that way.

Candace kept talking, as if he'd answered. "It's just...this is serious, this time."

"Thirty years ago you were serious about ice cream." She'd wasted her first wish on dessert. Her second was for help deciding what college to go to. Her third was for "enough" money. Who wished for "enough" money? When was she going to get stupid like the rest of her kind? If he had to be chained to her for another fifty or sixty years....

"I'm not kidding, Skragg. I have a real problem."

From another part of the house, a human whooped with excitement. Blimp whooped back.

Skragg said, "Is someone else here? If anyone else learns about me, our deal's off."

Candace stared at a wall as if she could see through it and into the room where the noise had come from. "Damn it."

Skragg was about to give Candace another lecture on the importance of not letting everyone on Earth know about genies, but the exhaustion and concern on her tear-streaked face stopped him and made him feel all the ways he hated feeling.

Candace said, "Wait a minute. No one can notice an imp." Her face squeezed into tired concentration. "Except me...."

"You're connected to me, so you recognize them."

"Would my family recognize them, then?"

"No. It's because you have my lamp, not...."

Skragg saw what she was saying. Whoever had whooped with excitement at seeing an imp, shouldn't have. He headed for the hallway.

Candace stood up. "Don't!"

"Don't worry, no one will know I'm here unless I want them to."

Skragg kept his head ducked down—stupid low human ceilings!— and marched down the hall. He could smell Shrimp and Wimp baking something awful in the kitchen, but ignored them. He sensed Blimp and an unusually musty human in a bedroom. He entered that room with Candace right behind him.

Then he stopped so fast Candace almost crashed into him.

There was a woman, a young adult by human standards, wearing pink pajamas and sitting in a motorized wheelchair. Her head lolled at an unusual angle, and her forehead bulged out in a way human foreheads rarely did. She was as round as Blimp, she smelled like she didn't bathe often, and her hair had been cut so short she hardly had any. She was staring at the imp, waving one flabby arm in a circle, saying, "Hi," again and again. Saliva formed a tiny puddle on her lower lip. She was smiling.

None of that surprised Skragg. Humans came in a wide range of shapes, sizes, and ability levels. What he'd never seen, until now, was an imp stand still for so long.

"Skragg," Blimp said without turning around. "She can see me. She can see me *for real.*"

The wheelchair-bound woman turned her chair to the right, which seemed to be the only way she could position herself to look at Skragg. Which she was doing. Looking right at him, even though he didn't want her to see him. "You're tall," the woman said in a high-pitched monotone.

Blimp moved to get in front of the wheelchair woman. "You're *beautiful,*" he said.

Skragg was too stunned to speak. He felt Candace dragging him back to the living room, muttering, "I don't believe this," again and again.

The other two imps came by to see what was going on. From the hall, they stared into the bedroom with exactly the kind of stupid look on their faces that Skragg feared was on his own.

Skragg sat in a wicker chair and made sure his flaming hands and feet didn't damage it. Candace sat on her brown sofa, curled into an upright fetal position.

Skragg felt the need to say something. "That's not Ruth." He'd seen Candace's sister, and the wheelchair woman was not her.

Candace kept staring. "Ruth was adopted," she finally said in a voice that sounded farther away than it really was. "A few years ago, she got married and adopted a teenager with problems. Two months ago they died in a car accident. Ruth and her husband I mean."

Skragg had figured out who she meant. "I won't fix death."

"I know."

So that's not what she wanted. "Was their kid in the accident? That's why she's in a wheelchair and brain-damaged?"

"No." Anger gave Candace's voice a surprising weight. "Melanie was born 'brain-damaged,' as you so crudely put it. Plus, orphanages aren't known for their medical care, you know? I'm sure she got worse the longer she was there. Ruth wanted to save some kid no one else would touch. Melanie has some kind of muscular dystrophy, she's mildly retarded, and she's schizophrenic. Not the paranoid kind, thank God. Just the regular kind where she hallucinates a lot."

Skragg had heard stories about humans who could see through magical defenses. It made sense. The perception-based magic that kept humans from noticing creatures like him worked directly on the brain. It might fail if someone's brain was different enough.

The imps were in the bedroom with Melanie, arguing. He'd never heard such worry in imp voices before.

"Ruth kept pestering me to be Melanie's emergency guardian," Candace said. "I kept refusing. When Melanie became an adult I finally agreed because, hey, she's an adult now, right? If she could make it to adulthood with all her problems, she'd never need me." She made a sound halfway between a hiccup and a gasp. "So when she turned twenty-one I finally agreed. I had the house inspected and did all the lawyer things, and I kept thinking what a stupid waste of time it all was, and then they died."

Skragg found himself unnaturally silent again. He needed to remind her, and possibly himself, of who he really was, and why he was there. "What wish would you like granted?"

Candace coughed. "Did you see her? She's happy. I've never seen her happy. Never."

"Most humans aren't happy very often."

Candace flung herself forward. "And she's a hundred times worse off than most of us! You could end that cruelty, right? But am I just being selfish? Do I want you to make Melanie normal for her sake, or mine? So she won't need me anymore? So she'll leave?"

Skragg wasn't sure what difference her reasons would make. "I can't make her 'normal.' I don't know what 'normal' is. But I can turn her into what she would have been if she'd been born without injury. At least she'd live longer."

"Longer?"

He flared his magical senses and studied the body of the woman in the wheelchair, two rooms away. "Her neuromuscular condition's killing her. She'll be dead within twenty years, probably less."

Candace sat quietly for a while. The unhappiness lifted from her only slightly. "If you took away her physical problems, what would happen to her mind?"

"It would work as badly as every other human mind."

"I mean, she probably can't count to ten. I know she can't read."

"That puts her just slightly behind a typical high school graduate." He folded his arms. "Look, I can give her the ability to learn anything she bothers learning. But I won't hand her all the world's knowledge."

Candace's eyes watered. "But is it *right*? To change her that much?"

Skragg, not knowing what else to do, retreated deeply into his caverns of sarcasm. "Oh no, Master. The only *right* thing to do is leave her a drooling schizo in a wheelchair and let her die soon."

Now the spluttering began. "You... you horrible...."

A whirring sound distracted them both. Skragg heard no sound from any of the imps, and that made the whirring more ominous.

Melanie rolled into view. Blimp was by her side, smiling angelically, and holding her hand. Wimp and Shrimp walked behind them, smelling of anxiety.

"Skragg," Melanie said. Her yellow-brown teeth showed as she smiled. "Can he stay?"

Blimp nodded with such enthusiasm, Skragg got dizzy watching his head bob.

"He's not human," Skragg said, because that was the one part of all this his mind could process.

Candace said, "He can't stay, Melanie. He has a home."

"I want to stay," Blimp said. "She notices me."

The immensity of the imp's request was sinking into Skragg like sharp teeth. "No."

Melanie started to cry. "He likes me."

Skragg assumed as much of his full nine-foot height as Candace's eight-foot ceiling would allow. He pointed a sharp, flaming finger at the imps. "You three. Go home."

For the first time ever, Wimp and Shrimp obeyed him and opened a portal to their homeworld. They tried to drag Blimp with them, but he held onto the wheelchair and wouldn't budge. Melanie cried louder.

Candace ran to Melanie's side. "Sweetie, listen. The imp has to go now. He wouldn't be happy here anyway."

Blimp said, "Yes I would!"

Skragg said, "I told you to go!"

Blimp clung to the chair. "I'll be a great man for her!" A cowboy hat appeared on his head. "See?"

"Blimp...."

"I'll be a perfect man! I'll run a big company and drop out of college and solve crimes and drink beer! I'll dunk basketballs!" The other imps were in the portal already, pulling Blimp by his feet. "I'll drive a truck! I'll shoot things!"

Wimp and Shrimp won their tug of war, and pulled Blimp through the portal. "Bye-bye, honey apple!" he cried out as the portal faded.

"Impy!" Melanie screamed, reaching out as Candace scrambled to get between her and the portal. The portal closed with a rush of air, and the imps were gone.

Melanie cried like she would never stop.

Candace, raging, turned towards Skragg. "Fix this."

Skragg saw his chance. "Is that your wish? I can solve this problem any way I want?"

Candace held Melanie's head against her own shoulder and grimaced. "No. That's not my wish."

"Then what is?"

"I haven't decided yet!" Candace sighed through her teeth as Melanie cried louder. "Skragg, I reverse your summoning. Go away until I'm ready for you."

Skragg bit off two words—"Yes, Master"—and went home.

At home, Skragg found more misery than he'd left behind. Blimp had buried himself head-first in the dry red ground. His feet were aimed towards the sky.

Wimp and Shrimp ran in circles around Blimp. "We can play Parcheesi, with real cheese!"

"We'll play submarine commander, and you can be the helicopter!"

"You two," Skragg said. "Don Juan and I need some time to talk, alone."

"We can't abandon our friend," Shrimp said.

"We have to stay together," Wimp said.

There wasn't any sense in asking why. Imps bonded into groups, and once bonded, stayed bonded. Usually, anyway. Skragg had never heard of an imp breaking such a bond, or wanting to bond that way with a human. "Then stay together, but further away."

The imps each hugged one of Blimp's upright legs. "Never!"

Skragg picked up Wimp in his left hand and Shrimp in his right, and brought their faces in front of his own. "I'm asking you politely, one magical being to another, to give me some time alone with your friend. Do you understand how important this is?"

At first, they just looked scared. But eventually, they nodded.

He put them down. "Then you two go play somewhere without him for a while."

Wimp patted Blimp's leg. "Don't forget to pay your insurance premiums." Shrimp patted the other leg and said, "Never put metal in your microwave." They wandered away, drooping like wilted plants.

Skragg yanked Blimp out of the ground, placed him upright, and sat in front of him. "Let's talk."

Blimp said, "I want to marry her."

"You just met her."

Blimp didn't answer right away, which was unusual. If the creature were anything but an imp, Skragg would have sworn he was thinking.

A ball appeared in the imp's hand. "Skragg? What shape is this?"

Skragg played along. "Round."

"And what color is it?"

"Yellow."

"How can you know that? You just met it."

Skragg felt like burying his own head, and staying that way for about a hundred years. "Maybe for imps, romantic love is that simple. But for humans, it's the most complicated thing in the world. And what gets them into trouble is, they want it to be simple. They want it so badly, they fool themselves into not seeing all the complicated parts until they've had three kids, two mortgages, and six affairs."

"I'm not human, Skragg."

This had to be the longest coherent conversation with an imp in the history of imps. "Melanie is. And romantic love has to be right for both parties involved, or it doesn't work."

"She can see me, Skragg! She knows what I really am!"

"That's because her brain doesn't work like other humans'."

"And she *likes* what I am!" The imp sighed. "No one else does."

Self-reflection? In an imp? "That's not true."

"You don't."

"I don't like anybody," Skragg reminded him.

"Well, the other imps don't like me either."

"Of course they do."

Blimp shook slightly, probably from the strain of rational conversation. "The tall one's bossy, and the short one acts like he's smarter than everyone else."

"Smarter? You all act like morons."

"You'd see it if you were an imp." Blimp made a chocolate cake appear and drop-kicked it far into the sky, where it burst into giant butterflies.

Skragg realized he could argue with this imp for the rest of their lives, and not resolve anything. "You're not marrying Melanie."

"Says you."

"Says reality!" Skragg stood up. "Do you honestly think you can spend the rest of your life in the human world?"

"The humans would ignore me. You know that."

"Yes they would, even when you turned one of their leaders into a cotton candy machine because you can't go ten seconds without messing with something. You'd cause more havoc than a war. At least with a war, they could defend themselves. You'd turn their planet upside down because you can't help it, and they'd let you do it because no matter what you did, they'd think the world had always been that way."

"No I wouldn't! I can control myself!"

"You can barely handle linear thought."

"That's not true!" But the imp was trembling like gelatin in an earthquake.

"It isn't? Count to fifty, slowly, aloud."

The imp crossed his arms. "One. Two." Huge beads of sweat grew on his forehead. "Three." His body shook like a ringing bell. "F...F...."

Skragg waited.

The imp leaped into the air. "Fire hydrant! Purple! Cinnamon buns!" He ran in a circle around Skragg. He grew a moustache that fell off his face, turned into a crow, climbed into a tiny jet plane, and flew away.

Blimp raced after his imp friends, screeching and crying.

Skragg tried to believe the problem was over. He failed.

The green man was gone. Melanie felt Candace push her back into her new room. She wanted her old room. She wanted her old mother. Everyone just *pushed* her everywhere, like she was a chair and no one could figure out where to put her. She screamed until she saw the bright colors that sometimes calmed her down, and they helped this time, but not much.

"Mean!" She banged her arms together. "Mean genie! Hates me!"

Behind her, Candace said, "No, he hates me. He doesn't feel anything about you."

Candace went away and came back with the terrible pill bottle and its terrible pills. Melanie clamped her mouth shut and put her fists up. Candace wasn't going to "make her better" without a fight.

Melanie watched Candace stare at her. All the bright energy flowed out of Candace as if *Candace* had lost her home and her mom. Candace could walk and was really smart and pretty and had everything in the world anybody could ever want, and all Melanie wanted was for the green man to come back. And the big genie said no. No, no, no.

"Just one pill," Candace said. "These pills keep you alive, do you understand that?"

Melanie understood *plenty* and didn't back down an inch.

"You'll get tired," Candace said. "You'll get tired of fighting and give in. That's what always happens. The stronger person always wins." She was looking at the floor when she said that. Then she said "Ruth" and left, taking the terrible pills with her.

The next morning, late for work, Candace was trying to help Nurse Gwen get Melanie to eat something. Melanie kept shoving the food away. Gwen said, "Go to work, ma'am."

"She has to eat."

"It'll be better when you're not here."

"Don't say that." Candace put her dress shoes into her purse so the heels stuck out. "Nothing gets done if I'm not here. I should have wished for a maid."

"What?" Gwen asked.

"Never mind."

Candace knew Gwen didn't like her very much. To Gwen's oft-spoken mind, Melanie belonged somewhere she could get round-the-clock care, and the chance to be with other special needs adults. Candace hated the term "special needs." As if the only way your needs could be special was if you were in a wheelchair.

"Imp," Melanie said like a whiny six-year-old.

A chill ran through Candace when she realized just how little patience she had for whiny six-year-olds, and how right Gwen probably was about where Melanie would do best.

Gwen knelt next to Melanie. "There's nothing to be scared of, dear. No imps or goblins are getting in here."

Melanie sobbed.

Gwen gave Candace an accusatory look. "Why is she suddenly scared of monsters? She wasn't like this last week."

Gwen was just the latest person Candace couldn't tell the truth to. Having a genie that only she could know about was a curse, not a blessing.

"You have no idea what scares her. But I can't take any more time off or I won't have a job left to go back to. Maybe you should think about that."

"She needs a group home. There's the American Association for Retarded Adults, the...."

"I promised my dead sister I'd take care of her. All I need is for you to keep her safe, okay? Because God knows I don't know how to do it."

Melanie, still crying, hummed "Here Comes the Bride."

Candace shouted, "You're not marrying an imp!"

Gwen gave Candace a look of such shock and confusion, Candace couldn't stay in the room anymore. She went out to her car.

Time and again Skragg had told her she was one of the luckiest people on Earth. Every ten years, she could have nearly any wish granted. Today she'd have traded all of it for anyone else's idea of bad luck.

In the human world, three days passed. In Skragg's world, where the sunless sky was always golden and bright, Skragg knew only that the imps had attempted to put on five different plays since returning from the human world, and all of them had gone nowhere because Blimp wouldn't stop moping.

Blimp was wearing a t-shirt that said, "I Suffer For Love." Blimp made heart-shaped flowers appear, then stomped on them.

Wimp and Shrimp came up to Skragg. "You have to do something."

"Does ignoring him count?"

"We can't even do plays anymore," said Shrimp. "Every story has to have love in it now."

"It's true!" Wimp said. "We tried to do *Romeo & Juliet!* He wanted to make it a love story!"

Skragg held his temper. "Look, there are things I don't know about imps. Is it normal for an imp to one day become serious?"

Both imps put their hands over their pointy little ears. "Never say the 's' word!"

Blimp wailed. His t-shirt now said, "Pain Is My Destiny."

Shrimp said, "And he won't stop watching the human world. He watches the same thing every time."

Skragg sighed. "Melanie, right?"

"He calls her names, like Love Bunny and Sticky Lumps!"

"How romantic."

Wimp said, "She sings to him! But not to us! And he sings back! The same song Melanie sings! He doesn't change the words or anything!"

Skragg snapped to attention. "They're *communicating*?" He marched past them and lifted Blimp off the ground. "What is the *only* rule about windows into other worlds?"

Blimp sighed. "Keep them shut."

"That's right! You can look and listen and smell all you want, but you never, *ever* reach into...."

Skragg had never heard an imp admit a rule existed. Though logic had always been useless with imps before, Skragg wondered if this time, it just might work. "Blimp, what would your life be like on the human world if you married Melanie?"

Suddenly, Blimp was wearing a tuxedo. "We'd have a ranch with horses and cows and we'd go sailing and we'd have a hundred children and we'd go dancing every night!"

"Melanie can't dance. Are you telling me you'd try to fix her?"

The imp looked utterly confused. "What's wrong with her?"

How could he explain? "She's different in ways that make her life very difficult. She'll never be able to do most of the things other humans build their lives around."

"I think she's great."

Skragg tried a different approach. "How would you survive in the human world? You have no money, no job, no skills, and you destroy everything you walk past."

"I can be a spy! Nobody notices imps, right? And when a bad guy throws me out of an airplane...." An open parachute appeared over his head, then floated down, covering them both.

Skragg incinerated it. "You know, I'm tempted to let you go through with this. You'll be happy for about an hour, then you'll see how much trouble you're in. If you're not going to fix Melanie, then you'll have to give her medications and follow all kinds of rules. You won't last a day. And then what'll happen?"

"I'll do anything for her."

"Yeah? Count to fifty, slowly, aloud."

The imp, still wearing the tuxedo, used a burst of magic to release himself from Skragg's grasp, and straightened his tie. "One. Two. Three." Then the sweating began. "Four. Five." He shook. "Six. Seven. Eig..."

Skragg waited.

"Eig..." Blimp's green face paled. "Eig...." He clenched his fists and yelled, "Egg salad!"

Applause and hooting came from behind Skragg. Wimp and Shrimp were cheering Blimp on.

Skragg told them, "This isn't something to be happy about."

"Of course it is!" Wimp said. "Now, forget about that human and stay with us," he told Blimp. "You're happier here."

Wimp and Shrimp scampered off, juggling eggs that turned into horseshoes that turned into rocking horses.

Blimp remained where he was, stared at the ground, and hugged himself. "Eight," he whispered.

Skragg wandered around his realm for a while, searching for any other possible solution. He found no answers anywhere. So he gritted his teeth and summoned a window into Candace's home. Then he rapped on that window with his spiky, wiry, fiery knuckles.

Candace lay in bed, not sleeping. A bright light appeared in her closet, where she kept Skragg's lamp. She got up and took the lamp out of its box. It had never glowed like this before, but instinctively, she knew what it meant. She rubbed the lamp.

Skragg appeared, his hands and feet lighting the room with a glow exactly like the lamp's. "We have a problem," he said.

"I know." Candace crawled back into her bed. "I thought I could do this. Take care of Melanie, I mean."

Skragg sat on the bed. "You fought against being her guardian all along. I think deep down, you knew you couldn't handle it."

"Which makes me a very bad person."

Skragg leaned towards the nearest wall as if he wanted to bang his head against it. "You can't design skyscrapers, either. Does that make you a bad person?"

Of course a genie wouldn't understand. "I can't keep doing this. I can't concentrate at work, I can't sleep…."

"You don't really need a job, you know. You'll always have 'enough' money, remember?"

"Having a job is about more than money, Skragg. And if I tried to abuse that wish I made, you'd find a way to ruin it. I know you."

Skragg didn't answer.

"Besides," Candace said, "having 'enough' money let me look for a job I'd really like, even if it didn't pay much. I run an office for a bunch of lawyers who handle domestic violence and family cases. They're great at working the system but they can't even keep their own briefcases organized, much less the office. They need me and the world needs them, and

I'm not giving that up. Meanwhile, Melanie won't stop crying over a smelly magical beast she saw once for five minutes."

"It's worse than that. They've been talking all this time, in secret."

Candace looked up. "He remembers her?"

"Imps form bonds instantly. I thought that only happened with other imps, but…."

"So this is something the imp *did* to Melanie?"

"Not the way you mean."

"Then what's going on?"

"Isn't it obvious? I think this is the first time in Melanie's life that anyone's ever liked her exactly the way she is. She's not an idiot, you know."

Candace remembered how Ruth had gone after the neediest orphan she could find. "I'm going to help somebody," Ruth had said. "Somebody everyone else will just let rot." Even to Ruth, Melanie had been more of a project than a daughter.

"You're probably right," Candace said. "But Melanie has three completely separate, incurable medical conditions."

"Incurable for you," Skragg said. "I could cure them. That would solve everything. She'd go off on her own, her 'boyfriend' would see her and get grossed out, and never think about her again."

Candace could no longer imagine any scenario in which she could use that solution and feel good about it. "You were right. Most humans are unhappy a lot of the time. How many people get the chance for the kind of happiness Melanie could have? Maybe this doesn't need solving."

"It absolutely does. I'm not putting up with that imp…."

Candace stopped listening to Skragg's scratchy, complaining voice. But this much of his rant got through to her: the imp was as miserable as Melanie.

When she let her mind float clearly, and she stopped worrying about how impossible everything was, she remembered the power of the genie at her command, and knew what to wish for.

It took Skragg a full week to stop seething. If a wish was selfish enough, it was absolutely within his rights to misinterpret it. Candace's wish was so complicated, he could alter it a thousand different ways. But was she abusing his power for excess personal gain? No. Not when he was honest with himself.

She'd done it again. He was stuck with her for another ten years.

Skragg got everything ready, then appeared in Candace's living room with all three imps: Blimp in the same tuxedo as before, the other two grumbling and worrying that nothing would ever be the same again.

"I don't see what's so special about her," Wimp said.

"Good," Blimp said.

Skragg pulled Blimp into Candace's kitchen. "Last chance."

The imp shook his head.

"Are you sure you understand?" Skragg said. "I'm going to make you human. Your life'll be so limited you can't even imagine it right now."

"My imagination will be better as a human? Won't my life be less limited, then?"

Skragg thought of ten sarcastic replies, then settled for patting the imp's shoulder. "Talk to me in six months."

The imp walked around him like a dog. "You aren't going to change how I feel, though, are you? I'll still be an imp on the inside?"

"That's the deal. But people will notice you now, and what you do will have real consequences. I saw the three-headed giraffe statue the other two put in Candace's neighbor's back yard. The neighbor probably thinks it came with the house. That kind of thing won't happen anymore. You're going to have to be very careful, which is why we can't let you remain an imp. It's also why you and Melanie will be living with Candace."

"I know," the imp said. "It'll be okay, Skragg."

"No word in any language describes what this is going to be, and if one did, 'okay' isn't it." The phrase "class six hurricane" came close, but that was three words.

Skragg had created a spectacular wedding dress for Melanie—one that decorated her wheelchair as much as her body. She was giggling and slowly spinning around and eagerly taking the medication Candace was giving her. That was part of the deal: no in-home nurses, at least not for a while, but Melanie would take her pills and see whatever specialists Candace took her to. And her new husband would go with her to every appointment.

Candace ran over. She was dressed in blue jeans and a sweat shirt. "Skragg, you've made sure this is going to be an official wedding, right?"

"It will be," Skragg said. "But that reminds me." He grabbed Blimp again. "What do you want your name to be? And it has to be a human name."

"I get a choice?"

"Any name you want."

The imp thought for a moment. "Jeremiah Sandstone Agnew Fistivius Bond the Tenth."

"No."

Melanie came over and took the imp's hand. "Lester," she said.

Skragg looked at Candace, who shrugged.

"Lester it is," Skragg said. "Is he taking your last name?"

"Ruth adopted Melanie under her own married name," Candace said. "So it'll be Melanie and Lester Cordon."

"Okay then," Skragg said. "Let's get this over with."

Skragg, tired of slouching, magically raised the ceilings in Candace's house to ten feet, then took his place at the head of the living room, between the flat-screen TV and a bookcase. Melanie slid into the space made for her, just a few feet in front of him and to his right. The imp waddled into the spot Melanie was staring at. Melanie took the imp's claws in her hand. Her face shone like a spotlight and the imp was still and patient. In the back, Wimp and Shrimp giggled nervously. A few of their green scales turned brown and dropped off, the imp equivalent of crying.

Candace stood behind Melanie with her hands out as if she were afraid Melanie's huge, heavy chair would tip over and she'd have to catch it. The complex expression on her face mixed melancholy, pride, relief, disappointment, and possibly a touch of jealousy.

Skragg leaned over to Candace and whispered, "They'll never survive without your supervision. Three people are getting married today, not two."

"I know. But we'll have enough money, right? Even with my new responsibilities, that wish still holds?"

"Enough for everything you really need, and yes, these two count as a need. I just don't understand why you're doing this."

The war of feelings in her face settled into a grim smile. "That imp is steadfast, loyal, and dumb. He'll be the perfect husband for her. I've made a lot of mistakes in my life, Skragg, but this isn't one of them."

Skragg was slightly amazed to find himself wondering what some of those mistakes might have been. He hadn't paid that much attention to her, even when watching the human world. In fact he usually watched everyone *but* her. He did, though, catch one tone in her voice she wasn't admitting to. "You wouldn't be happy with steadfast, loyal, and dumb. You'd want more."

She wiped her eyes and said nothing.

Everyone was waiting for him to start. Candace was still deeply conflicted and the fears and desires he sensed in her made his whole body itch. He whispered to Candace, "Do you know where that belief about genies and three wishes came from?"

Candace shook her head.

"Hardly anybody *ever* makes it past three wishes without abusing the magic. What every human really wants, deep down, is to remake the world the way they think it should be. Usually that means they should be the richest and most famous person ever. Or they want to rule the world because they think they have all the answers."

Candace choked off a laugh. "That's me, all right. All the answers." She stared at Melanie. "I can't talk to anybody about this. Not at work. Not anywhere. Who'd believe I've got a genie? I don't tell anybody anything. I wish…."

Skragg aimed every bit of his attention right at Candace. If she asked for another wish now, that would be a second wish in the same ten-year span, and a clear violation of the rules. He'd be free of her.

Candace said, "I wish I knew the right way to use a genie."

It was not, Skragg understood, the kind of wish that would break his bond with her. In fact, it produced the opposite effect.

Skragg watched "Lester" and Melanie giggle and play some kind of game involving singing and making their hands move along Melanie's wheelchair like crawling spiders. Melanie's whole face glowed like the lamp in a lighthouse. Lester's eyes were just as bright, and focused entirely on Melanie. Even Wimp and Shrimp stood mesmerized.

In a low voice Skragg said, "This is the right way."

And he couldn't take much more of it. "How does this stupid ceremony start again?"

Candace said, "'Dearly Beloved, we are gathered here today—'" and Skragg gagged. "Never mind. I'll wing it."

Skragg took a deep breath and filled the room with his booming, raspy voice. "Merely Tolerated, we are gathered here today to infuriate every traditionalist on Earth. Imp, do you have the ring?"

Blimp let go of Melanie's hands and looked scared, then thoughtful. He summoned a hula hoop and placed it around Melanie and her wheelchair. Melanie laughed.

Skragg sighed. "Now, Lester."

Blimp looked around the room.

"That's you," Candace said.

The imp's face went from excited green to embarrassed red. "Ready."

Skragg glowed with power. The imp grew to almost twice his original height, and slimmed down a little, and his tough green hide melted away into flesh. Dark hair grew on his newly human head. A five-foot-four pudgy human male in a perfectly-fitting tuxedo stood before them all.

Skragg let Lester's human nose stay as warty as the imp version, because he sensed Melanie liked it that way. "Melanie, do you accept Lester as your husband?"

Melanie banged her clenched left hand against her wheelchair twice. "I do."

"Lester, do you accept Melanie as your wife?"

"I love her," he said.

For his first human words, those weren't bad. "Then by my astonishing power as an awesome, butt-kicking Elder Genie, I now pronounce you two married."

Magic blasted across the entire planet. Paperwork was filled out, photographs appeared, computer files were updated. Every government office in the world had every official record about the marriage anyone would ever need.

Lester kissed Melanie. Wimp and Shrimp waved their arms, and fireworks streaked across the room, bounced off walls, and turned into freshly baked corn muffins. It was probably some kind of protest, but right then, Skragg didn't care.

He looked to Candace. She was staring at the still-embraced Lester and Melanie with eyes so deep Skragg thought he could have reached into them.

She stepped next to him but didn't take her eyes off the bride and groom. "What's horrible is, I'm happiest that I don't have to take care of her anymore."

"Are you kidding?" Skragg asked. "Now you've got *two* people you need to watch every second."

"No," she said. "He'll be everything she needs. They can live here as long as they want, but he'll be her guardian, not me." But her worry was as deep as her eyes.

"There's nothing awful about knowing your limits, Candace. Everyone has them." He lowered his voice again. "Speaking of which, these two won't be giving you grandchildren. I don't know what an imp-turned-human would produce and I don't want to find out."

She nodded. "Thank you. Please don't go yet. You're the only one who could ever understand and I need to talk to somebody about all this."

"You know how this works. I granted your wish. Now I get to leave."

"And do what?" She faced him squarely. "Look me right in the eyes and tell me you've got something better to do."

Skragg couldn't.

Lester finally broke his embrace with Melanie, but kept holding her hands. "Skragg," he chided in his new voice, "you forgot our vows. We wrote our own."

Skragg rolled his eyes. "This I've got to hear."

The room quieted. Lester took a deep breath, and so did Melanie. Together, they counted to fifty, slowly, aloud.

Lending Luck

Cheryl Rydbom

EVEN IN EARLY evening, the full moon shone brightly, causing the trees to cast eerie shadows that the torchlight couldn't penetrate. Fireflies danced and the priestess spoke the ancient words, but Raelin wasn't listening. Instead, she stared numbly down at the white silk cord binding her wrist to that of the man—the stranger—beside her. Somehow her two-day leave had turned into a handfasting ceremony.

Raelin wiggled her cold toes, in an attempt to dislodge damp blades of grass. Her attention shifted to the deep shadows of the forest. Nervous energy plucked at her spine as she listened to the night. Nothing sounded wrong, but that didn't mean anything. After fighting for years in the war against the Fomori, she knew that there was always the slight possibility that one of the soul-devouring, black-scaled demons, could slip through the Line. There were too many of them and too few clansmen. She eyed the shadows warily, knowing that if one was there, she wasn't in any position to stop it when it attacked.

She bit back a snarl of frustration, flexing the muscles in her wrist. The ceremonial knot was too tight. She couldn't pull free if something happened. The cord would have to be cut. That was a problem. Her mother had taken her sword before the ceremony, and her knives were with her motorcycle back at the house.

Her gaze settled on the altar. Outlined in candles, strewn with flowers, it held the priestess' tools. Raelin relaxed. Right in the center, next to a silver whistle, was an athame clearly made of Blessed Steel. The blade glowed a silvery blue, even in the firelight. *Now* she had a plan.

"Raelin?"

Her name drew her attention back to the priestess, although after four years at the Front, she was more used to her surname. Judging by the priestess' countenance, it wasn't the first time her name had been called.

At her unapologetic bow, the priestess smiled faintly and said, "Raelin Shayla Mallory, do you willingly and with an open heart, enter this binding to last a year and a day…"

Again, the words blended into noise, and Raelin's attention went back to the night. The ceremony was a farce. No one really expected a lifer to raise a family. Not a female lifer. Raelin had already given her soul. She'd chosen the warrior's path and had the blessing of the Morrigu, Goddess of War, Fate, and Death. Tradition might dictate that her people wed and produce the next generation of fighters, but Raelin had always assumed she'd be exempt.

The silk around her wrist belied that assumption.

A crow cried out from its perch at the top of a nearby tree, causing her to jump. The priestess was no longer speaking. The old woman's rheumy blue eyes narrowed at her expectantly. Raelin glanced at her mother for insight. Her mother had squeezed her eyes shut tight as she strangled a bouquet of wildflowers.

Enlightened, Raelin said, "I do?"

At her words, her mother opened her eyes and expelled some air, the priestess clicked her tongue, and the crow cackled. Raelin didn't check to see what her betrothed thought. She still hadn't looked at him. It didn't matter what he looked like. In her mind, he was either stupid or ugly. Why else would a perfectly sound man tie himself to a perfect stranger, much less a lifer?

"You may seal the binding with a kiss," the priestess intoned.

Raelin frowned. She already had to hold his limp fingers. Now they had to kiss? When she didn't move, the priestess pursed her lips. Resigned, and shoulders sagging, she closed her eyes and lifted her chin toward the man. Lips brushed hers in a chaste, impersonal kiss.

She felt a surge of hope. A man desperate for a woman wouldn't have held back like that. Maybe he was caught up in the same traditions and requirements that had snared her. Perhaps he'd be okay with the letter of the vows. She could remain just as faithful to him from the Front as she could from her mother's house. At the end of the year, they could tell the priestess it hadn't worked. No marriage, no babies.

Raelin flashed the priestess a wide, teeth-baring smile, startling the wrinkled old bat.

While her mother fiddled with the knot binding their wrists, Raelin finally gave into curiosity and looked at her betrothed. He was tall and broad, but that much had been obvious. He wasn't ugly. He was even attractive, with dark eyes, strong, angular features and wavy, black hair.

But while his hands were calloused and flecked with marks, if any were blade scars, they'd long since faded. Even his nose was perfectly straight. No evidence of battle marked his skin, unlike hers. Angry red lines crisscrossed her arms. Her knuckles were slashed and her nails were broken. Worst of all, her face was marked: her first year at the Front, a Fomori had clawed her from jaw to temple.

She was lean, hard, and scarred.

The man's billowing, traditional linen shirt hid his frame. Not ugly, but probably soft and fat. Definitely a poor match for a lifer.

Of all the ill-gotten luck, she'd come home to find her mother and the priestess waiting with the man they'd handpicked for her. She should have stayed at the Front. They wouldn't have come for her there.

The long buried memory of a young boy surfaced, eyes round and earnest as he quoted his papa, "Luck never gives; it only lends."

She scowled. She'd always hated that proverb, but it seemed fitting today. She supposed that Luck was cashing her out. What had been that boy's name again? Cal? All she could remember about him was that he'd called her something dreadful.

She glanced up and found the man studying her with the same mild curiosity that she'd been studying him.

"Do I measure up, Rae-Rae?" he asked, with just the smallest hint of a grin.

Raelin's eyes narrowed. Was he mocking her with his casual familiarity? She opened her mouth to return the insult, but then snapped it shut, flushing. She didn't know his name. The priestess would have said it during the ceremony, but she couldn't recall hearing it.

The cord dropped to the ground.

She pulled her hand free from his.

"Nice to meet you..." she trailed off, giving him an opening.

He raised a dark eyebrow, but only bowed in acknowledgement.

Caleb Pennant pulled off his helmet, and leaned forward on his bike to peer around the trees. He hadn't really expected Rae to fall into his arms in rapturous bliss after their handfasting, but he'd hoped that she'd stick around long enough to talk.

Instead, she'd bolted as soon as her mother untied the silk cord.

Now he sat, hidden by shadows, outside the Mallory house, feeling like a stalker. He cursed his own particular hell, love at first sight, or technically, love at second sight. He cursed the fact that Rae had been so tied up at the Front that they hadn't gotten a chance to talk before the ceremony. And he cursed the mess that he now had to fix.

But when she'd come into his shop, just two months ago, for a simple oil change, he'd lost his heart without even exchanging two words with her. He'd only learned her name later and recognized it. By then he'd been so afraid that some other man would claim her that he'd forgone courting and had immediately petitioned her priestess.

In hindsight, he probably should have approached her first.

When Mrs. Mallory pulled into the driveway, she glanced in his direction but didn't wave.

A few minutes later the front screen door banged open and Rae stomped out, saddle bags flung over her shoulder, and scabbarded sword clutched in her hand. Gone was the ephemeral wood nymph from the ceremony, replaced by a goddess of death.

Caleb's pulse quickened. She was beautiful.

"Raelin Shayla Mallory!" Her mother stood on the tiny porch, hands on hips, her toe tapping.

Rae looked skyward for an instant before returning to her mother. With her head drooping and shoulders slumping, Caleb could finally see his childhood friend in the grown woman. She had looked the same then whenever she'd been scolded.

He got off his bike and wove through the tall, scraggly pines toward the women as Rae wrapped her mother in a hug.

"Tell my betrothed…." She pulled away, not finishing the sentence.

He cleared his throat. "Tell me yourself."

She whirled, automatically stepping between the threat and her mother. Moonlight caught on the silvery blue of her knife. It had appeared in her hand as if by magic. He froze, but did not back away.

Her mother laid a gentle hand on her shoulder and whispered something. Recognition flashed, and Rae sheathed the knife with obvious exasperation.

Caleb wanted to tease her until she laughed, but he'd been warned that she was not the carefree girl he remembered from their childhood. Four long years at the Front would do that to a person. He'd only served his two obligatory years and still had nightmares about the demons, five years later. How much worse would it be for her?

So instead he stood silent and frowning, waiting for her to speak.

Finally she said, "I'm going back to the Front. I'll try to come home at the next full moon. We can discuss the handfasting then."

Mrs. Mallory sighed heavily and went back into her house without another word, her progress followed by two pairs of eyes.

Caleb waited until the door closed. "I go where you go."

"What?" Rae blinked at him. Her cool, detached mask slipped, and he saw a little more of the girl.

"That's typically how betrothals work," he said as he fought to keep from smiling.

"Look," she said, edging away. "I'll honor my vow, but we aren't going to work. We won't be getting married. It's not you. I'm sure you're a lovely person. It's just that I'm not marrying anyone."

She took the last few steps to the gravel drive, and dumped her bags onto the back of a bike that looked like it was being held together by duct tape and prayers. Without even glancing up, she said, "I'll see you around."

Caleb jogged back to his bike, pulled on his helmet, and waited. When she pulled out onto the road, he flicked on his lights and followed.

Raelin swore steadily during the long ride to the coast. She kept willing him to go home, but the single headlight in her mirror never faltered.

When she pulled into the war camp's makeshift garage, parking her dilapidated bike beside other piecemeal motorcycles, her temper had peaked, but the shiny, Italian motorcycle that pulled in beside her choked the words in her throat. It was worth more than her mother's house. Was he insane bringing it to the Front?

The war camp was the last line of defense against the Fomori. It shifted to compensate for any new incursions. Everything here was temporary, inexpensive, and expendable. Equipment, bikes, lifers.

She gaped between the bike and the man. Its extravagance was out of place in the garage, but he didn't seem to care.

"Who's your war chief?" he asked.

She answered automatically, still staring, "Erik Syrus."

He nodded and gestured for her to lead the way. "I know of him, but you should probably introduce us."

"Nice bike," she said as they walked, managing to convey both her admiration and scorn.

He chuckled, his smile wide enough to reveal dimples.

Raelin's hackles rose. He'd trapped her into a handfasting, followed her home, and now was laughing at her?

His smile vanished. "Forgive me. It's just that I knew you'd say that."

She clenched her fists. "And what is that supposed to mean?"

He opened his mouth, closed it, and then tried again. "Maybe I'm just a good judge of character."

"Lieutenant?" The war chief's sentry saluted.

Both of them glared at the boy and he seemed to shrink down into his boots under the weight of their combined stares.

Raelin returned his salute. She hated scaring the kids. This one was so fresh from civilization that his leather armor had squeaked when he raised his arm. "I need to talk to the war chief."

"Is that Mallory, boy? Send her in," a voice boomed from the drab, olive tent.

Gas lamps lit the room in a soft, warm glow. War Chief Erik Syrus stood hunched over a large, tattered map taped to an old wooden table. The furrow between his eyebrows was deeper than usual.

"Mallory," he said, without bothering to look up. "You're back. Good. I need you in the field tonight."

"War Chief?" she asked, surprised. Technically, her leave did not end until tomorrow.

"Something's not right," he said. "I need your eyes out there."

He tapped a spot on the map, and both Raelin and her betrothed stepped forward to take a closer look. The extra shadow caught the war chief's attention. "Who's this?"

"He's my...." Raelin trailed off, glancing at the big man. "We're...."

"Caleb Pennant." He held out his hand in the modern custom.

The war chief's eyebrows rose and he all but tripped over the table, extending his own hand and elbowing Raelin out of the way. She stared between them, perplexed, as she rolled his name over her tongue, committing it to memory. It sounded familiar.

"Is there a problem with the requisition?" Syrus asked. "Tell me it's not the funds."

"No, War Chief, everything is still on schedule. My family is minding the shop while I'm here. You'll get your blades." Pennant smiled and released the war chief's hand. "I'm here with Raelin. We were handfasted this evening."

The war chief blinked, eyebrows furrowed. Raelin's face got hot.

"What'd you do to piss off the gods, boy?" the war chief finally asked, with a bark of laughter. "The region's most talented swordsmith paired with a lifer."

Raelin sucked in some air, startled. The swords. That's why his name was familiar. Caleb Pennant was the only crafter of Blessed Steel in the New World. Before he'd opened his smithy, the various American outposts had been supplied by Old World smiths, at great expense. If the rumors were true, he forged the weapons at cost, refusing to profit from the Front. He also owned an auto shop, which everyone within driving distance was quick to support, including Raelin's own mother. Her mother drove two hours there and back just to get her car serviced. Raelin had even gone along the last time, but she hadn't seen him.

She blanched, remembering that on that trip, her mother had told her that the Pennants had once lived next door, and that Raelin had followed the youngest son around like a puppy. Now that Pennant son was looking at her, intently, almost challengingly.

"Well...." The war chief laughed again and clapped her on the back. "Congratulations, Mallory. Now collect a team and go. I need to know what those soul-suckers are up to tonight."

She shook herself and saluted. "Yes, War Chief."

She nodded at Caleb Pennant and left without a backward glance.

Raelin felt a little lost when she ducked into her tent and lit the lamp. Not that anything in there had changed, but that everything else had. She dragged her footlocker out from under her cot and pulled out her fighting gear. By the time she'd donned the odd, but comfortable, mix of leather, Blessed Steel chain mail, and Kevlar, she felt a little more grounded.

It said a lot about her night, that she wanted to be on the other side of the wall, fighting the Fomori. The demons attacked the Line night after night trying to break through to feast on the unsuspecting masses. She'd dedicated her life to stopping them. She needed that purpose after the evening's ceremony.

As she strapped on her weapons, she searched her childhood memories for Pennant, but none of the young, blurry faces matched the big man. It was disconcerting to think that they'd been friends once.

Raelin was distracted as she headed for the wall to meet her team, so distracted that she missed the towering, black shadow that stepped into her path.

"Good scout you'll make tonight," said the smith, with soft chuckle.

She scowled. He was the last person she wanted to see. "Not now, Pennant. I've got to go."

He held up a hand. "Please, this will just take a second."

She ground her teeth.

"Syrus won't let me join your team. He seems to think I'm out of practice hunting Fomori." He looked a little angry, but Raelin couldn't help feeling relieved. She wasn't up for tourist duty.

He reached into his jacket and pulled out a large satin sachet. "I have a handfasting gift for you."

Reluctantly, she took it, catching a whiff of dried flowers. It was heavier than one would expect from a bag of herbs, but it was beautiful, intricately embroidered with white runes. It was not, however, something you gave a lifer.

She forced a smile. "Thanks."

"Open it."

A blending of scents hit her, clean and pure. "Nice. I smell lavender. What else?"

"Acacia and columbine," he answered with a touch of impatience. "It's not just a bag of potpourri."

She reached two fingers in, fishing through the dried flowers until she hit something solid. The oblong object was the length of her hand. It sort of looked like a large pocketknife, but it glowed the faint blue of Blessed Steel. She raised a quizzical eyebrow. Only traditional weapons and armor could be crafted with that metal.

He took it from her, ran his thumb down its length, then flicked. A silvery blue blade whipped out.

"A switchblade?" she breathed. "Out of Blessed Steel? Will it work?"

Pennant thumbed the catch again and the blade vanished. He held the knife out to her and she took it with reverence.

"Honestly, I don't know. Everything about it is made of the divine, but I've had no way to test it," he said.

She ran her thumb over the hilt, finding the catch and tripping it. The blade leapt free as smoothly for her as it had for him.

"Do you know what this means?" she asked, excitement building. "That you can make modern weapons blessed by the gods?"

"It's just the one knife for now, Rae." Pennant grinned and his deep dimples flashed.

She looked between him and the knife. It *was* the perfect betrothal gift for a lifer. She was suddenly aware that he was too close and that it was getting hard to breathe. Standing in his shadow she felt five years old and nothing like a warrior.

His smile vanished. "What's wrong?"

She wanted to take a step back, but that would be weak. She closed the blade and returned it to the pouch, still struggling for air. "I can't accept this, Pennant. I don't want to be bound to you."

He took it from her outstretched hand, but then he stepped even closer to drop its long cord over her head. It fell heavily against her chest. She opened her mouth to protest, but he said, "It's the autumnal equinox. It's a full moon. I am Brighid's chosen and the Morrigu was in attendance tonight."

Raelin paled. She had heard the crow. Could that have really been the Goddess of War?

Pennant caught her face between his hands, and tipped up her chin. "I know it's not what you wanted, Rae, but you spoke the words. We are bound."

She locked eyes with him, feeling an odd mix of fear and awe. And then his lips touched hers. She tried not to react, not to move, but while their first kiss had been impersonal and forgettable, this one held heat and promises. His mouth moved slowly, seductively. His lips were soft. His hands on her face were gentle, but under that, she could sense his strength, his steel. Her lips parted, almost against her will, and then she was kissing him. And it felt right. It felt like they fit, and she forgot about everything but him.

Until, nearby, a dark, masculine laugh turned into a cough. Raelin stiffened and Pennant pulled away, a growl rumbling up through his chest. The war chief was walking toward the gate, pointedly not looking at them.

Raelin cursed.

"You can say that again," said the smith, but his eyes were twinkling.

She felt her lips curve up into a smile and stamped it down. She glared at him instead, holding up the sachet. "And what am I supposed to do with all this? Use it for luck?"

"Just keep it close tonight." He caught her chin between his thumb and forefinger before she could slide away. "Surely you remember what my papa always says about luck, Rae-Rae."

Caleb stood on the wall, watching Rae lead her small band of six through the gate and into the night. His lips still tingled with the kiss and he was itchy to pick a fight with Erik Syrus for interrupting it. It was all he could to do hold his tongue, while she went into danger without him.

"It's what she does, Pennant," Syrus said, standing beside him.

"Who is going with her?" Caleb didn't really care. He just needed the distraction.

Syrus squinted. "Four second years and two first years." He paused then added, "If Mallory thought it would be dangerous, she'd have brought another lifer and left the first years behind. She's obsessed with protecting the kids, making sure they all make it home."

"Who makes sure that she comes home?" asked Caleb.

The silhouettes of the team blended into the forest's shadows, vanishing. Syrus was silent for several long minutes.

"Your priestess didn't randomly pair you with Mallory, did she, son?" he asked.

Caleb's shoulders sagged. He sent a quick prayer of protection chasing after Rae. "No, it definitely was not chance."

Waves lazily lapped at the rocks far below. A quick glance at the stars told Raelin that it was nearly midnight. Only five hours since she'd been betrothed. She licked her lips.

How could this have happened to her? Memories of little Cal kept resurfacing. He'd had those same dimples back then and she'd been jealous when her mother told her that they were something you were born with. She remembered that he could name any car just by hearing its engine. He'd tugged her braids and teased her, but he'd told the best stories.

She had cried when his family moved away so his dad could open an auto shop.

And now they were handfasted and blessed by two goddesses, if he was right. His betrothal gift told her that it wasn't an accident. It wasn't priestesses arbitrarily matching up unpaired clansmen and women. He'd known her name and her calling, and had still chosen her.

A crow's cry tore through the night. Raelin glared up into the black trees. If goddesses were going to follow her around, at least they could be quiet.

She stared down at the shoreline, from the high cliffs, and knew that something had changed. Her team never should have been able to get so close to the Fomori stronghold. Even alone, she'd never been this close. Not at night. On every other night, the demons were out in droves, first testing the Line for weaknesses, and then just before dawn, just before the sun banished them, they rushed the gate.

Uneasy, she gestured for her team to fan out in the shadows along the cliff. The Fomori stronghold was built on the shore. It extended up into the sea caves, and down into the ocean's depths. They were nocturnal and amphibious. With every setting sun, they slithered out of the water to hunt for blood and souls.

Time passed, but the only night creatures Raelin heard were crickets, owls, and rodents. The ground was damp and cold beneath her and smelled of mulch, with just the hint of rotting fish.

Fish.

She raised her nose to the wind and the smell of dead fish grew. She crept toward the cliff's precipice, staring down into the water.

A yellow-white light suddenly blazed from the depths. Raelin's breath caught in her throat, even as she scrambled back into the shadows. Hundreds of Fomori hung suspended in the water. They hung in unmoving obeisance all *facing* the light.

The Fomori were afraid of light, ultra-sensitive. Outside of Blessed Steel, artificial light was her clansmen's only real defense against them.

She leaned out again. Something dark and massive burst through the light from the depths of the sea. Muscular arms stretched out from broad, heavy shoulders while water cascaded down in a waterfall that dwarfed the rocky cliffs. A wail rose from the ocean's depths. The towering form solidified into a decidedly masculine frame. Horns sprouted from his head, while powerful legs separated from the geyser. A spear appeared in his right clawed hand and a shield in his left.

He threw back his head, mouth wider than any human's, and bellowed at the moon. The Fomori, no longer unmoving, writhed in what could be either ecstasy or agony.

Raelin froze. Every muscle in her body locked, her blood turned to ice, and she ceased breathing. She knew who he was and for that one instant, she was immobilized by terror. Only one being, one god, could keep the Fomori from their relentless, mindless hunger for humanity: Balor, the Demon King.

The crow screamed, jolting Raelin into action. She raised her fist and signaled for her team to take flight.

The shrieks and cries of a thousand Fomori rent the night and the ground shook with Balor's rage. They'd heard the Morrigu's warning and taken it as a challenge.

Raelin and her team fled.

The trees conspired against them, branches slashing their faces, roots tripping them. Raelin ran behind the last of her team, one of her first years. He kept looking back over his shoulder, his eyes too wide, stumbling on the uneven ground.

"Just run!"

He didn't hear her. The next time he looked back a root sent him sprawling. Raelin tried to yank him up without breaking stride, but he fought her.

When the first Fomori reached them, Raelin whirled, sword naked, and swung at the tide. Each slash connected, but it was like fighting the sea. There were too many. Claws ripped at her chain mail while stones and crude spears thudded against her Kevlar.

The first year's grunt of pain reminded her that she wasn't alone. She had a boy to protect. She groped at her hip, sword still swinging in wide arcs and drew a flare gun. It had two shots. She fired one directly into approaching horde.

As Fomori cringed away from the fiery missile, Raelin spun toward the boy and dragged him to his feet. He looked at her with glassy, uncomprehending eyes.

She gave him a little shake. "Run!"

He didn't react. She smacked him. Nothing.

A Fomori snarled behind her.

"Hold the Line!" she barked.

He blinked and recognition finally flared. She shoved him toward the gate and he ran.

She tore after him. From the corner of her eye, she caught movement. The Fomori were flanking them. When the first launched itself, Raelin dove, intercepting it. The boy kept running.

Her sword plunged into the demon's scaly spine. She rolled and tried to stand, but five more took its place. She swung wildly, trying to buy room, but she only got to her knees before they closed in too tightly.

The rotting fish smell was so strong that Raelin gagged. She inhaled through her mouth and could almost taste them. Her world shrank to the tree at her back and the horde in front of her. She moved to block a reaching claw with her off-hand, remembering, just in time, that she still held the flare gun.

She twisted her arm, protecting the fragile plastic. A Fomori's sharp nails grazed the weapon, as they ripped through the leather of her gloves to catch in the blessed chain links. Raelin swung her sword, severing the claw, and with a quick, silent apology to the goddesses and the smith, fired the last flare into the night sky.

"*There?* Did you see that?" Caleb asked, pointing to the arcing streak of pink light.

It was the second flare. They'd almost missed the first. It hadn't even cleared the trees.

"What the hell?" asked Syrus.

An alarm sounded. Lights flared, illuminating the clearing between the gate and the forest. Two clansmen broke from the trees, sprinting toward the gate. Syrus descended the ladder to meet them. Caleb hesitated, straining to see Rae. A third clansman broke free of the shadows. One of them *had* to be her.

He slid down the ladder.

One of Rae's second years had already collapsed in the relative safety of the garrison. She was gulping water when Caleb joined Syrus.

"Easy, easy." The war chief was squatting beside the girl, looking almost paternal. "What did you see?"

The girl's face was streaked with mud and paint. Terror had turned her lips gray. "Don't know, War Chief. Never…There were so many."

The next three clansmen were even less forthcoming. All were terrified, all were incoherent and Caleb was furious with them. He paced by the open gate searching the shadows for Rae. As each clansman broke free of the forest into the safety of the light, he grew angrier.

The fifth clansman, a second year, stumbled through the gate, looking just as terrified as the others, but kept his feet. With wide eyes, he scanned the crowd until he found Syrus.

"I think that it's Balor," he said, jaw so taut the words almost didn't come out.

A lifer, crouching next to one of cowering kids, snickered. A few others nervously joined in.

"At ease!" snapped Syrus. The laughter and chatter died and he handed the boy a canteen. "What did you see, son?"

The boy took a shaky breath, then a swig of water, rinsing his mouth and spitting. "It was insane. All the Fomori were in the ocean when Balor rose. Did you see the light? It didn't hurt them. They even liked it."

Icy tendrils wrapped around Caleb's heart. He knew the story of Balor. He'd even tried to scare Rae with it when they were kids. He'd been so proud of himself, telling her about how the god-king of the Fomori appeared every five hundred years, bringing death to the clansmen who stood against him.

Rae had just focused on the single grain of hope from his retelling. That if they destroyed him, the clansmen would have seven years of peace before the Fomori would recover enough to plague them again. She'd wanted Balor to come.

A few more lifers rolled their eyes and shook their heads. Believing in the demons was one thing, an absentee god was another. But Caleb knew enough not to discount it as a children's story. His people lived the myths. He knew that better than most, working Blessed Steel under the watchful eye of Brighid. Gods and goddesses were real. Balor, God of Death, was undoubtedly real, and Rae was out there with him.

The last member of her team, a first year, stumbled through the gate, ashen and visibly shaking, his armor was torn and his weapons gone. Caleb was the closest, so he handed him his own canteen.

"Where's Rae?" he asked softly.

The boy stared at him blankly, and Caleb cursed. "Raelin Mallory. Your lieutenant. Where is she?"

Blinking his too-round eyes, the boy mumbled, "She told me to run."

Every muscle in Caleb's body went rigid. Through clenched teeth, he asked, "What?"

The boy took a ragged breath. He tried to meet Caleb's eyes but flinched away from whatever he saw. Caleb jerked him up by his armor. The canteen hit the ground with a dull thud. Water seeped into the earth.

"Where's Rae?" he roared, inches from the boy's face.

The boy's composure crumbled and he sobbed. Caleb threw him up against the wall, shouting for an answer. Hands grabbed at Caleb's arms, trying to pull him back, but he shrugged them off.

"Pennant!" Syrus' authority cut through Caleb's fury.

Caleb stared at his hands still clutching the boy's leather shirt and released him. The boy crumpled, arms going protectively over his head as he cried.

Raelin woke in utter blackness with a huge headache. She'd been dreaming about crows turning into crones and boys changing into men and then back into boys again. Nothing had stayed constant, everything had moved, flowed, changed. Even rocks had become demons and mountains, gods.

She shook it off and had to fight a wave of nausea. She sat up slowly, clutching her temples, and wondered if she was blind.

Blind was better than dead. She could live with blind. Her knuckles brushed a bit of slimy rock above her head. Bits of memory intruded on her present as she explored her surroundings. Hordes of Fomori. A three foot ceiling. Caleb Pennant. Balor. A jagged, rocky floor puddled with sea water. Balor. Cal. The pervasive smell of rotting fish. Balor? Balor!

Why was she even alive? Fomori didn't leave humans alive. They were desperate to feed. Her dead body should be lying in the forest, her soul devoured.

Two glowing red globes flared several feet away and she jumped, scrambling away from the demon.

"Small blessings," she reminded herself, as she frantically groped for a weapon. She was not blind and not dead.

But her sheaths were empty and her armor was destroyed. The Kevlar was mostly intact, but the leather was shredded, and all of the blessed mail was gone.

The Fomori hissed at her and Raelin recoiled, madly scraping at the ground, searching for anything useful. It clicked its tongue and hissed again. Its eyes narrowed and widened with each sound.

It was trying to talk to her. Raelin shuddered. The beast inched closer and she backed against the wall. Trapped and, except for the creature's glowing red eyes, blind.

It narrowed its eyes again and it hissed long and low. It took a step closer and she lashed out with her foot. She connected, but the demon didn't so much as blink. It took another step and she kicked again. This time the Fomori caught her ankle and twisted. She thrashed, trying to pull her leg out of its taloned grasp.

Its eyes suddenly vanished, taking her sight. It moved, and then she was being dragged. Panicked, she kicked harder. The Fomori twisted her leg so savagely she howled. Her head cracked against the uneven, wet, stone ground. When the pain subsided, she struggled again. Same result.

After what seemed like miles, the Fomori released its grip on her leg. Wet and aching, Raelin struggled to get her bearings. The stench of fish was overpowering, but the tiniest hint of a breeze teased her skin. Around her, demons hissed and snarled, while somewhere in the distance, waves crashed against rock. But mostly, flickers of red light winked in and out.

There were hundreds of eyes.

She bit back a curse and once again blindly searched her surroundings for a weapon. There was nothing. No rocks, nothing loose.

The horde's snarls, hisses, and growls morphed into a collective hum. She froze, mind frantically trying to come up with an escape plan.

The hum steadily increased in pitch until it drowned out thought and she was vibrating from it. Just as she reached her hands up to cover her ears, the room exploded in vicious white-yellow light.

The Demon God roared triumphantly and the Fomori howled. Raelin shielded her streaming eyes enough to see past his unholy aura. Her heart stuttered. His single onyx eye was fixed on her.

"The gate is not opening again tonight," said Syrus. "If you won't go home, at least take this sword and try to stay out of the way."

The sword was well made, but Caleb knew instinctively that it hadn't been one of his. Syrus stepped onto the ladder.

"What about Rae?"

"You can't do anything to help her." Syrus paused, looking up at him. "That's what the second flare meant...."

Caleb snarled. "I damn well know what a second flare is supposed to mean, but she's still alive. I'd know if she wasn't. We're bound together."

Syrus didn't react and Caleb wanted to hit him, although he doubted it would help. Terrifying the boy hadn't helped. Playing sentry wouldn't help. He needed to get to Rae.

Then, very quietly, Syrus said, "If Mallory is out there, she's on her own. If you go, we lose the only man who can forge the weapons that will keep us fighting."

Caleb shook his head. "I taught my father and my brothers. They'll carry on."

"They too have been blessed by Brighid?"

Caleb hedged, "She has no objection to them working her metal."

Syrus' steady gaze wrung a more thorough answer from him. "They can work my designs but no more."

The war chief let a long pause fill the distance between them before he said, "Honor your goddess as Mallory honored hers."

Caleb stared out across the illuminated field, watching the horde of demons writhe in the forest's shadows. There was no way to tell how many waited. The Front's defense of floodlights suddenly seemed flimsy, laughable, but he couldn't make himself care.

Rae was out there alone.

"Fuel needed at the southern tower," called a sentry.

Someone tried to crank an old Jeep waiting nearby. It was loaded and ready to move, but the engine wouldn't catch. A girl swore and Caleb glanced down at the small group of kids that had gathered around it. The girl's high pitched oath had almost made him smile. He had no doubt that Rae would swear like that.

He slammed his fist into the wall and cursed. He could play sentry or he could be useful. With an oath of his own, he jumped off the wall, forsaking the ladder. He shoved several milling kids out of the way and stuck his head under the hood. He quickly tightened the loose battery cable and signaled for the girl to crank it again. The engine sputtered once before roaring to life.

He let the hood fall closed. Two things happened at once. The horde screamed, thunderously charging, and a sudden sparkle of silver caught Caleb's eye.

The ground shook as thousands of feet bore down on the wall. Sentries shouted and floodlights blazed. The girl behind the wheel gestured wildly for everyone to get clear.

For an instant, Caleb stood transfixed by Brighid's tiny silver whistle hanging from the rearview mirror. Then he bellowed and people scattered. He all but dragged the poor girl from her seat and took the wheel.

The gate shuddered.

He revved the engine.

The girl screamed at him, but he ignored her.

The gate buckled, then exploded in a shower of Fomori and debris. Several of the floodlights went out in a burst of sparks, leaving behind patches of darkness.

Caleb threw the Jeep into gear and floored it, flying toward the gaping hole, mowing down demons. They bounced off his windshield and tore at the frame, but he didn't slow. They only noticed him when he got too close. They were too interested in getting through the wall.

When he finally cleared the horde, it didn't take long to reach the cliffs, but all he could do was stare down at the shore. He didn't have any equipment to scale the rocky cliff face, but there was no doubt in his mind that Rae was down there. Alone.

He paced the precipice searching. Desperate and resigned, he squatted beside the most likely spot. He'd have to pray for protection and climb without gear.

A crow cawed, first close, then a few seconds later to his left. Then a little further. Caleb rose and followed the goddess.

Raelin fell to the ground, forehead pressed against the stone in supplication. It didn't matter that Balor was the reason so many of her clan died every year. It didn't matter that his minions wanted nothing more than to rip the souls from the innocent, ignorant humans. He was a god, and she was just a girl. Around her, the Fomori prostrated themselves in adoration.

He roared and the cavern rumbled. Raelin screamed as his voice ripped through her, pain exploding in her head, in her eyes, in her heart. Mortals were not meant to be in the presence of gods.

Something tore into her back, ripping through the remaining leather and dragging her into the air. Her body felt like it was burning, consumed by pain. Then she was being shaken, arms, legs, head snapping, flailing. Her chin cracked against her chest cutting off her scream.

A whiff of lavender filled her nose. The subtle aroma masked the stench of fish and a sudden influx of strength coursed through her veins.

The smell teased Raelin's memory and distracted her enough from Balor's presence that she remembered Caleb's gift.

The god shook her again. The smell of flowers grew and her pain diminished. The smell was buffering her from pain and his godhead. She gulped for air as she dangled like a misbehaving puppy, then batted awkwardly at her chest, praying that the sachet was still there, hidden behind her shredded leather.

It was. Raelin took a shuddery breath. Hope could be just as dangerous as despair.

A crow's cry, magnified by the ocean, bounced around the chamber. Balor stiffened, then roared. Raelin grasped at the distraction, clumsily drawing out the satin bundle. It wasn't easy. Every time the crow shrieked, Balor answered, shaking her and tearing the cord from her grip. By the time the bag cleared her collar, she was drenched in sweat and trembling. Her fingers fumbled at the noose even as she tried to mask her movements from the demons.

Below her, they writhed as their lord thundered. He shook her again and again, but desperation overrode her pain.

Finally, the switchblade slid into her hand in a puff of dried petals. The smell of lavender blended with sunshine and summer flowers as her thumb found the catch. The hilt felt so small, so puny, so ineffectual compared to the god.

"Raelin!"

The sachet fell against her chest, forgotten as she combed the cavern for the speaker.

Caleb Pennant was pinned against a wall in the far corner, surrounded by stalactites and a sea of black scales. He'd drawn his sword, but the demons kept circling. There were hundreds of the creatures between him and her.

He met her gaze and her heart stuttered. *What was he doing here?*

Balor screamed, shaking her so hard the switchblade almost slipped from her grasp. She tightened her grip and looked back at the smith. He held the sword correctly, but he was too slow, too out of practice. He'd get himself killed. She had to get to him.

He shouted something else, a single syllable. Balor roared and more of his minions turned on the smith, their red eyes focusing on him like a sea of lasers. Pennant swung his faintly glowing blade in a wide arc. One demon went down, while the others inched back.

"Sling!" Pennant's voice sliced through the demons' din.

The god went berserk, shaking her and showering her with his burning saliva. The sachet bounced against her, spilling dried herbs, wafting scent. *Sling? Sling what?*

The early memory of a dimpled, curly-headed boy telling her childhood self about a slingshot, perfectly aimed at a god's single eye, surfaced in her mind.

She clutched the knife. Pennant shouted again, and Balor answered with another burst of rage. She used the violent momentum to surge up and lunge at his face. At the last instant, she flicked the catch, and the blade plunged with sickening ease into the Demon King's single eye.

Balor howled as sweet-smelling, gold ichor fountained from his wound, drenching Raelin and blinding her. He flung her away and she crashed to the ground, rolling to an aching halt. She dragged herself to her knees. With one hand, she patted the ground, searching for the switchblade; with the other, she scrubbed her face.

When her eyes were clear, she saw Balor clawing at his own face, spraying the cavern in luminescent fluid. Her knife, still wedged in his eye socket, gleamed a hot, bright blue. The hilt was too small for his massive, taloned hands, and he only drove it in deeper.

The Fomori ignored her, creeping closer to their crazed god, their collective communion broken as he stumbled, drunkenly, around the chamber. The embedded switchblade flared brighter with every passing second.

Raelin pushed to her feet and ran. She had to get to Pennant.

Balor's agonized cry tore through the chamber again and the ground shook. Bits of the cave came loose, crashing around her. A heavy body crashed into hers, throwing her to the ground and pinning her in a salty puddle. She panicked, thrashing wildly.

The weight disappeared. "It's me. It's Caleb."

She threw herself into his arms as Balor shrieked again.

Pennant and Raelin huddled together while the cavern shook, rocks fell, and Fomori hummed. All of the demons had cocked their heads to the side, their red eyes staring quizzically at their master.

The switchblade blazed like the sun and Balor dropped to his knees. The Fomori closest to him scaled him like a mountain. He swatted at the creatures clinging to his body and sent one flying, limbs splayed and shrieking to crash with a squelch against the wall. More of his minions surged up his legs.

Balor, The Demon King fell. He smashed down face first with a resounding thud. The rock walls rippled with the impact. Brilliant, pure blue light burst from his head. The Fomori, with a last deafening keen, vanished, leaving behind a wisp of black acrid smoke.

The cavern went dark but for puddles of still glowing ichor and a glint of silvery blue across the chamber. In the distance, waves crashed.

Pennant rocked her against his chest, tucking her under his chin. She could hear his heart beating a furious cadence.

"Your papa must have been wrong." Her breathing was erratic. "We can't be indebted to luck. We used too much and we're still here."

He stroked her gnarled braid. "Perhaps all this was a betrothal gift from the goddesses."

Moonlight streamed brightly through a few wispy clouds. Babies wailed and fireflies danced. Raelin stood before the priestess clutching the hand of her beloved, while the old woman bound their wrists together with a white leather cord.

Raelin's toes were bare on the ground, and she took pleasure in the chilly evening. Candles on the makeshift altar flickered merrily in the cool breeze. The priestess spoke of beginnings and fidelity, but Raelin wasn't really listening. Caleb's big hand squeezed hers, his thumb teasing her with small caresses.

"Raelin Shayla Mallory, do you vow to love, honor and cherish this man? To remain faithful…."

She rubbed her free hand over her slightly rounded belly. Six more years of freedom to live and grow and raise a family. Six more years to prepare and train. A lifetime to love her husband.

A crow cackled. The priestess raised an exasperated eyebrow and her mother sighed, looking heavenward, but Caleb's dark eyes twinkled.

"I do," she said, smiling up at him.

Angel's Touch

Alicia Wright Brewster

EXHILARATION RACED THROUGH Kaia's body. Her webbed feet and articulated toes, her craggy horns, her distended belly, and every inch of her flaming red skin tingled. Around her, a twenty-foot high ring of fire roared, casting shadowed replicas of her monstrous form across the concrete floor. Before her, in the center of the blazing ring, a human soul writhed in agony.

Kaia had chosen her present for to enhance the fear of this particular human soul. As a child, the soul's body had suffered a recurring nightmare about a beast such as this. Fear oozed from the soul, and Kaia gave a gleeful smile at the scent of fresh suffering and the musical tinkling of its screams.

She raked her ragged claws across the soul, and her smile widened as it shrieked. Like the fire, the blood was nothing more than illusion, meant to enhance the suffering of the soul, which would, after a life on earth, equate blood with pain and suffering.

Ah, now it smelled of regret, also familiar to Kaia. She sighed in contentment.

Suddenly, the flames disappeared, and the dark cavern filled with white-blue light. A circle of seven beautiful humanoid creatures, surrounding Kaia, now stood where the fire had been raged.

Angels. Their features looked human, but these creatures had unblemished skin and perfect, symmetrical faces. The bare-chested men each wore white pants, and the women wore long, flowing white dresses. A white-blue light emanated from them. As if affected by the brightness, the soul's fear waned.

A male stepped forward from the circle, tall, with tan skin, chin-length black hair, and eyes greener than Kaia ever thought possible.

"Release the human soul." He spoke with such authority that Kaia had

84

stepped backward with one webbed foot, before she remembered that this was her domain.

She narrowed her gray eyes, the only part of her she was unable to change at her will. "You have no place here. Remember the rules!"

The angel took another step forward, and Kaia matched him with a backward shuffle.

"I know the rules. Do you?" he said. "A human sold this soul for the life of his daughter. This is forbidden."

"The soul is mine, purchased from my master. I did nothing wrong."

"And how do you think your master obtained it?" He stepped closer as he gestured toward the soul.

Kaia's stomach knotted. This angel appeared to lead the others, which likely meant he was strong, ancient. A lowly torturer, she couldn't match him if it came to violence.

She clenched and unclenched her clawed hands to lessen their trembling. "That's not my concern." Her voice feigned confidence. "And you have no place here. We don't interact. You don't come down here. We don't go up there. It is written!"

"This was a righteous human, and its soul belongs to the Maker. So my place is between this soul and you."

Kaia stepped in front of the soul, fearing her master's wrath more than she feared this creature. "You can't have it."

"Must you make this difficult, demon?"

She concentrated on the rhythm of her breathing, and raised her chin in defiance.

"Very well." The dark-haired angel strode toward Kaia.

Her body tensed as she prepared for battle. He placed his hand on her misshapen shoulder and pushed her aside. At his touch, her resistance disappeared, and her mind emptied.

Then the creature was gone, along with his followers.

The darkness returned, and the circle of fire roared about her again. But the human soul was gone.

"You have performed your duties nobly." All eyes regarded Alonis as he spoke, and the human soul he had rescued from the demon lay nestled in his hand. He stood on the beach of a small island not yet discovered by humans, with six angels facing him. Alonis towered above the tallest of the others by a few inches. His green eyes swept over the small crowd, focusing on each angel in turn. "Thank you all for—"

"Why did we risk ourselves for this soul?" A blonde angel interrupted, his voice so low it would have escaped human ears.

Alonis approached the angel, and the others stepped aside to let him pass. He extended his hand as if to touch his brother's arm. "Sorin—"

Sorin ducked his shoulder and stepped backward. "Your touch will not work on me. I already belong to the Maker."

"I don't want to coerce you, Sorin. But please, remember our purpose." He fought the urge to yell at his brother. This same fight—Alonis making a decision and Sorin arguing with it publicly—was getting old.

Sorin raised his voice to address the entire group. "Don't you tire of our purpose? Why are these humans Favored over us when we are the obedient ones?"

Alonis bowed his head of black hair and said the same thing he'd told Sorin a hundred times before: "Envy is beneath you. Serve the Master well, and you will earn his Favor for your next life."

Except for Sorin, the others nodded and murmured their agreement.

Sorin bared his teeth, revealing sharp incisors. "The human sold this soul to a demon, and you put us all in danger to recover it!" Sorin unsheathed his sword and directed it at Alonis. He stepped forward, pressing its tip into Alonis's throat. The blade entered his neck but drew no blood.

"Out of the question." Alonis stepped out of the sword's reach. It couldn't hurt him at the moment, but his temper stirred in his chest.

Sorin lunged forward, but Alonis stepped to the side, leaving Sorin off-balance. Alonis waited as he recovered.

When Sorin was poised to strike again, Alonis beckoned him forward. "Come, brother. Can't you defeat me even with my sword sheathed?"

A few of the other angels laughed, and Sorin's face flushed red. He lunged forward.

Sorin feinted to Alonis's right and then went left, but Alonis rolled forward toward the outside of Sorin's outstretched sword arm. As he passed Sorin, Alonis struck him on the wrist. Sorin dropped the sword with a howl. Before he could recover, Alonis circled back and swept his legs from under him. Sorin hit the ground, the air rushing from his lungs.

Alonis stepped away from Sorin's prone form and crossed his arms over his chest. "Are we done now?"

Sorin rose from the sand, and his face broke into a too-wide smile. "It appears we are, brother." He extended his hand for Alonis to shake, but when they shook, Sorin held his grip for a few seconds too long. "So then, what shall we do with the soul, fearless leader?"

Lannair, a female, suggested, "Let's return it to life. Give it an opportunity to prove itself, to prove it deserves the Maker's continued Favor."

"Do any of you object to this?" As Alonis spoke, he looked at Sorin and raised his brows. Sorin shook his head. "So be it. You're all dismissed for now. Again, thank you."

After the group dispersed, Alonis sat on the sand and meditated, letting the sound of the waves lull him back to calmness. He pinpointed several humans in need of his direction. One in particular stood on the verge of a choice that, if made wrongly, would lead the human down a path away from the Everlasting.

Alonis went to him.

He found Franklin with his head bowed over his unconscious wife's hospital bed. A collection of worn monitoring equipment beeped next to her. Invisible for the moment, Alonis felt Franklin's anger as soon as he entered the room.

Franklin felt the doctors hadn't done enough. He felt that his wife, Clara, hadn't received the care she needed because he couldn't afford the best treatments.

He fingered the gun in his pocket.

Alonis could see the possible outcomes. Franklin intended to kill himself. But when Clara died—and she would die—Franklin's anger would overtake his sorrow. Instead of turning the gun on himself, he would find the doctors who had treated Clara. Franklin would interrogate them, one by one at gunpoint, about their actions and their decisions about Clara's care. When their answers didn't satisfy him—and they wouldn't—Franklin would kill them all. And then, in prison, Franklin would curse the Maker. He would forsake the Maker.

He would lose his soul.

But Alonis could see another possible outcome too. Franklin might go home and cry until he slept. For months, he would draw into himself, refusing to interact with the world. And then one day, he would wake up and, though the pain wouldn't be gone, Franklin would be ready to continue living. He would remember that Clara had taught him he was worth loving, and he would look for love and happiness again.

Alonis could feel all of this as he breathed in the scent of Franklin's sorrow. And although he couldn't make the choice for Franklin, Alonis could grant him a single moment of clarity, with which would come a lasting bit of peace.

He reached out and touched Franklin's cheek, and Franklin felt peace.

When Alonis moved his hand away, Franklin's pain returned. But hope remained. Alonis had shown him the right direction, and now the choice belonged to Franklin.

Outside in the hallway, Alonis leaned against the wall and slid down to the floor. After a few minutes, he tried to transport himself back to the beach. He felt his consciousness return to the beach for a moment, but he couldn't complete the transportation. His body wouldn't follow.

He must have used too much power in his touch this time; Franklin had had so much anger inside him.

Having given up on transporting at the moment, he rested on the floor, invisible to the passing humans, until his energy returned. Then he sought out other humans who might benefit from his touch.

Kaia could hear the souls screaming, even though she was too far away for her ears to pick up the sound, and even though the screaming had long since ended. The imagined sound of their screams vibrated in her bones and prickled at her crimson skin. The noise stabbed at her like a thousand knives as it rippled across her body.

She threw back her head and screamed with the echoes of a hundred souls she had tortured.

Kaia could always hear them, ever since that angel had touched her. She understood now why interactions between angels and demons were forbidden.

This was the fourth cave where she'd hidden. This one was tucked in a hollow of a mountain, high above the ground and high above the underground. And yet, it was as if she were still with the tortured souls.

She smelled her own fear and regret. She'd never felt them before, and she wouldn't have recognized them except for the familiar scent. Her nose no longer found it a sweet smell; it stung her nostrils and burned into her brain.

Kaia grabbed her head and squeezed. Anything to stop the screaming! But the wails in her memory continued all through the night.

Alonis could feel someone in pain, as he could feel the pain of all of those he had touched. But he couldn't pinpoint the source. It felt wrong. His gift was one of peace, but this person felt nothing that resembled peace.

The pain drew him to it.

He found a familiar-looking, red-skinned demon curled in a ball toward the back of a cave tucked deep in a mountain. She clutched her ears with clawed hands and whimpered to herself. Alonis recognized her from the under-ground, but he couldn't believe it was *her* pain that had drawn him here.

"Demon, where is the human?" he demanded.

She flinched at his voice. "Please, no," she whispered. "Please, the noise, the screaming. No."

As he approached, he could feel his empathy grow stronger, as it did any time he approached someone he had touched. He halted midstride. "Did *you* summon me here?"

"No," she whimpered. "No."

Alonis took another step toward her and felt empathy wash over him with such strength that he almost fell over. "You did!" he said. "*You* summoned me here."

He reached toward her but then drew his hand back, surprised at his initial instinct to help her. "Demon, you have no place to summon me. You know the rules."

Her head snapped up to peer at him with gray eyes, the only remotely human aspect of her monstrous form. "You and your rules!" she spat at him, saliva spraying from her black lips. "Isn't there a rule against what you've done to me?" She took a step toward him, and he retreated a step. "*What* have you done to me?"

He stammered. "I touched you. But I did not know…I didn't…You're not human. It shouldn't have…."

"Spit it out!"

He gathered himself. "My touch grants clarity, and with it comes peace. Usually."

"Is this your peace—what I'm feeling now?" She took another step toward him, baring pointed teeth. "Take it back, angel. I don't want it."

"I can't."

"Take it back!"

"I can't remove the clarity I gave you. To do such a thing, I would have to turn back time. And that's beyond me."

The anger in her gray eyes turned to devastation. Her shoulders shook, and tears fell. "No." She collapsed to the ground, shaking her head and muttering to herself. "No, no, no."

Alonis couldn't help himself; his nature won out. He fell to the ground beside her, wrapped her in his arms, and rocked her as if she were a small child. She stiffened, and her sobbing stopped.

He pulled away from her.

"No," she said again, forcefully this time. She grabbed for his retreating arms, breaking his skin with her sharp talons. "Hold me."

He held her until well past sunrise. When Kaia opened her eyes in the morning, a sliver of light had already brightened the entry of the cave. She clenched her eyes shut again when she caught him staring at her.

He knew she was pretending to sleep, but he didn't care. His duty required him to help those to whom he was drawn. True, this was the first time he had been drawn to a demon. But who was he to decide whom he should help and whom he should leave to suffer?

As he peered at the demon resting in his arms, he contemplated what it meant to be a Saving Angel, charged to save human souls. There was no human soul here—only a demon. Alonis shook his head to clear it, but he couldn't banish his ambivalence. For now, he'd do his sworn duty. He would bring peace to the one who'd drawn him here. Tomorrow, he would meditate on whether this was the right thing to do.

Alonis squinted as he emerged from the cave in the morning. His head spun, and his limbs weighed him down. He tried and failed to transport away. So instead, he walked a fair distance from the cave and leaned against the mountain, letting it do the work of keeping him upright.

His eyes fluttered shut and stayed there until he was strong enough to transport again. By then, the sun shone high in the sky.

After the angel left, Kaia uncurled herself from her dark corner of the cave and stretched out her legs, arms, fingers.

Fingers?

She'd been too focused on her agony to change her form. But her hands had changed. A curtain of hair tumbled across her back as she stood, and she was surprised to find that it was now a glossy chestnut brown instead of matted black. She fingered the top of her head and found that were her horns were gone as well.

Her skin was still red, her feet remained webbed, and her monstrous shape still had far too many joints and sharp angles for any humanoid form. She had been comfortable in her demonic skin. Now, it was a skin she didn't recognize.

She grimaced as she ran her fingers through her soft, brown hair. She concentrated on changing her shape, tried to return her hair and hands to her chosen demonic form, but she was still too weak.

Kaia dragged herself to the edge of the cave and looked out over the world. She could see farther and sharper than any human could. Many miles away, a small town sat in a valley. A man, a woman, and two young children played in the yard of a modest home. The woman picked up the smaller child and spun him around. He stretched out his arms like an airplane in flight.

The vision changed in her mind, and Kaia saw the same family in her ring of fire. She imagined herself torturing their souls. She ripped each one to shreds, starting with the children, so the parents could watch. Her hair was matted black again, and claws tipped her hands. In her vision, she threw back her head and laughed, relishing the pure joy of it.

In the middle of her laugh, tears filled her eyes. Kaia hugged her arms around herself and shook her head. Was that what she wanted—to torture that family? No. She didn't think she wanted that, but she couldn't chase the evil thoughts away. Her hands still tingled with anticipation when she imagined torturing souls, yet the thought of causing them to suffer brought tears to her eyes.

She couldn't stay stuck in between like this.

Kaia squeezed her eyes shut and concentrated again on changing her form. She would leave her hair and hands as they were now and change the rest of her. After thirty seconds of trying, she gasped with the effort. She opened her eyes and looked down at herself. Her skin was still red and her shape still grotesque.

With a sigh, she returned to her corner of the cave.

Soon after the sun set, the angel returned. He hesitated at the entrance to the cave, shifting from foot to foot. At first, Kaia pretended not to see him. After a few minutes, he turned to leave.

"Angel?" she said.

He froze, still facing away. "Demon."

"Kaia."

"Excuse me?" He turned to look at her.

"Kaia. That's my name."

"Oh." Was that a smile that touched his lips just for an instant?

"I thought you might prefer to call me by name, rather than 'demon.'" She paused. When he didn't speak again, she added, "Shall I just call you 'angel'?"

"No. You...you can call me Alonis. That's my name. Alonis."

He was even more beautiful when he stuttered. He was flawed, just like her.

"Alonis. Why have you come back?"

"Do you want me to leave?" He took a step toward the cave entrance.

"No!" She leapt to her feet. When he flinched, she slowly sat back down. "Are you frightened of me?" She tilted her head to the side in a question. "You weren't frightened of me in the under-ground, and I was more of myself then. I don't want to hurt you now."

He smirked. "You couldn't hurt me even if you wanted to."

There was the confident creature who had cursed her unwittingly in the under-ground.

"I believe you. So why do you fear me now?"

"I'm not frightened…just uncertain."

"Come over here next to me." She adjusted herself to sit cross-legged on the dirt floor of the cave, facing the entrance.

Alonis sat down across from her. He peered into her gray eyes with his green ones. He reached toward her, and she bridged the remaining distance and placed her hands in his. As soon as she touched him, everything became clear. Only this time, she concentrated on sorting through it all.

She was Kaia, a demon by birth, born only a century ago. As a babe, she had been taught the arts of torture and fear. She had reveled in them, for what else was she to do? She'd known no other way. When the angel had touched her, she had seen the world with a new clarity. She now recognized the pain she'd caused.

That awful part of her could stay in the past. One by one, Kaia allowed the souls she'd tortured to confront her in her mind. Through the night, she faced her demons. She felt the suffering she'd brought to human souls, and her screaming filled the cave. Alonis rocked her in his arms and wiped her tears, murmuring comforts.

Kaia sealed the memory of each soul away behind a wall in her mind that she erected just for this purpose. Behind the wall, she locked her desire to harm, her love of suffering, and her guilt.

Kaia had the most beautiful eyes. Even when he had muscled that soul away from her in the under-ground, Alonis had noticed her striking gray eyes. Now that she was changing, he could see her every emotion in them. Her eyes truly were the windows to her…to her what? If she had a soul, it was the soul of a demon. And that fact alone meant that Alonis probably didn't belong here. What did he hope to accomplish by coming back?

Nothing. He hoped to accomplish nothing. Months had passed since he'd first held her in the cave. He'd continued to come back here every few days because he'd been haunted by her lovely, pain-filled gaze. Every time

Angel's Touch

he closed his own eyes to meditate, her gray eyes had floated in the darkness of his vision. He wanted to see happiness in them. He wanted to see her, even if he couldn't guide her to the Everlasting.

But now, it wasn't the pain in her eyes that kept him with her. It was the twinkle in them.

"What do you feel?" he asked her, when a sliver of the sun's light cut across the cave entrance.

She smiled with full, pink lips. "I feel peace. I feel new."

"You've had enough of me now that you'll be fine when I leave." Regret filled his chest as he spoke. Their time together was ending, but it was too soon. He'd never before met anyone—demon or human or angel—who worked so hard at becoming better. He admired her and felt more useful and more appreciated than he'd ever felt before.

She clutched his hands. "I'd like you to stay," she said, her eyes smiling as much as her lips, "if that's okay with you."

He nodded, and couldn't hide a smile of his own.

Throughout the morning, she asked him questions. At first, the questions focused on his duties as an angel. Then she shifted to lighter topics. What kind of foods did he like? What was his favorite color? What was his favorite place in the whole world? These questions had nothing to do with his duties. For a few of them, he had no answers, and she pushed him to find some.

With every question she asked, his heart felt closer to being complete; his *self* felt closer to being complete.

After a time, Alonis rose to his feet, extracting his hands from Kaia's. "I must go. I am summoned."

She stood with him, and his eyes widened as he took in her full appearance. During the night she had changed.

"Tell me, Alonis," she said with a coy smile and mischievous eyes. "Do you always go where you are summoned?"

"Of course." He'd been too focused on her face to see it before. But now, his gaze wandered downward to her ample breasts, narrow waist, and shapely hips, all covered in smooth, bare skin. He flushed and turned his face away. He'd had sexual desires before, but never so strong and never toward a demon.

Alonis turned back to her. For a moment, Alonis froze, staring, trying to understand what he was feeling. He had a connection with this woman he'd never before experienced. She listened to him, cared about his feelings, seemed to want him for more than just what duties he could fulfill.

93

"Then I will summon you tonight," she said.

Tonight couldn't come too soon.

When Alonis arrived back at the beach for a team meeting later that day, the usual group of angels was already there.

"Good to see you, brother," said Sorin. His voice sounded flat, and Alonis suspected the sentiment in his words was a false one.

The others reformed their circle around Alonis, staring at him expectantly. He turned to Lannair. "Report please."

"I've touched exactly one hundred charges since our last meeting. Thirty-seven chose the right path." She hesitated before continuing. "I lost sixty-three of them." She stared at her feet, a blush climbing across her pale cheeks.

Alonis shook his head. "Your numbers were better at our last meeting. What happened?"

"I don't know." Her voice was just above a whisper.

"Take Quon with you for your next twenty touches." He turned to Quon, another angel in the group. "Make sure she's interceding before her charges are too far lost." Quon and Lannair both nodded.

Alonis turned back to Sorin. "Report please, brother."

Sorin crossed his arms over his chest and flashed a smile. "How about *you* report for once. Tell us about your demon charge."

Lannair, Quon, and the other three stared at him with wide eyes. Shock registered on their angelic features.

"Demon charge?" asked Quon.

"Alonis has been visiting a demon—regularly—for the past four months." Sorin stepped to the center of the circle and clapped Alonis on the shoulder. "Haven't you, brother?"

"She summoned me," Alonis said. "And I've done more good with her than I ever have with any human."

"You've done *good?*" The circle reformed around Sorin as he spoke. "What good could possibly come of helping a demon?"

"The cycle of existence. She's a demon now. But when her current life ends, she may not be. Perhaps a bird, a butterfly, even a human. Every being is a potential human, and so every being is capable of being saved."

Sorin laughed, and the sound dripped with bitterness. "How dare you?" His voice was low with menace. He stepped close to Alonis, put his nose only a few inches from the other angel's. "A demon could never gain the Maker's Favor."

"That's not for us to decide," said Alonis. Sorin opened his mouth to speak again, but Alonis held up a hand to cut him off. "End of discussion." He turned to Quon. "Report please."

"I've touched one hundred twelve humans since we last met. Seventy-nine chose…." Quon's eyes strayed to Sorin, then back to Alonis. "So this demon—she has tortured souls?"

Alonis sighed, frustrated that this conversation continued. But he nodded in answer to the question.

"Does she really deserve to be saved?" Quon asked.

"We could ask that of every human charge."

Quon's gaze wandered across the shoreline as he considered this. "Okay. But there are only so many of us Saving Angels. We can't touch everyone. Why this demon, instead of a human who will never get that same opportunity to be pushed in the right direction?"

"She summoned me. It's not for me to decide. Would you have me turn away from a charge right in front of my face, to seek out one who hasn't cried out for help?"

"I guess not…Seventy-nine of my charges chose the right path. I was unable to save thirty-three." Although Quon finished his report, uncertainty danced behind his eyes.

Over the next year, Alonis visited Kaia most days, between performing his duties. She didn't need him anymore, but he needed her. When he went too long without seeing her, the percentage of human charges he was able to save suffered. He was just *happier* when he saw her.

At first, they continued to sit on the cave floor and talk about everything that came to mind. When Kaia became restless in the cave, Alonis taught her how to dress as a human. Then he showed her his favorite places in the world. They walked hand in hand on the beaches of Fiji; they ran across the Irish countryside; they explored the nooks and crannies of architectural structures in Chicago, Dubai, and Athens.

On most nights, Kaia collected a souvenir, usually something plucked from nature. But sometimes, she scored a gift shop bauble left on the ground, abandoned by a careless human.

Among her treasures were a crystal replica of the Eiffel Tower, a stuffed animal from a theme park, a rubber spider from a haunted house, a seashell from a beach, and a flower from a garden. She cherished each one and placed them around her cave for decoration.

One day, in an art museum, Kaia took particular interest in a sculpture of a nude man. She circled the sculpture several times, marveling at its perfection. It looked much like Alonis, with its unmarred face and perfectly formed musculature. Until recently, her experience with humans had been limited to torturing souls. She'd never before examined the living human form.

Each circle about the sculpture brought her closer, until she stood within a foot of it.

"Is this how human men look underneath their clothing?" she asked. Alonis shook his head. "This is an ideal depiction."

She turned to him and reached up to push his hair away from his face. She shifted her gaze back and forth between Alonis's face and the sculpture. "It looks like you."

He smiled, and Kaia felt a flutter in her chest. Alonis didn't smile enough, carrying the troubles of the humans he'd touched. If only she could touch him and give him peace, she would take his pain away as he had taken hers.

She trailed her fingertips along his cheek as she continued to examine his facial features. His lashes were so long and dark that the green of his eyes against them shocked her every time he blinked. But she rarely saw joy there.

She turned to the sculpture again and circled to its back. Kaia ran her hand across its smooth buttocks and announced, with a wide smile, "This is my favorite part!"

Alonis chuckled, showing her every one of his white teeth. Then he clasped her hand in his own and moved it away from the sculpture. "The humans prefer that you not touch the artwork. It crumbles."

Her mouth made an "Oh" as she stepped away from the sculpted man. Several museum patrons scowled at her from about the room. But she had made him laugh, so let them stare.

"Let's go somewhere else now," she said, too excited about her victory to end the day so soon.

Alonis led her outside the museum. He wrapped her in his arms, and a second later, they stood inside a deep canyon of red rock. Kaia tilted her head upward and spun a circle, awed at the hugeness of it.

"This is my favorite place," he said. "Humans call it the Grand Canyon."

"I love it." She grabbed his hand and dragged him away from human eyes, deeper into the canyon. There, she shoved him to the ground and walked a slow circle around him, unclasping the buttons of her blouse. Bit by bit, she bared more of her pale flesh. Her chest, her breasts, her navel. He reached out for her, but she giggled and slapped his hand away. She tossed her blouse at him and pushed her pants to the ground. This time, when he reached for her, she let him pull her down.

They made love for the first time in that crevice deep in the canyon. She didn't have a clue what she was doing, and neither did he as far as she could tell. But being that close to him was how she imagined heaven, a place she knew she'd never see.

When they had finished, she danced naked at the edge of the canyon, singing an old bar song they'd come across in their travels. Alonis lay back against the red rock and watched her. His smile warmed her through to her soul.

Kaia whistled to herself as she rearranged the knickknacks in her cave, which now felt like a happy home—especially when Alonis was around. She could almost imagine that the two of them lived there and could one day have a family like the one she'd seen in the small village nearby.

Of course, that could never happen, since neither of them could reproduce, and he had too many responsibilities out on the world. Still, the dream made her smile. And that was enough.

Although it was late in the afternoon, the cave suddenly went dark. Kaia spun toward the entrance. Standing in the entryway was a demon, blocking the outside light.

She stiffened. From the large ears and long, hooked nose, she knew he was a Chaser demon, born and bred to track and catch prey. If he was here, that meant *she* was his prey.

He rushed toward her before she could react and transport away. His fingers wrapped around her wrists, long talons cutting into her skin.

"The master is looking for you," he hissed in her ear.

Kaia flinched away from the stench in his breath. "I won't go back." She'd come too far to return to what she used to be. She'd die before she went back.

Her body trembled as she struggled to get away, but he pressed his claws deeper into her skin. Her wrists dripped blood onto the cave floor.

"So you defy the master?" he asked, pushing her against the back wall of the cave. She had nowhere to run. Tears rolling down her face, she nodded. "Then you accept the consequences." He disappeared, leaving her trembling on the dirt floor.

***

97

For their next meeting, Alonis met his band of angels on the otherwise uninhabited beach. Kaia had told him how the Chaser had threatened her, and his nerves teetered on edge. He owed the angels his attention right now. Then he'd return to Kaia and comfort her.

When Alonis arrived on the beach, the other angels were already there waiting, with Sorin in front. All had their swords drawn.

"This cannot go on, Alonis," Sorin said.

"*What* cannot go on?" Alonis crossed his arms over his chest.

"You can't continue to entertain the affections of that demon."

Alonis tightened his jaw but didn't respond. At first, Alonis had gone to Kaia out of a sense of duty. But any duty he had toward her had long since been fulfilled. Yet he continued to be drawn to her.

"Or are you doing more than merely *entertaining* her affections?" Sorin raised a suggestive eyebrow.

Alonis narrowed his eyes to slits and spoke in a low voice. "That's not your concern."

"Then whose concern is it?" Sorin nodded toward the angels at his back. "Because we are all concerned. How can you lead us when you spend your nights with our enemy?"

"Enough!" Alonis said, his voice rising. "You have questioned me too much! You forget your place."

Alonis's entire body tensed. With his power, he pushed, and the angels' swords became heavier. He had yet to visit any humans today, and his power was at its strongest. One by one, the angels buckled under the weight, and their swords fell to the ground. None of them were as powerful as he was, which was why he was in charge.

Sorin, too, dropped his sword. He bent over as if to retrieve it, but instead scooped up a handful of sand and threw it in Alonis's face. Sand burned Alonis's eyes. Sorin slammed into him, knocking him to the ground. He pressed his knee into Alonis's chest.

"You disappoint me," Alonis whispered from the ground.

"I tire of sport," Sorin hissed. "This will not stand, Alonis."

Alonis placed a single hand on Sorin's chest and pushed. Sorin sailed through the air, past the shore, and splashed into the ocean.

He came up from the water sputtering. "This will not stand!" he shouted as Alonis disappeared.

Alonis didn't go far, just to the other side of the small island. There, he meditated late into the night.

Sorin's point wasn't lost on him. The thought of never seeing Kaia again, never touching her soft skin, never kissing her full lips, never running his fingers through her wavy hair, made his chest ache. Yet the thought of neglecting his duty to his Maker made him ill. If the angels didn't respect him, he could not fulfill that duty to the best of his abilities. But the Maker valued love above all else, so how could he turn his back on it?

Alonis pondered the conflict between his duty and his feelings for Kaia. He felt Kaia summoning him, but he didn't go to her. He needed to figure this out. He wanted to give her his whole self, and he couldn't do that with his feelings in turmoil.

As the sun's rays cut into the cave, tears stung Kaia's eyes. Why had he not come? What was he doing? Was he hurt? Was he upset with her?

She paced back and forth at the mouth of the cave, trying to decide whether she should search for him. Sometimes she wished she could sense Alonis the way he could sense her.

By afternoon, she had decided. She clothed herself in human garments and left the cave. Kaia transported to all the places he had shown her; the beaches, the countryside, the tall skyscrapers. But he was in none of these places. Then she remembered another beach that he'd shown her once, one that he'd said had special meaning to him.

As she arrived on the beach, Kaia saw Alonis walk across the sand, the wind whipping his hair as he moved. Her heart raced, as it always did when she saw him. She opened her mouth to call his name, but she stopped when he joined a group of other angels.

Tucked away behind a palm tree, Kaia watched Alonis engage a blonde angel in conversation. The two of them gestured wildly as they spoke. After a minute, Alonis turned and walked away.

"This will not stand! This isn't over!" the blonde angel yelled to Alonis, but Alonis disappeared, transporting himself elsewhere.

Kaia watched the blonde angel meditate after Alonis left. Like Alonis, the angel had a beauty unreachable by humans. But Kaia knew evil, and as a consequence, she knew good too. Maybe this angel saved human souls according to his duty, but he was definitely *not* good.

Just as she turned to leave, the Chaser demon who'd visited her weeks before showed up on the beach. Sorin didn't attack him or flee; instead, he stood from the sand, and the two of them walked side by side along the shore.

Kaia crept behind them from afar. She couldn't hear them, but from Sorin's gesturing and animated facial expressions, she could tell that he was furious about something. The demon nodded as Sorin spoke. Before they both disappeared from the beach, they shook hands and smiled.

When Kaia returned to the cave, Alonis was already there. "Where were you?" he shouted.

Her eyebrows drew together. She'd never seen him this upset before. "What's wrong, my love?"

He inhaled sharply. "I'm sorry. I was worried."

"But why? You can feel me. You knew I was fine."

"You're not fine. You can't hide it from me; you're worried. Even if I couldn't feel you, I can see it in your eyes."

Despite her anxiety about what she'd just seen on the beach, his concern brought a smile to her face. She stood on tiptoes and wrapped her arms around his neck. "I'm fine, my love, now that I'm with you." She kissed him on the tip of his nose.

His jaw relaxed into a small smile, and Kaia felt his heart rate slow. He tightened his arms around her waist, drawing her up toward him, and kissed her hard on the mouth.

When he released her, she was breathless and light-headed. But when she looked at him, she saw continued worry in his eyes. "What's wrong?"

His shoulders sagged. "I argued with one of my brothers. Sorin. Then I helped four humans. Then I argued with Sorin some more. He's so determined to be in charge, power-hungry. Always fighting me for leadership. I'm starting to think there's no boundary to what he'll do to take my place." He sighed heavily. "I think we should leave this cave for good."

She looked around at the place she'd made her home. The knickknacks from their travels decorated the cave, so that everywhere she looked, she recalled something she had experienced with Alonis. She didn't want to leave, but she knew he was right.

He also had to know what she'd just seen. "I think I just saw one of your brothers make a deal with that Chaser I told you about," she said. "A blond angel. Is that Sorin?"

His beautiful green eyes widened. "Yes. Sorin is planning something rash; I'm sure of it. And that can't be good for us. We leave *now!*"

"Where will we go?"

"I don't know. Away from here. Sorin is planning something rash; I'm sure of it."

Kaia bustled about the cave, gathering her souvenirs into a sack. When she looked up at him after grabbing the final item, he had drawn his sword and stood facing the mouth of the cave.

Demons, maybe ten of them, blocked their exit. With them was the Chaser demon she'd seen twice before. Terror slid around in her stomach as Kaia's gaze landed on the blond angel she'd seen on the beach. Sorin. He stood at the edge of the group, an evil grin playing across his beautiful face.

Kaia grabbed Alonis's arm and transported them to a small warehouse where she had once collected a soul. After they had inspected the place and assured themselves that they were alone, she asked, "What now?"

"I'm thinking." Alonis's gaze jumped back and forth between the two exits.

"You know they don't need doors."

"Well, I have to do something! Guarding the doors keeps my mind occupied."

A horde of demons suddenly appeared in the warehouse, blocking their route to one of the exits. There must have been twenty of them this time. Again, Sorin stood at the edge of the group. Kaia grabbed Alonis's shoulder and tried to transport them, but she couldn't move them.

"I can't transport," she whispered through clenched teeth.

He spoke without turning his head, focused on the demons before them. "Neither can I. There are too many of them. They're blocking our powers." Alonis pushed Kaia behind him and took a few small steps backward, ushering Kaia toward the other door. "*Run.*"

"I won't leave you." Kaia recognized several of the demons as Chaser demons. They were too fast. Even if she ran, she wouldn't escape them. One of the Chasers disappeared and reappeared by the door, blocking their remaining exit.

At first, they attacked one by one, and Alonis cut them down easily. The monstrous demon bodies piled up between them and the remaining demons, and Kaia began to feel hope. They were forming a barricade!

The demons must have realized this tactic was not working. They began to attack in pairs, one approaching Alonis and Kaia from each side of the demon-body barricade. Alonis backed up until he pressed Kaia into a wall. She could hardly breathe. But from their position, Alonis could continue to hold the demons off.

They were winning!

Alonis's movements slowed. He'd used his power on humans today, he'd said, and she could see the wear in his movements.

The demons crushed into them until Kaia could see nothing of the warehouse except for Alonis and the demons surrounding them. A towering monster propelled Alonis away from her. Another demon seized her and pinned her arms behind her. It wrenched her arms upward, lifting her off the ground. Pain shot through her shoulders. Kaia kicked backward, and her feet met unmoving muscle.

"Angel," the demon holding her called. "Look what I've got."

Alonis shoved the monster, sending his attacker careening into a wall. He raised his sword at the demon holding Kaia. "Put her down!"

The demon ran a hair-covered hand up her stomach, stopping just under her breast. "So tell me, angel…" Although he addressed Alonis, he whispered with his lips touching Kaia's ear. "…just how sweet is this little demon? She must be pretty sweet to make you risk everything. Maybe I'll find out just how sweet she is." Kaia squeezed her eyes shut and concentrated on not panicking.

She opened them just in time to see a shock of blond hair moving toward Alonis. "Alonis!"

He heard and reacted, but too slowly. Alonis's sword plunged toward his attacker just as Sorin stabbed him through the heart. The two angels slumped to the ground, each skewered by the other's sword.

"Alonis!" she screamed again, wriggling to break free of her captor. This wasn't right. He couldn't be dead. She had just found him. She had just found *life*.

His body lay motionless, his eyes wide and lifeless.

Seeing him lie there brought physical pain. Her chest felt like it was about to split in two. Tears sprang to her eyes and rolled down her cheeks. Her demon captor dropped her and laughed—a deep sound that vibrated through the room.

For a brief moment, she considered lying down on the floor with Alonis and letting them kill her too. But no, he would want her to survive.

Only a few demons remained, so she succeeded in transporting herself. She didn't have a destination in mind, but she found herself back in the Grand Canyon, in the hollow where she and Alonis had made love for the first time. She could still see the remnants of her footsteps in the dirt, making a circle around where Alonis had lain on the ground waiting for her to give herself to him.

Kaia crumpled to the ground and wept until she was too exhausted to push any more tears from her eyes. Her chest felt hollow, empty. That space Alonis had filled in it was now an empty hole that would never be full again.

She pushed herself up from the ground and readied for the demons to find her. She didn't know how she could enjoy this world without Alonis, but she would try because that's what he would have wanted. He'd done so much to make her what she was now, and it was her duty to preserve it if she could. That's how she would repay him.

When the remaining demons arrived, Kaia had transformed her fingers and toes into claws. She could barely see the demons through her bloodshot, cried-out eyes, but she set her feet apart for balance, lifted her arms in front of her in a fighting stance, and beckoned them forward.

"Come."

Kaia took two of them down with her before she died.

***

Minutes later, a baby girl was born in a small town nestled in a valley. Her gray eyes were full of emotion from the moment she left the womb.

At almost that same moment, a baby boy was born in the same town. His mother remarked at how his eyes were the greenest she'd ever seen.

Alonis and Kaia had earned the Maker's Favor.

Dancing with the Rain

Timothy Buller

"MORE COFFEE HERE, Ben," said Frank.

I grabbed the pot and filled his cup. It was a slow Tuesday afternoon at Hickman's Diner, Aspermont, Texas, and there were only two customers. Frank Wolfe was a deputy from the County Sheriff's Department. Sitting at the table with him was Jon Stevens, a farmer. Frank usually had some good stories from the Department, but today Jon was talking about the drought.

"They'll call this 'the great drought of '53,' one day," he said. "We've had less rain in the past four months than we normally get in a week. I'm not sure how much longer this town can handle it."

"Aspermont will be fine, Jon," said Frank, pointing at the sky through the large windows at the front of the diner. "In fact, it looks like the weather's turning right now."

Dark clouds were rolling over the town, causing a shadow to creep across the diner floor.

"I'll be damned," Jon muttered. "Those weren't there just a few minutes ago. It don't seem possible."

"It must be possible, because the clouds are right there," Frank said.

Jon kept his eyes on the sky through the window, but waived me over to refill his coffee. I topped off his drink, and took the empty pot to the kitchen to start another batch. The grill hissed as Alan Hickman, my boss, set beef patties on the hot surface.

"Looks like it's going to rain," I said.

"'Bout damn time," he responded. "Starting to get sick of all these rising food costs. It gets harder every year to keep this place running. Last thing I need is a drought to put me out of business."

I walked back out to the front windows in the dining room. The clouds were a deep shade of purple. The low grumble of thunder was overhead, and lightning flashed in their billows. The bell on the door chimed when I opened it, stepping out under the diner's awning to get a better look at the oncoming storm. A sudden crack of thunder startled me, and rain began to fall.

That's when I saw *her*.

A young woman was walking in the middle of the street, and she was absolutely beautiful.

From the look of her features, I guessed she was Japanese. Strands of long dark hair ran down her face, the rain making them stick to her cheeks. She was wearing a green dress, simple and sleeveless, with a high neckline and a long skirt. The wet material clung to her skin and hugged the curves of her hips. The girl twirled once in the downpour, and laughed. It was an innocent laugh, and it made me chuckle.

She stopped in front of the diner, and I realized I was gawking. With a graceful stride she came close to me, wearing a beautiful smile. Her eyes were the right height to meet mine, and when they did I was captivated. They were blue, and for a moment, they looked like swirling clouds with speckles of gold lightning.

"Hello," I said, but she didn't reply. Instead, she took my hands and walked me out into the road. Lightning flashed, and thunder sounded off like brass cymbals in an orchestra. Placing my right hand on her waist, and taking my left in hers, she prompted me with swaying. I led her in a waltz, the rain and thunder our only accompaniment.

Surprised and speechless, I searched for something to say as she turned into a spin.

Then, as if the song on our imaginary radio had ended, she stopped, and placed her arms around my neck. She stood close to me, like you might with someone you were familiar with.

"I'm Ben, " I said.

"I know who you are, Ben Johnson."

"You know my name?" I asked, surprised. "Have we met before?"

"No, we haven't met." She looked up with a slight tilt of her head and scrunched her mouth to one side before saying, "You can call me Amy."

"Okay, Amy. Thank you for the dance, but would you like to come inside?" I wanted to find out more about her, and how she knew my name, but I also wanted to get out of the rain. Besides, Alan might not be too happy if he caught me in the street when I should be working.

She shook her head. "I like the rain. It's pure, and cleansing. It washes away all of our bad starts, and leaves us to try again, until we are who we are supposed to be."

I hadn't expected such a deep thesis on rain. I decided to chance a scolding from Alan if it meant a few more minutes talking to the mysterious Amy.

"Then tell me how you could *possibly* know my name."

"Your father told me about you," she responded. "That's why I'm here. You look like him, Ben. He had the same emerald eyes."

I am the spitting image of my father; sandy colored hair, green eyes, even the same height and build. But I was eight when he died, and she looked no older than me. At first I was angry. Maybe she thought she was being funny, or maybe someone had put her up to it. But as I looked into her eyes I felt she genuinely believed what she said.

"My father? Amy, how could you know him," I asked. "He died twelve years ago."

"That is a long story, which I promise to tell you, " she said. "But not tonight. I can meet you tomorrow, at the cemetery. Will you come?"

It was a strange request from someone I had just met. Why the cemetery? Why couldn't she explain now? Part of me wanted to demand answers. Ultimately I decided to go along with her request.

"When will you be there?"

"I will be there when you are," she said, as she began walking down the road again.

I watched for a moment before turning back to the diner. The encounter struck me as odd, and if she hadn't been so beautiful I might not have humored her. But she *was* beautiful.

Jon gave me a grin when I entered, but Frank was focused on his coffee.

The kitchen door swung open, and Alan emerged carrying two dinner platters. One look at me soaked to the bone and he asked, "Why were you out in the rain, son?"

I didn't think, "I was dancing," would be a good answer, so I kept my mouth shut.

"Well don't just stand there and drip," he said. "Go get cleaned up. And get a mop for this floor before someone slips and breaks their neck."

I couldn't get Amy off my mind for the rest of the night. I had never met anyone that stunning. And she was mysterious. She knew my name, and said she knew my father. My mind was racing with possible explanations, but none were plausible. I would just have to go to the cemetery and find out who she was.

***

I followed FM 2211 straight through the flat farmland of Stonewall County. Other than a few scattered trees and farmhouses, the Double Mountains, two mountain ridges to the south, were the only things obstructing the skyline for as far as I could see in any direction. Soon I arrived at the cemetery, and hopped out of the truck with an apple in hand.

There was no sign of Amy. The cemetery wasn't very big, and only a few trees surrounded it. The air was fresh, and there was the lingering smell of grass after rain, though there was no sign the rain had fallen here the night before.

Memories flooded my thoughts while I waited. We buried my mother here a year ago, next to my father's plot. I walked over to their graves and was surprised to see someone had placed a bundle of bluebonnets at mother's headstone. Bluebonnets were fairly common throughout the area, but we hadn't seen any with the drought.

Bluebonnet was also a nickname dad had used for my mother. He once said that bluebonnets were the most beautiful of all flowers, and my mother was the most beautiful of all women. So it made sense to compare them. No one else had ever called her Bluebonnet, and I didn't know anyone in town that would have visited her grave. Dad was the only one I could imagine leaving the flowers, and that sent a chill up my spine.

Choosing not to think about the bluebonnets, I sat in the shade of one of the trees and ate my apple. It was still early in the day, maybe ten, and soon my head was bobbing with the weight of boredom. I dozed for a minute before my neck snapped straight again. When it did, I saw Amy walking towards me.

She was as beautiful as I remembered, and wearing the same dress from the night before. Her hair was in a braid now, draped in front of her shoulder with a row of bluebonnets tied into its folds. One look at her face was enough to send my heart racing.

"I'm glad to see you again, Ben. I enjoyed our dance," she said, as I stood to greet her.

"Yeah, I don't normally do that sort of thing." The words sounded distant in my mind. I wasn't even sure if I had said what I thought I said.

"You really should do more of those sorts of things," she said, before turning and walking to my parent's headstones.

I followed, eager to hear how she knew my father, but she only stood silent in front of his stone.

"Last night you knew my name, and you said my father sent you. You even knew what he looked like. How?" I asked.

"First tell me what you know of your father's death."

"He was a Marine, stationed at Fort Mills on Corregidor, an island in the Philippines. The Japanese attacked on December 29th, 1941, and he died in the first aerial bombardment."

"Your father didn't just die in an air raid, Ben." Amy turned from the grave and took my hands into hers. "He was more than just a casualty of war. He was a very brave man. Special."

As she spoke, I felt drawn into her eyes in a way I cannot explain. In them I saw a swirling storm, like a hurricane. The clouds seemed to surround me. But I passed through them, and saw a man in the darkness of night. He was a Marine, and he was running towards a building. I could hear the sound of bombs over head, and could see debris being tossed into the air.

Once inside, I realized the building was a hospital, and the Marine was my father. My heart ached when I recognized him. He ran to each room as if searching for something precious. I felt connected to him somehow, and could feel he was frantic. Finally, he found a Japanese boy, no older than six or seven, scared and crying in the corner of a room. He took the boy in his arms and ran for the door. I heard him say, "It'll be okay. Don't worry, I've got you." There was a sound like a whistle, a deafening boom, and a flash of light followed by the darkness of dust and debris.

The darkness faded, and I was back in the cemetery.

"What...What just happened?" I asked, my body trembling. "Where was I just now?"

I felt weak, so I let go of her hands. I sat on the ground, pushing my hands through my hair, and rocked back and forth to try and calm my body from shaking.

Amy placed her hand on my shoulder and knelt next to me. "I showed you what your father was doing when he died," she said. "He was saving a boy that he didn't even know. The boy's caretaker, realizing he was missing, asked a soldier for help. Your father ran after him as bombs were falling all around. He was more than brave, he was compassionate."

"That was how he died?" Tears were building in my eyes.

Amy took my hands again. "May I show you?"

I closed my eyes for a moment. When I opened them again, I could see down into the ruins of the hospital. My father was face down. The thought that I was looking at his corpse horrified me. But then he gasped, and rolled over. Underneath him lay the boy, shielded from the blast and debris. Slowly, the boy stood, then took a few steps away. He stopped and took the hand of a figure standing by the partially fallen doorway. It was a woman.

I gasped when I realized it was Amy.

She wore a bright blue kimono that illuminated the surrounding area with blue light. Her hair was done up in a fancy bun, like the beautiful geisha women I had seen in pictures. But there was no joy on her face. Her lips were pressed together in a somber frown.

"You saved his life," she told my father. "But now I am afraid you are dying. It is not often I see such courage in men. Let me do something for you, on behalf of this boy."

"Safety," he gasped. "Get the boy to safety. Make sure he lives."

"I have offered you a favor and your concern is still with the boy. I assure you he will be safe. But what of you?" she asked. "What do you need?"

"Ben...my son. He will need...."

He was struggling to speak now, and I felt it wouldn't be long. I wanted to reach out to him, tell him I love him. Tell him I missed him.

"He needs to know that I love him. That I'm proud of him. That...I'm sorry I won't see him grow up. He needs to be strong. Please...help him to be strong."

That was the last thing he said. The vision faded back into the present. I was in the cemetery again, and my father was gone. Tears were streaming down my cheeks. I sat, weeping and holding Amy's hands. After a few minutes, I was able to compose myself.

"Why now?" I asked. "Why not then? Why not come to me when I was a boy, when I needed that strength and assurance?"

"You did not need me then," she said. "You had a mother who was still there for you, who would comfort you. Now she is gone, and now you need to know."

"Didn't she deserve to know how he died?" I asked.

"How your father died is not as important as how he felt about you," she said. "Your mother was already confident in your father's affection, and he knew that."

She stood and helped me up to my feet. Looking back at the graves I noticed the bluebonnets again.

Amy must have noticed what I was looking at. "I thought it was something he might do," she said. "He loved her, and these were her favorite."

"What are you?" I asked, wiping my eyes. "This is beyond anything I understand. I thought you were a young woman, but I saw you with my father. That was twelve years ago!"

"I am Ameonna, a spirit of rain and clouds," she said, as if that answered my question.

"A spirit?" I asked. "Like an angel? Or a demon?"

"Did you think there was not more to this world than men?" She asked. "Spirits, like myself, we see how all things are connected. Men see only themselves. Your father saw more, and I honor him for that."

I let my gaze fall to the ground and attempted to contemplate what Amy had said. How could she be a spirit? She certainly looked human.

"I don't think I understand," I said.

"You see me as human, but this is just a form I take." Amy held her hand in front of her chest and it began to change. Starting at her fingers, and moving up her forearm, her skin evaporated into a cloud. The cloud outlined the arm that had been there, solidifying into flesh at her elbow.

I rubbed my eyes, half expecting it to be an illusion. But nothing changed. "How...?"

"You may see me as a cloud as well," she said, "for that is another form I take. But you can also see me in the rain."

Drops of water began to fall from her arm, slowly at first, but it built into a steady downpour between us. The water splattered from the ground onto my shoes and pants. I stared at the tiny storm extending from Amy's arm with my jaw open in amazement. It frightened me, but it excited me more. It lasted for a matter of moments before the rain slowed to a stop and the cloud dissipated, leaving Amy's arm whole again.

"That was unbelievable," I said. What she showed me could only be described as a miracle. Even to see my father, despite the grief of watching him die, to hear his voice again was a wonderful thing. "But I still don't understand how it's possible."

"You don't need to understand. You just need to accept it."

Nodding, I wondered if there were other moments she could show me of my father. What else was she capable of?

"Why don't we take a walk?" she asked. "I saw a pond not far from here that needs my attention." She took my arm and we walked out of the cemetery. Even with all that had happened, what I had seen, I felt comforted with her arm around mine.

While we walked, Amy asked, "Why are you here, Ben? You know why I came to Aspermont, but why are *you* still here?"

"I don't know," I answered. "I guess I stayed for my mother. She got sick when I was seventeen. Alan and I did all we could for her, but the cancer won eventually. There's Alan, too. He did his best to step in after the war. He was a friend of my father's and wanted to help the family. He even lived with us until mom died. She and Alan never married, but he was like a stepfather to me."

"You don't want to abandon him," Amy said. "It's very noble of you to want to stay with him. He took care of you and your mother. But it's your fear of moving on that's really keeping you here, not your concern for Alan."

Amy's words resonated in me, and I knew they were true.

"You showed me why you're here," I said, "but I don't understand it. You're Japanese. My father was a Marine. He was fighting your people, so why would you help him?"

"Would you limit me to where I'm from? I do not like war, or those who wage it. I do not pick sides, but your father chose the life of a boy over his own, and that is moving." Amy paused a moment before continuing, "Many in Japan believe I came from Mount Wushan in China, the descendant of a goddess. You see me as Japanese because it was Japan that defined me. But, if you go far enough back, all spirits are tied to the same beginnings. It is the same with men, and though they look different, and speak differently, they are all brothers. I will help all who are worthy, despite the land they call home."

We had reached the pond, but it didn't resemble much of a body of water. It was very shallow, and the banks were dry. Amy ran into the middle of the pond, leaving me standing by the road. The water reached just below her knees.

"It needs more water," she called. "It needs life!"

Amy raised her hands, and swirling clouds formed over her, appearing to extend from her hands. They darkened as they spread to cover the pond and its dry banks. Then came a sound like muffled thunder. Amy spread her arms wide, but she was no longer in the water. She floated above it, slowly spinning, her feet well over the surface. My mouth gaped with awe at the sight. Despite what she had already shown me, this was an amazing scene that I could never have imagined. Then rain poured down, as if a waterfall had been released from the heavens, and came crashing through the clouds. I could feel the spray of the cool water from where I stood by the road.

As the rain fell, the water in the pond became clean and clear. The bluebonnets washed out of Amy's hair and floated to the banks where they took root and spread out in all directions. Amy lowered back down into the water, which now came to her chest. The rain stopped as suddenly as it began. The clouds cleared allowing the sun to shine over Amy's pond once again.

Amy laughed and waved for me to join her. I took off my shirt and ran into the cool, welcoming water.

We splashed, and swam, and played for a time, and then I settled on the grass in the sun to dry. Amy stayed in the water, but stood close to the bank. The pond had been a welcome distraction, but my mind turned back to what Amy *really* was. I thought I should be cautious, guard myself from infatuation, but then I looked at her beautiful face and ignored my worry.

"Will you be leaving now?" I asked her. "You've shown me what happened to my father, I imagine you've done what you promised." I didn't want her to leave.

"I told you, Ben, that I came to you when you needed me. There is more to my promise than what is obvious." Then she asked, "What do you want to do in this life? What do you want to see?"

"I guess I would like to see other parts of the world," I answered, "like my dad did in the Marines. He sent me some letters when I was a kid, and told me the Pacific Ocean was breathtaking. He said he would take me to see when he came home."

"He would still want you to see it." Amy waded out of the water and I put my shirt on before we walked back to my truck at the cemetery.

"I will leave you for now," she said, "but I will see you tonight, at the diner. I'll come inside this time, and maybe we can talk more?"

"I'd like that," I told her.

She turned and walked back the way we came. I watched her for a moment, and then jumped in the truck.

When I looked back she was gone.

Amy kept her word and came to the diner that night. She sat at a booth in the corner, and I brought her a hot chocolate. Alan didn't let us give free food or drink to customers, so I paid for it myself. It was a slow night, and I had time to sit and talk with her.

"I've never had hot chocolate before," she said, "but I like it. I rarely drink anything, but there were times I would go to teahouses just to witness the art that went into making the tea. It's a beautiful use of water, and they've been perfecting the art for centuries."

"How old are you exactly?" I asked. The question popped into mind when she said "centuries," and I asked it before remembering it was rude.

She laughed. "Old enough."

In my vision at the cemetery I had seen her with my dad. That was twelve years ago, but she didn't look a day younger than she did right now, sitting across from me in the diner.

"Amy, why were you on that island where my dad died? You said you weren't helping the Japanese in the war, so why would you be there?"

"Do I need a reason, Ben? Must the rain explain where it falls? Or the clouds say why they follow the wind? I was there, and that is all." Her posture stiffened, and she avoided eye contact.

"No, I want to know more." The only way I was going to understand her was if I pushed her to open up to me. "You came to me. Not randomly, but because you said I needed you. You were there when my father died, and you showed it to me. You saw me as I watched, and should know how deep and personal it was for me. Help me understand why you're here. Tell me how you happened to be where my father died."

Amy sighed and relaxed her posture before looking me in the eye.

"You saw that the boy was Japanese, didn't you?"

I nodded, but it hadn't occurred to me at the time.

"He is how I found your father." She paused, and I thought she might not finish explaining. "I found him in Japan," she continued. "His mother was dead, and his father abusive. So I took him. We traveled to the island so no one would recognize him. I had always desired to be a mother, but I didn't know how. I often left him with women from the island to care for him. We were there for several years before the war reached us. Your father did something I couldn't. He put the boy's life before his own. In that moment your father was a better parent to him than I had been for the past three years. So I took him back to Japan, and left him with an orphanage."

Amy picked up her hot chocolate and took a sip. I suddenly felt guilty for pressing her to share something so sensitive.

"We don't always get what we want, Ben. I wanted to be a mother, but if it was meant to be, that was not my time," she said.

"You said you descended from a Chinese goddess, so can you ever have your own children? Have a family?" I asked.

"It is possible," she said, "when I'm ready."

Her answer gave me the childish hope of someone who believes in love at first sight.

When my shift was over, Amy walked me home. That became our routine. Each morning I drove out to the pond, where we would talk about life, my father, Japan, and anything else we could think of. Sometimes we would play in the water, or lie in the bluebonnets to watch the clouds. Each night she would meet me at the diner, drink hot chocolate, and we would talk as time allowed. Often, she would touch my arm or hold my hand as we spoke. Every day I found myself longing to see her more.

About three weeks had passed when Alan called me back to the kitchen one evening, and Amy was left alone in her booth.

"You've been spending a lot of time with that girl," said Alan. "Are you sure that's wise, son? No one seems to know anything about her, why she's here, or who she is."

"I know her," I said. "Amy's a great girl. Shouldn't that be enough?"

Alan just shook his head. "You don't get it, do you? It was one of her kind that killed your dad. You think your mom would have approved? You think it don't bother me?"

"I'm sorry if you don't like her, Alan, but I know mom would be okay with it. Amy had nothing to do with the war." I wanted to tell him what she had shown me, and why she was here, but it wasn't my secret to tell.

"I've done my best to be like a father to you since your dad died. I know I'm not him, but this is who I am. I worry that you're chasing after some girl you don't even know. I just don't want you to get hurt. Frank's been hearing things over at the sheriff's department. Strange things."

"What kind of strange things?" I asked. Fear was creeping in the back of my mind that people knew there was more to Amy.

"I don't know exactly, Frank was vague." Alan waived his hands dismissively as he continued. "You're missing the point though, Ben. This girl is raising suspicion around the town, and you're sitting in here entertaining her every evening. I'm not sure why I allow it, seeing as I don't pay you to sit and talk."

"Wait, what suspicion is she raising?"

"Damn it, Ben!" Alan raised his voice in frustration. "Would you just trust me on this? She's no good for you, and I don't want you seeing her anymore!" Rubbing his forehead, Alan sighed. "Ben, you know this diner was handed to me by my father, and someday I'd like to hand it over to you. You're the closest thing to a son I've ever had, and I don't want you jeopardizing your life by spending time with the wrong people."

Amy had said in the cemetery that I felt obliged to Alan, and now I realized she was right. Knowing what I needed to do, I took off my apron and handed it him.

"There's more to my future than this town or this diner. " I said. "And I hope that Amy is always a part of it. If you're not okay with that, then I'm sorry."

I went back to Amy's booth and helped her up. "Let's go somewhere else," I said.

As we drove, I told Amy about Alan wanting me to take over the diner, but I didn't mention the things he said about her. I told her she was right about my being afraid to leave town. She listened with a comforting hand on my shoulder, letting me say what I needed.

We reached the pond, and got out of the truck. There was a blanket in the cab, which I threw over the tailgate so we could sit.

"I've been meaning to ask you, what do you do when we are not together?" Alan's comments had reminded me that I didn't know.

"I do this," she answered, gesturing to the pond. "I look for places that need me, and I bring life."

"I guess you've been doing the same for me," I said. "Helping me see more to this world."

She smiled, placed her arm in mine, and laid her head on my shoulder. "You're becoming your own man, Ben. It can take time to find ourselves, and we don't always know what the journey will look like, but you are taking steps towards being who you are meant to be. Your father would be proud. *I'm* proud."

Amy had come to mean so much to me over the past few weeks, and I knew that she was everything I could want in a woman...even though she wasn't *really* a woman. She was strong and independent, but also soft and kind. She had been encouraging me in a way no woman ever had, and I had fallen for her.

Amy stood and took a step towards the pond. I stood up behind her, and when she turned back toward me my arms were waiting. I wrapped them around her and pulled her in close. Leaning in, I kissed her, and as I did she placed her hands on my cheeks. She tasted sweet, like the apple from that morning in the cemetery.

She pulled her lips away and I saw sparkles in her eyes, like stars reflected in water. There was only one thing I could say. "I love you."

Amy pushed me away, gently, and walked over to the edge of the pond. A moment before we were kissing passionately, but now it seemed something was wrong.

"Why would you love me?" she asked.

"Because you're beautiful," I said, "and you encourage me to be better. You kept your promise to my father and have shown me wonderful things. I'm in love with you, Amy."

"Those are just things I've done, and how I've appeared. It's not who—or what—I am." she said, still facing the water.

"There is more to us than what we've done, but what we do is a reflection of who we are, just like when you brought life to this pond." She turned back towards me as I spoke. "Amy, when I look at you I see a brilliant, beautiful person, and I can't help but love you. Do you not feel what's between us? What do you see when you see me?"

Rain was beginning to sprinkle as Amy walked back to me. She placed her hand on my chest and said, "I see an honest man with a good heart. I see pure intentions. I see so much in you, Ben."

That next moment was brief, but it felt long enough to plan a future with her. I wanted her desperately. She kissed me, and the rain began to fall faster. She pulled my shirt over my head, and I loosened my belt. Reaching the buttons on the back of her dress, I unfastened them, letting it fall around her ankles. Her skin felt soft against mine, her body was warm in my arms. I lifted her onto the blanket in the bed of the truck, and pulled myself on top of her, still kissing passionately.

Whispering in her ear, I said "I love you."

When she whispered it back, the sky lit up with lightning, and thunder rumbled above us. Laying with Amy that night, our bodies intertwined in the open air, the taste of rain and sweat on her neck, the sound of her breathing in my ear; it felt like a fire had ignited, consuming us under the stars. I believed it could burn forever.

The sun had dried the blanket and my clothes by the time I awoke. Amy was already up, standing ankle deep in the water of the pond. She was wearing my t-shirt, which revealed her smooth legs. Her hair was free in the wind, and she held some bluebonnets in her hands. When I sat up she said, "Good morning."

Her smile was wide, and her face seemed to glow in the sunlight.

"That was...an interesting evening," I said. Realizing that "interesting," didn't express how happy I was we had been together, I quickly added, "I mean it was a great evening. Really great."

She laughed at my inability to communicate. "You're cute in the morning," she said, which made me blush. We had just slept together, but her words still affected me like a giddy boy. She walked over and kissed me, but then her smile faded.

"Ben, you should know that last night was very special to me. But I must ask, how do you think our love will continue? Where do you see us going from here?"

"Well," I said, "I think we should do whatever it takes to make this work. For starters, I'll probably need to find a new job. You could move in with me, and we could get married. Whatever it takes."

She laughed. "I am Ameonna. I do not need houses or money. And what is here for us? Would you leave this town? Perhaps even leave your country?"

I assumed she meant moving to Japan, and I knew that I would. "It's not about us settling here," I said, "It's about being together. This is what my mind sees when I think of a future together, because this is what I know. But I would leave Aspermont if it meant we were together."

She laughed and kissed me again. "It may not be easy, but we can try.

Tonight, I could spend time at your house, to show you that I am willing. You may need money if we are to leave, so perhaps you should inquire about a new job."

I grinned. "Wonderful. But first, I'm going to need my shirt back."

I drove home and cleaned myself up. There was a grocery store across from the diner that I knew was hiring, so I decided to start looking for a job there. Looking around I realized the house probably wasn't ready for a woman to stay there, so I took a few minutes to clean it up before heading out.

Once at the grocery store, I glanced over at the diner. Through the front window I saw Alan. He was talking to Frank, Jon, and Gary Winchester, another farmer. The conversation appeared heated, and Alan was shaking his head. I noticed Frank had seen me, and he pointed in my direction. The conversation stopped, and now the whole group was staring at me. A knot grew quickly in my stomach.

The four men came out of the diner, but Jon and Gary stopped at the sidewalk while Alan followed Frank across the street towards me. Concern was written in Alan's wrinkled brow. Frank almost bumped into me, stopping with his face inches from mine.

"Where's your girlfriend, Ben?" he asked, hands on his hips. "I want to ask her some questions."

"Just a minute now," Alan put his arms out and stepped between us. "Let me talk to him first, would ya?" He turned toward me. "Ben, son, you need to let us know where she is. I know you feel strongly for her, you said as much yesterday, but I don't want you getting hurt."

"What's going on here, Alan?" I asked.

"I told you the sheriff's department had been hearing things. Well I think you ought to know just what they've been hearing." Alan stepped aside. "Tell him, Frank."

"Yeah, we've been hearing things all right." Frank paused, narrowing his eyes before he continued. "Strange things. One man said he was on his porch when he noticed a Japanese girl suspended up off the ground over his crops. He went in and got his wife, but when they came back the girl was gone. But it was raining though there had been no clouds only moments before."

"That's silly, Frank," I said. I was hoping to convince them they were paranoid, and get them to change the subject all together. "What does one old farmer have to do with Amy?"

"He ain't the only one who's seen things, Ben, I've got a dozen more reports just like that. Even Jon and Gary have had their own encounters." Frank pointed at the two farmers across the street. "Jon there was driving into town last week when he saw your girl walking on the side of the road. He stopped and offered her a lift because it was raining, but she declined. Then he gets into town to find her talking with you in the diner, not even wet. Jon lives five miles out. There's no way she would have beat him into town. Then Gary shows up and says he seen her that night too, but he lives ten miles the other direction!"

"You're crazy, Frank! Why don't you guys just head home before you make fools of yourselves." I needed to convince them to drop it before they could confront Amy.

Alan stepped back in. "We know she's not normal, Ben. Did you think I couldn't overhear you at the diner? Those nights when we had no customers, and it was just the two of you talking? I heard you say she was a *spirit*, Ben. A *spirit!* If it's true, she is too dangerous to let her stay around here. She needs to go. Now, I'll only ask once, will you help us?"

"Look, I know Amy, okay? " I was starting to feel desperate. " She's a good person. She hasn't hurt anyone. She's not a danger!"

"She ain't a *person*, Ben! She's a *thing!*" Frank stepped right up to my face again, and it was all I could do to not punch him across his jaw. "This town is my responsibility, and I will protect it from the danger she poses. If you ain't going to help, then be sure you don't get in the way."

"Frank! Alan! *Look!*" Jon yelled from across the street.

I turned to see Amy standing in the road, only twenty or thirty feet from us.

"Where the hell did she come from?" asked Alan. "She wasn't there a moment ago!"

I rushed to her, and grasped her shoulders. She was clearly confused by my abrupt actions. Her eyebrows arched and lips parted like a question was on the tip of her tongue.

"Amy," I said softly, so the others couldn't hear, "you need to go. These guys figured out what you are, and now they're scared. You should go to the pond. I'll talk to them, tell them they have nothing to fear from you."

"Scared?" She asked. "I have brought life to this area. It was dry, and dying, and I poured into it. Why would they be scared? I *helped* them. "

"I know that, Amy, and they will too. They just don't see it yet. They don't understand."

I looked back and saw that the four men had formed a line across the road. Frank had his pistol drawn, and Gary held a shotgun. They were walking slowly toward us.

"Ben, come away from her," Alan called out. "It's not safe!"

Amy pushed past me and moved toward them. "What would you have of me?"

The four men looked around at each other, and Frank stepped out to be their spokesperson.

"We don't know what the hell you are, but you're not welcome here. Leave or we'll be forced to open fire."

Above, the clouds grew darker, and thunder rumbled through the sky. The rain intensified, and so did the wind.

Amy took a few more steps forward. "Would you tell the clouds where they can form, or the rain where it can fall? You do not control these things, nor do you control me." She stretched her arms out and lifted up from the ground, wind twirling around her like a small cyclone.

The sight was enough to scare Gary. He dropped his shotgun and ran.

"Mankind is all the same!" Amy's voice was booming now, like it was thunder. A flash of lightning crashed incredibly near. "You would destroy what you do not understand. I do not fear you, but you will all tremble in my gaze!"

The rain was coming down almost sideways now, and the wind raged around us. The three remaining men held their arms over their faces and braced against the onslaught.

I forced my way though the weather and stood in front of Amy. She looked so terrible, her eyes glowing with light, her hair whipping in the wind. I yelled out to her, "Amy!" But she didn't respond. I reached up and touched her hip with my hand. "Amy! Stop it! You have to come down! You're only feeding their fears!"

"Shouldn't they fear me?" she cried, her voice echoing in the unnatural torrent. "They would see me destroyed if I do not succumb to their will!"

"Would you destroy *them* instead?" I remembered what she told me about men and war. "Is that what makes you better than them, that you're stronger, or more powerful? This is not who you are. You're strong, but compassionate. You're powerful, but wise. And I love you because you do what is right."

The rain let up, and Amy floated slowly down into my arms. Her eyes were clear again, and I held her, my back to her attackers.

I heard Frank and Alan move closer. Looking over my shoulder I saw that Frank was pointing his pistol in our direction. His hand was trembling.

"Stand aside, Ben," he said. "I'll do what has to be done."

"Please, Ben, do as he says," said Alan.

Amy spoke softly in my ear. "He is afraid, and he will pull the trigger. I won't be able to stop him if he does."

"Then I will give my life for yours," I whispered. "Because I love you."

"Last warning, son," said Frank.

"Ben, step away," said Alan.

"Alan, if you ever cared for my parents, or for me," I said, "then end this...*please.*"

Frank pulled back the hammer on his pistol.

"That's enough, Frank!" Alan suddenly yelled. "Put your gun down. We aren't going to win this anyhow. Last thing we want is to kill one of our own."

Frank didn't move. His hard eyes stayed on Amy, his hands still shaking. In that moment I was terrified, not of death, but of being separated from Amy.

But then, slowly, Frank lowered his weapon.

"I won't let this town suffer over this, Ben," he said. "I want her out of here. *Now!* Understand?" He holstered his pistol, picked up Gary's shotgun and walked back to his patrol car, never taking his eyes off Amy.

Letting out a pent-up breath, Alan glanced at me. "I hope you know what you're doing, Ben." Turning, he went back to the diner.

"You act more like your father every day," Amy said. She touched my check and I saw sadness in her eyes. "I can't stay, Ben. I can't do this. Men will never understand my kind, and I can't put you in danger again."

"It's okay, Amy. No one got hurt."

"No, it is not okay," she said. "I knew that this could happen. But when I look at you, I just want to be with you. I've been selfish. You've given me a taste of what it is to be loved, but I'm afraid a taste is all I am meant to have."

Tears burned down my cheeks. I didn't want her to go. I didn't want to believe she was even suggesting it.

"You said you came to me when I needed you most. Well I need you now, Amy. You are my strength." I was sobbing now. Amy lifted my chin to look her in the eye. She smiled at me like she had when we first danced in the street.

"You don't need me, Ben. You're strong on your own." She kissed me, and I could taste our tears mixed with rain on her lips. Pulling me close she whispered, "Goodbye."

And then she evaporated like a cloud in my arms, leaving me alone in the middle of the road.

Falling to my knees, tears welling in my eyes, I whispered, "Goodbye, Amy. I'll miss you so much."

Thinking of Amy, I stood and looked at the still, clear water of our pond. My suitcase was packed and waiting in the truck. The plan was to drive to California and book passage to Japan. I was going to look until I found her, no matter how long it took.

Rain began to fall, slowly at first, disturbing the pond's calm surface. Soon it built into a steady downpour, much like that night at the diner when I saw Amy for the first time.

Holding out my right hand, as if to place it on Amy's waist, and my left held up as if to take her hand, I let out a deep breath. Moving my feet, I led the rain in a waltz, alone by the side of the road. For a moment, if only a second, I felt her hand in mine and heard her laugh.

It was in that moment I knew the rain had accepted my invitation, and I was glad she had taught me to do this sort of thing.

A Single Touch

Julie Luton

THE VAN DOOR slammed shut with a screeching protest, abruptly cutting off a woman's screams. A man and woman jogging nearby reported later that the abduction happened so quickly they barely turned in time to witness the event. After a shocked pause, the man ran toward the van, while the woman, her face pale with distress, kept her eyes glued to the license plate to memorize its numbers.

Neither attempt did much good. Early morning shadows concealed most of the license plate, so the woman only saw the first three numbers. The man made it just half a block before the van sped by him, swerving momentarily in his direction and causing him to stumble in panic.

At the end of the block, an abandoned poodle dragged her leash, racing after her kidnapped mistress. The dog's forlorn howls echoed in the city streets long after she disappeared from sight.

Silence fell in his small office after Matt finished telling Lucie and Sam, his distraught sister and brother-in-law, the grim details of his niece's abduction. His hazel eyes burned with rage and with tears he couldn't let fall. As a private investigator specializing in missing persons, his professionalism was sometimes the only thing that kept his clients from falling apart. Today was no different, even if, on this occasion, it was harder to remain detached. After talking them through their despair and fear, he promised he'd call the second he heard anything. Matt's sister hung on his brother-in-law's arm as they left, and Matt ached to be there for her, too. Still, he knew his job was to find his niece, not to provide comfort.

He gathered up the case reports littering his desk and shuffled them together without glancing at the picture on top. The most current family photo of his niece remained seared on his retinas; he couldn't bear to see Laurel's big brown eyes and corkscrew curls framing her open smile. He could only hope Laurel still lived.

Unless, of course, she was better off dead.

Matt picked up his cell phone, scrolled through his contacts, and dialed. Moments later, the sugared tones of a woman's voice sashayed out and cocooned Matt. "Hello, this is Cinnamon. How can I help you today?" Low and sensuous, Cinnamon's voice entranced. Matt understood why men apparently paid fortunes merely to talk to her.

He shoved the case to the background for one moment. Relationships, even business ones, demanded finesse, and small talk was a necessary evil. Cinnamon's phone sex business paid well, and she never took money for helping with his cases, so he always took a little extra care. Besides, he genuinely liked talking to her. "Hey there, Cinnamon. How's business?"

Some of the syrupy sweetness left her voice, and Cinnamon answered briskly. "Matt! It's been a while. Business is fine; can't complain. It's great to hear your voice, sugar, although I'm sure you're not calling with good news. You taking care of yourself?"

Shrugging, Matt replied, "I'm okay. I've been busy, but nothing that was up your alley. At least not until today."

"Sorry to hear you need our services. What happened?"

In a few broad strokes, Matt outlined the case. "Third kidnapping in six months and the same MO each time. A young woman snatched off the street in front of multiple witnesses. A black van used in each case. The Kansas City police can find absolutely no forensic evidence or a connection between the victims."

Cinnamon asked, "You said three kidnappings, right? Have the police found any of them?"

After hesitating, Matt answered reluctantly. "Yeah, they found the first two bodies after a month of captivity each, but it's nothing you want to hear details about."

Cinnamon breathed softly through the phone. "I see."

"Look," Matt said. "I hate to ask since I know how your sister feels about this kind of shi...er, stuff. But the police have nothing. The clients are, uh, family friends. They think I'm some kind of miracle worker, and I, well, Cinnamon, the girl's only seventeen. She should be choosing where she wants to go to college, not...." Matt's voice trailed off, unable to voice his fears for Laurel.

Cinnamon didn't respond for a moment, but Matt knew she wouldn't say no. Even if she wanted to, her sister wouldn't let her. The delay wasn't even a calculated attempt to make him beg; she just genuinely hated things like this, especially when she knew what it would do to her sister.

Finally, she said, "Send me what you have and I'll talk to her."

"I'll send it by courier. You'll have it within the hour." He hesitated, not wanting to burden her with his relationship to the missing girl, but frantic with worry for his niece. "Cinnamon, there's no time to waste here. The police think the kidnapped girls were kept underground somewhere near here; their last hours were hell on earth. We need to find this girl as fast as we can."

Her tone annoyed, Cinnamon said, "You'll get her best work; you always do. It'll take as long as it takes."

Matt ran a hand roughly through his wiry black hair. "I know it. I just wish I could see her myself. It would make things easier."

Without answering, Cinnamon hung up the phone.

Matt muttered, "Hell, that didn't go well."

After the package arrived from Matt, Cinnamon walked down the hall of the town home she shared with her sister, her steps slowed by what she was about to ask Brianna to do. Again.

She stopped outside the music room and leaned her head wearily against the door, the majestic chords of a Rachmaninoff piece filling the air. She delayed entering as long as the music danced and spun around her, but when quiet fell, Cinnamon took her cue. She knocked once then opened the door. Brianna sat on the upholstered piano bench, her silvery blond hair hiding her face.

"Hey, Bri." Cinnamon said. She brandished the envelope. "I have a package from Matt."

Tucking her hair behind her ear, Brianna swiveled on her bench. "Matt sent me something? That can't be good." She paused a moment, and then asked wistfully. "Did you talk to him? How is he? Is he going to call again soon?" Brianna gave her head a swift shake. "Never mind. What's happened?"

Cinnamon shrugged helplessly. "I thought I'd let you look first to see if you want to help."

"I haven't had a choice in a long time, Cinnamon. You know that. If I can help, I have to." Brianna held out her hand for the envelope. "Let me see."

For one crazy moment, Cinnamon considered taking the package and escaping out the front door where Brianna couldn't follow. Then Brianna couldn't read, couldn't suffer. Instead, Cinnamon dumped the contents of the envelope beside Brianna. "He gave me the highlights. It's a seventeen-year-old girl. It'll be awful for you."

Eying the items piled beside her, Brianna responded. "It's always awful. The only thing that makes it bearable is helping someone else." Brianna didn't touch anything yet. She just looked. A hairbrush laden with strands of dark hair drew her eyes first. Next to that was a small photo. The curly-haired girl looked happy, her brown eyes clear and her smile bright. Lying near the photo, a chunky necklace with a striking stone hanging from the silver chain twined around a well-worn pink dog collar.

Carefully sliding the envelope under the girl's possessions and taking care to touch nothing with her bare hands, Brianna stood. "Not here. This room is too full of music, and it's distracting."

Cinnamon gathered the items and led Brianna to the small library where books overflowed the shelves. Brianna settled down on the mahogany-colored chaise occupying a corner. Cinnamon placed the items next to her sister, and then sat at the antique rolltop desk with note paper, ready to record whatever details Brianna gave. She could hear Brianna's deep inhale and slow exhalation. After a few minutes, Cinnamon turned around to look at her sister. Her pale blue eyes sightless as she focused deep within herself, Brianna stared straight ahead as she touched the items one by one.

"Seems to be taking a long time." Cinnamon said, the words loud in the quiet room.

Brianna answered, her voice slow and deeper in timbre than usual. "I can feel her around me but can't quite reach her. She's shielding herself somehow."

"Matt said the kidnapper kept the other victims underground somewhere," Cinnamon said. "Could that be interfering with your gift?"

Brianna shifted her blank-eyed stare in Cinnamon's direction and blinked once. Her eyes darkened in color and intensity until once again Brianna's dark blue gaze looked at Cinnamon.

"No, I don't think so. I think this is some kind of internal block. Does it say in the file if she's a sensitive of some kind?"

Shaking her head, Cinnamon answered, "Doesn't say. Matt might know. I should call him."

Brianna's face lit up. "I'll call him. I can describe what I'm talking about rather than relaying through you."

Her tone sympathetic, Cinnamon still spoke disapprovingly. "You know what happened the last time you two spoke."

A blush appeared on Brianna's face as she looked away. "I won't let it happen again. I have it under control this time."

"I doubt it, Bri, but you're an adult. Call him if you want." She tossed Brianna the phone and left, grunting a "be careful" in her direction.

Brianna looked at the phone uncertainly. Talking to Matt on previous occasions had made her feel a bit like she was walking outside during a thunderstorm. His emotions had swirled and swept by her, frightening her with the sound and fury. But oh, it was exciting!

She exhaled slowly and then dialed. The phone rang only twice before it connected and Matt's gruff voice answered.

"Matt Graysen Investigations."

Brianna sat still, a little taken aback by his abrupt tone. "Hello, Matt? It's Brianna."

She could almost hear him sit up straighter, and she winced. He probably thought she had news.

"Did you find her?" he asked in a rush. "Where is she?"

Brianna answered, "I'm so sorry, no, not yet. I need some help first."

"Oh, sorry," he said, "What can I do to help?"

Brianna asked, "Is Laurel a sensitive?"

Sounding puzzled, Matt answered after a slight pause, "Not that I know of. Why?"

"She's blocking me or something. I can't tune into her frequency."

He snorted. "What is she, a radio station?"

"Something like that, I guess," Brianna said uncertainly. "That's the way I think of it. I get bits and pieces of what someone broadcasts." Her voice low, she added, "Sometimes I get things they've stuffed in the crevices of their minds; stuff they wouldn't want anyone else to know."

"Got it. Sorry. The description just sounded a little strange. You've never explained exactly what it is you do. I just know you're never wrong."

Annoyed by his "strange" comment, Brianna responded, "That's because it isn't easy to describe. It's part of me the way breathing is part of me. Forgive me if I sound weird to you."

Matt sighed. "Brianna. I wasn't making fun of you. I was honestly curious. I appreciate you explaining your gift to me. What can I do to help?"

Somewhat mollified, she said, "For some reason, I can't get a connection from ordinary objects like I usually can. I need something more, something directly tied to her on a personal level. The only thing I can think of is a friend or family member who has contact with her on a regular basis." She hesitated and whispered, "Please, it has to be someone who isn't so agonized by her disappearance that their emotions are too out of control. It...hurts me...if that much emotion is so close to me."

"I know you can read objects and people, but I didn't know their emotions had that much impact on you."

Brianna spoke, her words hurried, "Never mind. Forget I said anything. Can you find me someone or not?"

"I can find someone right away. Just tell me where and when do you want to meet."

"My apartment. One hour. Is that okay?" Brianna asked.

"The sooner the better. One hour it is."

Exactly one hour later, Matt buzzed the apartment from the lobby.

Cinnamon's voice echoed out, "Who is it?"

"It's Matt."

"Who else is with you?" Cinnamon asked.

"It's just me. Look, let me come up and I'll explain." Matt waited through the long silence.

"Okay, I'll buzz you up," Cinnamon said through the speaker.

Riding to the top floor, Matt waited impatiently until the elevator shuddered to a stop. Doors opened directly into the living area. The interior of the room was dim, lit only by lamplight. Across from the elevator, curtains shrouded what Matt guessed were floor to ceiling windows. A chocolate brown leather sofa and chairs occupied the main seating area, accented by a few upholstered ottomans and straight-backed chairs. No knick-knacks or photos cluttered the surfaces. Although it appeared expensively furnished, the space looked little used. Obviously, the sisters spent their lives in other parts of their home.

As movement flickered to his left, Matt turned to find a woman staring at him. But he had no idea if it was Cinnamon or Brianna.

"Hello, Matt. It's good to meet you finally."

When he heard her voice, Matt recognized her instantly. "You too, Cinnamon."

She was heavier than her sultry voice let on, but she was also magnificent. Her hair hung in loose waves to her waist and shimmered with highlights in the lamplight. Her eyes were luminous, so dark they appeared almost purple in color, and were ringed by thick lashes. She wore a clingy, colorful robe that enhanced voluptuous curves. She smiled at Matt. He felt warmed and welcome, a friend whose arrival was happily awaited.

Cinnamon smiled wryly. "Sorry if I've been a bit snappish; I'm just worried about Brianna." She turned away, motioning for him to follow.

Feeling increasingly like his niece's time was running out, Matt strode quickly down the hallway, passing a library overflowing with books and a powder bath. As they passed a bedroom door, Matt saw a huge wooden sleigh bed with brightly colored, sumptuous-looking bedding. Clothing littered the floor, and the scent of cinnamon wafted out. He wondered if Cinnamon chose her name based on an apparently favorite scent.

The second room housed a white baby grand piano, accented only by the black keys on the keyboard. A thing of beauty, the instrument took up almost the entire room, leaving only enough space to circle around the bench. Posters from local theatrical productions decorated the walls.

He turned to the last bedroom, and his heart thudded in his chest. For over a year, he'd worked with these women, acceded to their somewhat mysterious ways. He'd wondered increasingly what it would be like to meet them, but most especially Brianna. Cinnamon's voice was beautiful, but something in Brianna's haunted him. Sometimes when they talked, she sounded fragile and almost broken. But other times, after they'd closed a case and he called to thank her, he'd heard a confident woman who captured his imagination, causing him to spend way too much time wondering what she looked like. Now, finally, he was about to meet her in person. He had no clue what he'd find behind the door. But he knew that Brianna offered the only hope for his niece.

"I thought Brianna would be more comfortable in here," Cinnamon said. Opening the door, she ushered Matt ahead of her. He walked in, ready to do whatever it took to find Laurel.

Then he saw Brianna and forgot to breathe.

Brianna stood near the bed. Her silvery blond hair framed a fine-boned face, and her dark blue eyes burned with a fire that ignited an answering intensity in Matt. While she wore only a simple white t-shirt with comfortable-looking stonewashed jeans and black flip-flops, her slim build enhanced by womanly curves still managed to look regal.

He thought, *She can't be real. No one is that beautiful.*

He'd imagined that she'd be pale, sickly-looking, a mere ghost of a person. Yet she appeared vibrantly alive, a flesh and blood woman who gazed at him as eagerly as he looked at her. She smiled, a little tremulously, and whispered hello.

Unintentionally, drawn as a moth to a flame, Matt stumbled forward, his hand outstretched in an unconscious desire to touch her, to hold her.

Only when Brianna jerked back, alarm plainly written on her face, did Matt stop his rush forward. He said, "Sorry, I, uh, don't usually charge at women that way."

Brianna waved airily, as if it was nothing, but Matt noticed her hand shaking. Confused by her reaction, he waited for her to speak. She said nothing, and the silence became awkward.

Cinnamon broke the tension. "Sorry, I would have warned you earlier, but we don't usually meet with clients. Brianna doesn't like to be touched. It's—how shall I put this?—upsetting to her. So please don't, under any circumstances, touch her. That's rule number one, okay?"

Nodding, Matt kept his eyes on Brianna's stricken countenance.

Cinnamon continued speaking, her melodious voice filling the room. "Rule number two is that you can never talk about this. You already know that one."

Again, Matt nodded. "My only goal is to find Laurel."

Appearing satisfied, Cinnamon looked at her sister. "You okay?"

"Yes." Brianna's face twisted slightly, and the slight tremors in her hands increased.

Matt suddenly knew she was deathly afraid of something, perhaps him. He clenched his hands to keep from enfolding her in his arms, comforting her, protecting her. He could do nothing to break the rules. Laurel counted on him.

Cinnamon said suddenly, "Brianna said she needed a family member. Why are *you* here?"

"Laurel is my niece." Matt ignored Brianna's soft exclamation of distress, figuring that Cinnamon was the first hurdle he had to clear. "I didn't tell you before because I didn't think it was relevant." He cleared his throat. "Also, it felt a little personal."

Cinnamon's face softened. "I'm so sorry, Matt. It might make it a little harder since Bri knows you. I don't want anything to distract her. What do you think, Bri?"

Matt didn't speak, didn't plead. He would if he had to; he would beg these women to help him save Laurel's life, but for now he simply waited as he looked at Brianna's delicate features.

Brianna eyes wandered Matt's face, and then she nodded. "A girl's life is at stake."

Matt loosened the fists he'd unconsciously clenched at his sides. "Thank you."

Jerking her head toward a table, Cinnamon said, "Let's get started."

Matt took a seat and made a conscious effort to relax. As he did so, he noticed the muscles in Brianna's shoulders relax, too.

Cinnamon settled herself on the bed, her robe a bright splash of color against the deep brown comforter. Neutrals dominated the room, but everything from the wall hangings to the furniture looked expensive. Candlelight made the room seem more intimate, and the faint scent of vanilla floated on the air.

Heaped on the table were Laurel's things. Matt's eyes lingered on the familiar items. Then Brianna hummed deep in her throat, pulling Matt's attention back to her instantly. Her eyes closed, and she rested her hands in her lap, loosely holding Laurel's hairbrush.

When Brianna opened her eyes, Matt jerked in his chair with shock. Before, her eyes had been startlingly blue, now they were a color so pale they appeared almost translucent. Her eyes closed again.

Cinnamon spoke, "Brianna's searching for your niece, trying to link with her."

Matt said, "Will it bother her to hear us talking?"

"No, until she finds Laurel, she'll sink pretty deep within herself and will only notice us with tremendous effort. The apartment could catch on fire and she probably wouldn't move. That's why it's important someone is always with her when she goes under. She's completely vulnerable."

"How can I help her?"

"Bri said your niece was blocking her somehow. I don't know how you can help with that. We'll have to wait and see."

Matt forced himself to lean back in the chair. "How long does this usually take?"

Cinnamon looked sympathetically at him. "It depends on what she finds. It'll take as long as it takes." She raised her eyebrows inquiringly. "While we wait, why don't you tell me about yourself?"

Matt smiled slightly. "I bet you say that to all the guys."

The good-natured expression disappeared from Cinnamon's face. She said, her voice stiff, "I was just making conversation, not working."

Matt kept his eyes on her face. "That's not what I was implying at all. I was just trying to lighten the mood a little bit, apparently not very successfully. I'm sorry. I'm just worried."

Cinnamon looked down. "Okay. I jumped to conclusions. I can be a little sensitive about my chosen profession."

Silence filled the room. Matt turned to watch Brianna for a moment, his attention caught by a change in her breathing. She hummed again and drew several deep breaths. Her hands twisted in her lap. Then she stilled. Matt turned back toward Cinnamon. "You want to know about me? I'm former military, and I opened my own shop because hunting for missing people seemed the closest thing to hunting terrorists. I didn't want to join the police or government. I've had enough of authority figures telling me how to do things."

Cinnamon's laugh rang out. "I can see that about you."

"I'm not very good at playing by the rules, and I'll do anything to get the job done. That's why I didn't flinch when I heard about Brianna through the grapevine."

Cinnamon nodded. "Why turn away from someone who might help, no matter how weird she seems?"

Sliding his eyes back to Brianna, Matt tried not to notice again how beautiful she was. "I don't think she's weird at all." He paused then smiled slightly. "Well, maybe a little different. I think she's wonderful, though. She's responsible for me finding four people in the last year. Four people returned home to their families just because Brianna is who she is. I'd be a fool if I ignored that kind of gift."

"And you're no fool."

"No," Matt said. "I'm not a fool."

Suddenly, Brianna arched in her chair, ending their conversation.

Cinnamon frowned, perplexed. "It sometimes can take a few minutes to connect, but she's really struggling."

Brianna's eyes opened. Her pale blue eyes gazed straight at Matt's face, but he had the eerie feeling that she couldn't really see him. She spoke, her voice low, "Matt, I need you to think about Laurel. Try to remember good times with her, not the fact that you're frightened for her. I need her to feel you here with me. She won't let me in; she doesn't trust me." She held out the hairbrush, and Matt touched it gently.

Then, supposing he looked as confused as he felt, Matt obediently closed his eyes and pictured Laurel moments after his sister thrust her tiny form into his waiting arms. He remembered her first Halloween dressed in a goofy bumblebee outfit. He pictured her learning how to dance, ride a bike, toss a football. He recalled piggyback rides and high fives. Finally, he simply wished he could see once more the beautiful, happy girl whose carefree exterior belied the serious amount of brains she hid.

He opened his eyes to see Brianna sitting before him with tears streaming down her face. Remembering Cinnamon's warning just in time, he resisted the urge to touch her,

She moaned, "Uncle Matt," her voice a higher pitch than Brianna's normal tone.

Matt surged to his feet. "Laurel, where are you? Help me find you! Please, I can't find you.."

Brianna trembled, but she didn't answer. "I'm afraid. Oh, no. Oh, no! He's coming; he's coming. I have to go." Brianna's voice rose to a scream. "Uncle Matt! Help me!"

Panic-stricken at the fear in Brianna/Laurel's voice, Matt reached Brianna's side and grasped her shoulders. He yanked her out of the chair, where she hung, dangling, in his furious grasp. "No! Don't go. Tell me where you are, dammit! Help me find you!"

Dimly, Matt felt Cinnamon beating him on the shoulder, yelling at him to stop touching Brianna. But he couldn't let go, couldn't think, couldn't hear anything but Laurel's abject terror.

Glancing up, he saw his reflection in a mirror across the room and froze in horror. He could see his hands, the knuckles white with fury, gripping Brianna. He could see Cinnamon trying to release her sister from his grasp. His face, set and frightening, glowered in the reflection as he held Brianna's trembling form.

With a start, he looked down and Brianna's eyes stared up at him, the pale azure replaced with an intensely anguished dark blue that banished his rage instantly, replacing it with fear for her safety. He set her gently on the chair and stepped backward, raising his hands in surrender.

Cinnamon rushed by him and knelt by Brianna, not touching her but staying close. She began crooning a lullaby, at first drowned out by Brianna's whimpering but slowly becoming more audible. Finally, all that could be heard was Cinnamon's beautiful voice, rising and falling in a mesmerizing rhythm. She pulled her robe over her hands to cover her skin and gently pulled Brianna to her feet. She led her to the bed and helped her lie down, pulling up the heavy comforter. Brianna closed her eyes and fell asleep in between one breath and the next.

Cinnamon rose to her feet and jerked her head toward the bedroom door. Matt left reluctantly, averse to leaving Briana. As the door closed behind them, Matt tried to apologize, but Cinnamon just held up her hand.

"Get out," she said.

He stared at her, stunned. "I can't leave. She made the connection. She reached Laurel. I have to ask Brianna what she saw, where Laurel is. I'm so sorry I hurt her, but I have to find Laurel."

Cinnamon advanced toward him, her face livid. "Do you have any idea what you've done?"

He shook his head. "I know you told me not to touch her, and I'm sorry. When can I talk to her?"

Cinnamon glared at him. "You can't ever talk to her again. You touched her. You poured all your worry and your rage and your hatred into Brianna. Do you know what she is?" She kept walking straight toward Matt, herding him to the elevator. "She's not just a psychic, she's an empath. That means she feels everything you feel. All your fears, all your hate, all your rage, every emotion bottled inside you, even the ones you hide from yourself, she gets them all. She can't hide from them, and she has no defense. She never has. Your emotions just exploded inside of her like a bomb."

Matt held up his hands in protest. "I didn't know! You never told me."

Cinnamon kept walking steadily down the hall. She spit out her next words. "She doesn't want anyone to know what she is. She feels like a freak as it is, without everyone knowing her business. Before she figured out what she was, she tried to commit suicide. It's taken her years to learn how to deal with her ability. She never goes out, rarely looks out the window, hardly ever meets with anyone personally, all to avoid exposure from the kind of emotion you unloaded with no warning."

They reached the elevator, and Cinnamon pushed the button. The door dinged open. "I was wrong, you know. About you not being a fool. Get out. Don't ever come back."

Without a word, Matt walked into the elevator and pushed the down button. Guilt ate at him like acid...guilt that he'd overreacted, guilt that he'd hurt Brianna. But more than anything, he knew he'd ruined his last chance to save Laurel.

Brianna stared at the ceiling. The candles had long ago sputtered out, but their scent lingered. The apartment was quiet, an all-enveloping silence that meant night had fallen. Cinnamon would be ensconced in her room, talking on the phone to her clients, the desperate men and women who bankrolled Brianna's way of life. Brianna couldn't afford to feel condescending toward them; instead she was grateful. Without them and the privacy their money afforded, she would have gone crazy long ago.

Every muscle in her body ached, especially where Matt had grabbed her. She delicately ran her fingers across her own skin, feeling the residual heat from his touch. Everything he felt had poured into her with no warning and no way to stop it. His towering rage, his love for his niece, his fear for Laurel's safety, even his lust for Brianna, all that became part of her in one surge. She had felt like she was on fire with emotion. She barely remembered him leaving. She'd retreated to her own mind, a place she'd learned long ago was safe, quiet...and boring.

Dear God, she was so bored with her life.

She wanted color and passion and laughter. She wanted happiness, and yes, even tears. She wanted something in her life rather than her own thoughts and muted emotions.

At Matt's touch, an entire world opened in front of her. All she'd had to do was reach out and take it. For a year, she'd wondered what it would be like to meet Matt...to see him, touch him, to be something more to each other than just voices on the phone. She'd even thought he might be wondering the same things, too. Instead, at the first opportunity, she hid herself away. She was a coward, and she despised herself for it. She wasn't a child anymore, afraid of her gift and of herself. She was a woman, and it was time she acted like one.

A soft knock interrupted her thoughts. "Bri? You awake?"

Brianna thrust the covers aside, stood up and walked to the door. She enjoyed the expression of utter shock that chased across Cinnamon's face as she watched Brianna open the door. "I'm awake. Call Matt and get him back here."

If Brianna enjoyed surprising her sister with her apparent good mental health, she absolutely adored the dumbfounded look that now took up residence on Cinnamon's face.

Stuttering, Cinnamon said, "Wha- what do you mean? I thought..." Her voice trailed off, her face anguished.

Brianna immediately felt ashamed of her enjoyment at Cinnamon's expense. "I'm fine. I need to find Laurel. I need Matt's help to do it. "

Cinnamon's face reddened. "Absolutely not, Bri! He touched you. He hurt you!"

"You're right; he did. But he didn't mean to, Cinnamon. He just let himself be swept up with all the heat and passion and emotion. It was terrifying...and wonderful. And really, it doesn't matter. What matters is a girl is being hurt. I can stop it. *We* can stop it. Will you help me?"

Cinnamon hesitated, then nodded. "If you're sure, Bri, then I'll help you. Always."

Brianna smiled at her gratefully and walked past Cinnamon. "I'm hungry." She allowed herself one small indulgence. As she passed by, she brushed her hand along Cinnamon's arm...the first time she had touched her sister in years. Cinnamon's answering smile was bright enough to light up the room, and Brianna almost staggered at the intense emotion pulsing from her. For a timeless moment, she shuddered as that intensity threatened to overwhelm her. Then, she straightened her frame, accepting the emotion as the gift it was.

She looked over her shoulder and smiled. "I love you, too."

Matt swirled the liquid in the plastic cup. He drained it in one gulp then poured another two fingers of whiskey from the mostly empty bottle. He gulped that down, too. He slumped in his chair, waiting for drunken oblivion to take him over, but even that appeared to be denied to him tonight. He'd called every source he could think of...every detective, every informant and every newspaper crime reporter. No one knew anything. He felt sick with worry for Laurel and disgust with himself over how he'd treated Brianna.

The lamp on his desk flickered slightly. He tapped it with his fingernail then sighed when the bulb popped and the light went out. He didn't move to fix the lamp, just grabbed the bottle and started swigging from it since now he couldn't see to pour.

When his phone vibrated, he nudged it with his elbow so he could see the readout, then grabbed it hastily.

"Cinnamon? Is Brianna okay?"

Cinnamon's husky laugh shocked him. "She wants to see you."

Carefully placing the whiskey bottle on the desk, Matt sat up straighter. "Does that mean she'll try to find Laurel again?"

"Yes, but she wants to do it now. Can you come back?"

Matt shoved his chair back and grabbed his coat. "I'll be right there."

Brianna felt Matt approach the room. Even shielding as she was, the extreme emotions surging through him shimmered into her senses. She put out a hand, steadying herself on the table, and drew in a deep breath.

She watched Matt as he walked toward her, and her breathing sped up. His energy both frightened and attracted her. He never took his eyes off her face as he moved, and she remembered momentarily that he found her beautiful. A flush heated her skin.

Matt walked to the table and took a chair, but he held up his hand as Brianna started to speak. "I'm sorry I hurt you, Brianna. You're amazing. You quite literally take my breath away."

"The feeling is mutual," Brianna wanted to say, but she couldn't, not yet. Her feelings were too strong, too overwhelming for her to acknowledge them with words. She contented herself with meeting his gaze steadily and allowing all her burgeoning dreams to surface in her eyes. She could only hope he would understand.

She watched as every muscle in his body tensed, and she swallowed hard as his eyes darkened slightly. His eyelids drooped, giving him a sleepy, sexy expression that sent Brianna's blood humming though her veins. He gazed at her a quiet moment, full of promise and passion. Then he cleared his throat and looked at her questioningly.

"You sure you're up to this?"

Brianna asked, "Does that matter? Laurel needs us to find her."

Matt nodded. "I'm ready to do whatever you need."

Taking up her place on the bed, Cinnamon sent Matt a somewhat half-hearted threatening look. Brianna shook her head at her sister and then ignored her, running her hands over the small pile of Laurel's belongings. She snagged Laurel's necklace and wrapped it around her fist. Closing her eyes, she breathed out slowly.

Emotions cascaded over her. Each memory attached to the necklace generated a corresponding emotion, and Brianna allowed those feelings through her shields, let them mingle with her sense of self. She sent those combined thoughts speeding outward, searching for Laurel. The girl was easier to find this time, but still shielded, too terrorized to allow a stranger into her head. She'd turned on a mental "do not disturb" sign that marked her as a sensitive protecting herself from attack.

Brianna didn't even bother trying to breach those shields. She turned her blind eyes unerringly in Matt's direction and held out Laurel's necklace so he could touch it. "Help me," she said. "Do what you did before. Let her know you're here and she can trust me."

Matt's love for Laurel flowed into Brianna, and she linked him to his niece. As she recognized Matt, Laurel dropped her shields, her relief at his presence surging through both Matt and Brianna.

Immediately, Brianna began mentally questioning the girl, trying to discover where she was. In Brianna and Matt's previous cases, the victims could describe their locations, but Laurel had been drugged and secreted away before she ever regained consciousness. Laurel's fear intensified as she realized she had no way to help them find her, and without warning, the link ended as her emotions overwhelmed her.

When Brianna opened her eyes again, she stared at an ashen-faced

Matt. His misery hung heavily in the air and Brianna fought to keep it from drowning her. Wordlessly, Matt shoved his chair back and started to pace in the small confines of the room.

"I'm not ready to give up." Brianna said it first in her head, and then out loud.

Matt stilled his movements, waiting for her to elaborate. Brianna pointed in the direction she sensed Laurel. "I mean, I can feel her. I know what direction she's in." She pointed at Matt with her other hand. "I know where you are." She drew her hands together and clasped them. "I just have to find a way to get the two of you together."

Matt said quietly, "You could take me to her."

Brianna shuddered and averted her face. She answered, her voice so soft it was barely audible. "I haven't been outside in years, but I remember what it was like, what *I* was like. The emotions, the thoughts, both good and bad, overwhelmed me so I couldn't function. If I tried and failed tonight, I wouldn't even be capable of linking with Laurel at all. We would lose the only connection we have. I'm sorry. It's too big a risk."

Matt nodded, his disappointment obvious. Brianna returned to her own thoughts, trying to work around her disability, to discover a new way to use her gift. Idly, she remembered one of Matt's memories, a laughing Laurel riding piggyback on her uncle's back. The thought percolated to the top, and Brianna struggled to capture its importance before it escaped. She sat up straight.

"I can't lead you there, Matt. But maybe I can carry you."

Matt looked at Brianna's small frame. "Uh, there is no way you can carry me anywhere."

She shot him an annoyed look. "No, Matt. I need to channel both of you long-distance. Inside of me, a piggyback ride of sorts."

"Can you do that?"

"Maybe. I need something personal of yours, something important to you that I can hold." She paused, and then met his eyes. "Matt, I'll be able to feel and see things you might rather I not know. If you don't want to do it, I'll understand."

With no hesitation, Matt pulled his dog tags over his head and dropped them into her cupped palms. The chain, still warm from his skin, slid into her hand. Brianna gasped and almost dropped it as the residual memories clinging to the tags invaded her defenses.

Anger, despair, exhaustion, fear...dark feelings created by years of a military existence cascaded through Brianna. She shuddered, her system almost shutting down in horror. Hastily shunting the dark memories off to the side, she opened herself to other, different emotions...memories of love, friendship, courage and loyalty that intertwined with the darker emotions.

Brianna breathed deeply, battling her awareness of the complex man who stood before her. He'd opened himself unhesitatingly to her examination, knowing she would see both the best and the worst of him. Afraid to acknowledge how much Matt affected her, Brianna closed her eyes, shutting him away from her, and slipped back into herself. She grabbed Laurel's necklace and held it in her other hand. She said, "Walk away from me, Matt. Let me see if I can track you."

She turned her head as he moved and heard Cinnamon's small sound of satisfaction. Brianna's connections with Laurel were dependent on the emotional upheaval of a girl suffering physical and mental distress. But Matt's nexus glowed steadily, a constant presence that filled her mind with his energy and determination.

Keeping her eyes closed, Brianna said, "Cinnamon, dial Matt's mobile. I can follow his movements and tell him how close he is to Laurel."

"Whether this works or not, I appreciate you trying," Matt said, his voice rough with emotion.

Brianna smiled. "Go, Matt. Find your niece. And please be careful. I...I want you to be safe."

Matt's answer was grim. "Don't worry. I won't risk Laurel's life by going in half-cocked." He lowered his voice, and darkness slid into Brianna as his rage, on simmer for days, threatened to boil over. "But after she's safe, if I find the man who took her, I'll be damned if I leave him for the police." He left without another word.

Her heart beating hard with fear, Brianna turned to Cinnamon. "I can't lose him."

"He'll find his way back. Just hold on tight to him."

Brianna sat unmoving in her chair, her attention focused on her connections with Matt and Laurel. Matt's energy burned inside her, although his emotions themselves seemed strangely repressed. Never having been in a combat or reconnaissance mission, Brianna could only guess his muted feelings were a result of a professional detachment.

She felt grateful for the distance. As much as she craved contact with Matt, his feelings overwhelmed her, leaving her defenseless. She wondered despairingly how she could ever overcome her fear of connecting with

A Single Touch

someone, then decided now wasn't the time to focus on it. Laurel's emotions remained quiet. Brianna didn't know if Laurel slept or just huddled in limbo waiting for a rescue she wasn't sure would come. After two long hours of guiding Matt's twists and turns, Brianna muttered, "Cinnamon, he's right there. He and Laurel are almost on top of one another." Deep inside herself, Brianna couldn't hear Cinnamon's response and had to trust her sister relayed the message.

Then, with no warning, Matt's energy signature spiked, and Brianna gasped as his rage flooded her. At that exact moment, Laurel's emotions crested, reflecting a fear that sent Brianna's senses into overload. The double whammy skyrocketed her heart rate. Brianna could dimly hear Cinnamon yelling her name, but she couldn't respond. All she could feel was Matt and Laurel, their emotions see-sawing rapidly, as they fought to save their own lives.

Matt staggered under the glancing blow from the metal pipe, his gun falling to the floor and sliding under nearby shelves. His ears ringing, he flattened himself against the dirt-stained, concrete walls of the abandoned tornado shelter. Laurel, shackled to an iron bed frame crammed into the tiny space, watched him, her eyes wide in her blood-stained, scratched face. He tore his gaze from her to focus on the man who stood before him screaming obscenities. Broad-featured with a huge frame, the man moved ponderously and Matt hoped he'd only need a few moments to subdue the bastard. He wished briefly for his gun, but one more look at Laurel's bruised face convinced him he'd enjoy the hand-to-hand even more.

The man turned suddenly and charged Laurel, swinging the pipe overhead in a move that would take her head off her shoulders. Surging forward, Matt tackled him, grunting as his shoulder hit the man's tremendous bulk. They tumbled into the edge Laurel's iron bed frame, and Matt's shoulder shifted agonizingly. As the man beneath him tried to flip himself over, Matt grabbed him by the hair and slammed his head repeatedly into the floor. A loud crack sounded, and Matt felt something give in the man's head. Matt sat up, cradling his dislocated shoulder. He watched the big man warily and checked for a heartbeat, but he felt nothing.

Three seconds later, Matt reached Laurel's bedside, and the expression of joy on her face made everything worthwhile.

Matt watched Laurel's wheelchair disappear down the hospital corridor. Her face grimy and tear-streaked but still glowing with an indomitable spirit, Laurel glanced back. She half-smiled, pain etched in lines on her face that hadn't been there before. Matt waved at her.

He watched his sister and brother-in-law, striding alongside the wheelchair, holding on tight to whatever part of Laurel was closest to them. His heart swelled with the certainty that, if love had anything to do with it, Laurel would be fine.

He stood unmoving in the corridor until they were out of sight. Laurel didn't need him, not right now. He felt lost, at odds with himself. The emergency doctor had pushed his shoulder into place, but it still ached, and the pain pills would have to wait until after he'd given his statement to the police. He glanced down at his shirt, streaked and bloody, and knew he should change. And shower.

And, even though he'd experienced it before, he probably should think about the fact that he'd taken another man's life. He was pretty sure, though, he'd never lose a moment's sleep over killing a miserable bastard with a penchant for torturing young girls.

Try as he might, Matt couldn't focus. Brianna filled his thoughts. He knew he'd hurt her; she was better off without him in her life. He should forget he knew her. Or at the very least, he should accept that she could offer him nothing but friendship.

In spite of his best intentions, minutes later he found himself parked on the street near her apartment. He sat in his car, bathed in the streetlight's glow, reluctant to approach the building. He'd bared his soul to her. What if she was afraid of him or refused to see him? And could he be with her if he couldn't ever touch her? He had to accept they had no future together.

He pictured Brianna again...her dark eyes that peered into people's souls and saw exactly who they were...her determination to keep going even though everyday life was a struggle...her smile that both broke his heart and made him believe anything was possible.

He left the car. Striding up the sidewalk, he stopped in surprise when he saw Brianna sitting on the stairs of her building. Cinnamon hovered nearby, gazing watchfully over her sister, but she neither moved nor spoke at his approach.

Brianna regarded him thoughtfully, her blue eyes serious. "You're all right. I knew it, of course." She showed him his dog tags still cupped in her hand. "But I wanted to see for myself."

"So now you know."

She looked down. "So now I know."

He sat next to her, carefully cataloging the distance between them so he wouldn't accidentally touch her. "What's next then?"

Brianna still looked away, but Matt saw a pulse beat heavily in her throat. "Something changed in me, and I don't want to hide anymore. Good or bad, I want a life that's something more than a princess hiding in her tower. It's going to take a while for me to figure out how to do this, and I can't do it alone." She whispered, "Matt, will you help me?"

He started to nod, to explain he would be whatever she needed him to be, do whatever she needed him to do, if only he could be near her. The words died in Matt's throat as Brianna slid her small hand into his. He heard her soft exhalation as he gently intertwined their fingers.

Brianna finally faced him, her expression glowing so radiantly that Matt caught his breath. She said, "You give me hope for the future. You make me *want* a future."

Matt smiled, feeling it spread across his face in celebration. He enfolded Brianna's hand more firmly, and together, they sat gazing into a night full of promise.

The Shimmer in the Woods

Leslie S. Rose

TIME HEALS NOTHING. The pain of my sister's death festers, waiting for its one true remedy, revenge.

I've traveled only the length of a fallen tree along the outlawed path when the crunch of a brittle leaf sends a warning. Something follows.

No one calls to me. I listen for laughter from the village boys who dare one another to cross through the forest arch and plant their boots along this forbidden trail. Nothing.

Mottled sunlight twists through the branches and falls in drops upon my arms, marking my intrusion into the forest. The knife in my hand glints from a shaft that darts between the leaves. My senses sharpen here in the wood, and I track the footfalls of the one behind.

I slow, preparing to confront the sneak. Nothing with good intent travels this path. I breathe in the savage air that clings between the trunks of ancient trees to give me strength.

My knife will speak for me. The knife whose blade holds a trinity of blood—my father's, the village mystic's, and mine in its steel. A knife that can kill things both natural and unnatural.

A knife to kill a witch.

Through a break in the skeletal fingers of high tree limbs, I see the lover's moon shining shameless in the late afternoon sky. Tonight in the village, new men who have gained their twentieth year, as I have, will take maids to their hearts and marry.

I will not. My life is pledged to a darker purpose. The lover's moon will light my way through the tunnel of trees so I can feed my vengeful heart.

Shushing sounds roll through the leaves, and a fat snake slithers around my boots without a whisper of fear. We are fellows of the wood now, wishing each other no harm.

There is a quick breath behind me. I whirl, holding my knife heart-high as my pursuer calls out. "Hansel."

"Louisa!" At the sight of her, I pull the knife back with such speed, it nicks my wrist. "Louisa!"

She runs to me and grasps my hand. "Don't go into the woods tonight, Hansel. Please."

I wipe three drops of blood from the knife against my breeches, and slide it back into its sheath. Louisa holds my sleeve. "Stay. You know dark things in this forest feed on the lover's moon."

"That's why I go tonight."

"Wait for a night less foul," she says.

I wrap my arm around Louisa, leading her back toward the arch of the trees that frame the opening of the outlawed path. She pulls away. "Come back with me to the feast."

I take her face in my hands. It's sprinkled with forest light under her braided hair. "No."

As she protests, I lift her into my arms and carry her away from the ancient trees. Instead of the pounding of fists on my chest that I expect, she lays her hand against my cheek and weeps.

"You'll be lost to me, my love," she says.

I stop and touch my forehead to hers. "I'm already lost."

"Gretel is lost, Hansel. Chasing the Witch this night will not make your sister live."

I set Louisa on a stump along the path near the edge of the woods and kneel at her feet. The village is close enough to smell the smoke of the cooking fires. The feast under the lover's moon will be grand. I have no stomach for food this night.

"The village mystic vows the only way to free Gretel's soul is to kill the Witch under a lover's moon," I say.

She seems to float down from her pedestal and kneels before me, taking my head in her hands. "You do not have Gretel's blood mixed in the metal of the blade. You cannot free her soul without that."

I grab her arms and give a shake. "I have my blood and the blood of our father. That is as good as hers."

A fresh wound rips into my scarred heart as I look into this face I love. A Witch doesn't die without a sacrifice. A death for a death is the price, my death for the Witch's death.

Louisa touches a finger to the newborn tear in my eye. Ten years past, it was Louisa who blessed the tears I cried for Gretel. She never told the other children about Hansel, the weak boy who wept in secret every night over his dead sister. "Gretel opened the oven door, my love. It was Gretel who let the Witch fly free when the hag should have burned to hell."

Harsh words. True words.

Worthless words.

I stand and walk away from Louisa, speaking to the woods, not her. "Gretel could not stand to take a life, no matter how evil."

"Would you have freed a pleading Witch?"

I turn to face her. "Never." Louisa's eyes compromise my resolve. I have to leave. This close to the open sky I hear birdsong. The notes call me home to the village, but I must dare the dimming path. "Go home," I say.

The sting of her slap across my face stays my progress.

"For the last five lover's moons since our fifteen year, you've sworn your love to me. This is not love. You leave me the way you left Gretel. Your twenty years show you to still be a boy, not a man."

I touch the ache along my jaw, since I can't soothe her jab to my heart. "Mercy, I gave you the love I have, but told you I had no heart to seal it. I have a nest of scars and woe where a man's heart should be."

"Leaving is how you celebrate your newly given rights to be a man?" Her anger gives a blush to her skin that holds me captive. "You have a man's right to grow a beard. You have a man's right to practice his trade out from under a master. You have a man's right to marry."

Stillness embraces the trees. Not a creature breaks the silence.

Louisa. My love. The only girl I would bless myself to call wife. Truth cuts more brutally than my knife. The girl I will never call wife.

"Don't abandon me under the lover's moon, Hansel."

Eyes as gray as a storm-bound sky pull me away from the forest and into Louisa's arms. My lips demand hers. Softness and urgency live together in one breath. I can't leave this. I can't leave her. I can't leave love.

The knife presses against my leg, reminding me. I am cursed to kill a witch, but still I press closer to Louisa. My lips move down her neck and caress the golden, silk strands that escape the twist of her braids. I love this girl.

"You'll stay," she murmurs.

I quiet her words with the most perfect kiss I can give, and then let her go. Her stunned surprise gives me few moments to slip back into the dappled light of the woods and my purpose.

"Wait," she cries. I shouldn't, but I do. There is something new in her tone. Understanding? Defeat?

She catches me. Her hand grasps mine and guides me to the high button on her blouse. With a tug she forces me to pull the brass colored button away from its fabric, and wraps my fingers around it.

"Take this into the woods with you. Do not lose it. You take me with you as long as it stays in your grasp."

"I will guard it with my life," I say.

Louisa opens the top of her blouse revealing the shining white skin below her neck. It seems to glow in the shadows. Her hands pull my head against her chest. "Hear my heart. It will beat strong for both of us, until yours is healed."

She buries her lips in my hair, and then walks away.

I watch until she is free from the darkening forest, and light from the setting sun touches her slippers. I clutch at my heart and look down, unable to bear her retreat. When I raise my eyes, she is gone, too quickly to have left the wood.

I turn and run. I know Louisa. She hides in the tangled trunks near the edge of the outlawed path, the Witch's path. Unless I outdistance her, she will come to me. I push my speed, charging deeper into the wood. I dart off the path behind an old woody giant. A glance behind does not reveal her pursuit. I dread her persistence.

I must still my gasps, or she will know where to follow. I close my eyes and picture sunny days playing with my sister, Gretel. We splash at the river's edge, muddying our socks. Father's wife scolds us, but we laugh at her. She punishes us with one piece of bread between us for supper.

I hold nothing but loathing for my father's wife. It was she who convinced him to leave Gretel and me in the forest. It was she who denounced our return. It was she who tricked us into the woods a second time with nothing to drop but bits of bread to find our way home. It was her hatred that drove us to the Witch's house of cakes and treats.

If I planned to return, I would not chance losing my way by leaving a path of pebbles or bread. I would slash the trunk of every tree, no matter how loud the tree hearts screamed, to mark my trail out of this godforsaken wood. This cursed wood. This Witch's wood that will claim my life tonight.

Not a sound follows me. No snap of twigs. No bite of broken leaf under Louisa's boot. I must be certain she has returned to the village. Sweet Louisa. Loyal girl. Loving woman. See me damned for breaking a true heart like hers. Why did I ever let love overtake my good sense? I did not have love to give. I fooled her with a liar's love.

Louisa will find another. An unscarred heart will find her. I drop to my knee and will it with my soul.

The Witch is destined to eat my heart, and Louisa would have nothing left but my severed heartstrings to hold in her hand. She is light and light will find her. By the next lover's moon Louisa will be bound to a man worthy to grow a beard, work his trade, and love a wife.

I will it.

I hate it.

The bits of sky peeking through the branches are slate colored now. The lover's moon casts webby shadows over the path even though it is not full dark. It was a lover's moon when Gretel and I found the Witch's house. It was a lover's moon when I fled down this same path, returning to my father's house without my beloved sister. I squeeze my eyes against the wicked shadows and I remember the haunted cries of other children lost to the Witch's kiln.

Sobs. Shrieks. Pleading.

I can't let my mind drift to horror. It will consume me.

I am convinced now that Louisa has not followed. Before I return to the doomed path, I pull my love's button out of my vest pocket and hold it against my lips. And as I do, there—off to my right a tree trunk flares with silver light to match my kiss.

I pull my lips away from the button and stare. The tree continues to glow. I kiss the button again. The light flickers for a moment and then snaps to a tree across the path, leaving an afterglow around the first trunk.

The light is beautiful, as if the lover's moon had sent threads to twine with the bark. I kiss the button again and again, winding the silver shine around me and down the path to light my way.

Is this enchantment sent by the village mystic to light my way to the Witch? Light floats around the kissed trees and fills the wood with a soothing energy. The hum breaches my flesh, filling my bones. It is kind, not an enemy. Dare I trust?

I move to the closest trunk and reach out a single finger to touch. The instant my skin meets the silver sparkle, the forest explodes in the blast of a cataclysm. In the burst, just before I am knocked off my feet, I see a vision of Louisa's face shining down from the glimmering branches.

The sizzle of fire rises around me, bringing the smell of charred wood. I leap up, drawing my knife and pivot to my left, my right, and behind. The stories of wood sprites and sorcerers fly through my mind. What has descended from the boughs to cause me mischief?

The lover's moon frees itself from the clouds to illuminate the trees. What moments before was healthy, sturdy wood is now blackened and hollowed. I run my hand along the ebony groove in a gray trunk and have to pull away. The heat from the scorch has not cooled. The true face of this evil wood shows itself. I will not sheath my knife again this night.

I move off the path to hide, waiting for my eyes to find their night talents. Here in the twisted trees a filthy dankness grips the air, and every breath fills my lungs with silt. Can the Witch hear me? Does she fly like the crow and peer down at me from the broken fingered branches. Was she the snake that skirted my boots within sight of the village?

I must be a creature of the woods. The demoness made me more creature than boy when she tried to fatten me up for her supper. I remember the bone I held out to her. The bone that was supposed to be my finger. The bone of my deception.

She is the one who need fear me now. I no longer fear the hag. I will take her out of this world.

A flicker catches my eye and I turn to look. Nothing. I move faster. Again, a flicker up ahead. I push for speed. The flicker follows me, disappearing when I turn my full gaze upon it. My blood chills. Benevolence does not dwell in the Witch's forest. No chit-chit of squirrels in the branches or rabbits swishing around the bulging roots of great trees fills this wood.

I stop and try to catch the light again. Does someone follow? Truly, no villager is mad enough to move this far down the outlawed path. They would not be allowed back into the village without confinement for three moons to see if they were bewitched after taking this cursed road.

This I know. This I've suffered.

It was only tiny Louisa who sang to me through the unchinked spaces between the wooden slats of my confinement cell. Only Louisa and my father cried tears for Gretel. The mystic warned that weeping over the Witch's supper would bring evil to the village and call the Witch.

But Louisa cried anyway. Sweet Louisa. Lost Louisa.

I kiss the summoning button. A tree sparks back to life next to me, and the silver shine returns.

This time I do not touch. I raise the button toward my lips, but a tendril of quicksilver darts over my hand and knocks the button to the ground. My hand warms where the streak of light touched it.

"Do not wake the others," wails a voice that deafens me.

I fling my hands over my ears.

The wail melts to a whisper. "I am too loud."

I hold my knife at the ready and search out my foe. For surely an inhuman glow in the wood is an enemy.

"Now you are too soft," I say to draw it out into the open.

A woman's voice croons with the gentleness of a lullaby. "You have dropped your charm."

I stay on guard.

"I will not harm you, Hansel," she says.

I will not trust this apparition who knows my name. Only a fool trusts the unnatural. My blade will kill all things natural and unnatural.

"Do not harm me or all will be truly lost," the voice warns, "and the child killer will walk free."

"You speak of the Witch," I say.

"I speak of the one who eats the bones and traps the souls of innocents."

My blood runs faster through my body. "She does this still?"

"Yes."

The mystic has sealed the road between the Witch and our village, but there are other paths, other villages, and other children. Oh, unholy Witch. Oh, murderess unchecked. Why have I delayed this quest? How many bones have been ground to dust between the Witch's teeth? How does this shining mystery know of the Witch's doings?

I challenge the voice that takes no shape. "How do I know you are not her servant?" The ground beneath me rumbles. A waterfall of thin branches pummels me from above. A merciless wind tosses dust into my eyes. "Stop, stop," I say.

"Do not dishonor me again, Hansel or I will leave you to your fool's quest with neither hope nor fellowship."

"You dare to demean honor, spirit? I go to avenge my sister. That is no fool's quest. Leave me to it."

I turn to go when I remember Louisa's button. I can't leave her precious token in a pile of molding leaves. I drop to my knees and skim the ground with my palms. I find the treasure between the layers of wilted spruce needles.

"Good," murmurs my shining bane.

"This is no business of yours."

A cyclone of silver liquid suspended in the air blocks my path. I am so taken with the beauty of the movement I can't step away. It is a dance of light and molten metal. Before my eyes the flurry takes the form of a woman's naked body without detail. She hovers not a hand's width above the forest floor. Floating fingers reach out and seem to pierce my chest, cradling my heart within their delicate grasp.

"You are a lover," she says.

My heart smolders, still safe within my body under her touch, but now it shines with a silver glow. Trails of light flow from her fingertips, crisscrossing its surface and glisten with each beat. The lover's moon breaks through the forest canopy and makes the creature more luminous. I am enchanted by the vision's touch on my heart. Images of Louisa dance before me and my heart swells, increasing its light. I am helpless to find reason.

"I have loved," I say.

"You love now."

"No more. I released her heart."

"You willed her to find another. I heard your spirit call out."

My heart takes on the weight of lead, even within the warmth of its new ethereal silver casing. The night woman speaks truth.

"I did," I say. Her hands drift away from my glowing heart, and I touch my chest to check its wholeness.

"Then you will rejoice to hear that I bound her to a lover in the very moment you filled the woods with light."

"What?" I cry. "On this night?" No. My Louisa even now married to another in sight of the lover's moon that should have been ours?

"You willed it. I granted your will. She is eternally bound."

I clutch the button to my breast as a tear trudges down my dirty cheek.

"Are you displeased, my Hansel?"

When I look up, the silver woman has taken on a bluish tone. She shines with the color of sadness in the cursed forest.

"What are you?" I whisper, feeling the pull of her enchantment, an attraction I've only felt before with Louisa. I revel in the familiar memory and have no desire to flee. "What will you do with me?"

The blue shifts back to silver and she moves so close I swear I feel her body, solid not light, barely touching mine. She blows an unseen breath across my face. My head lolls back and then drifts slowly forward. I feel Louisa's warmth in this creature. Cruel.

"I am your Shimmer, here to aid you on your journey."

Do lips graze my cheek? I pull away. The broken connection gives space for my wits to return. I shake my head, fighting the enchantment.

Shimmers. This is one of the folk who are said to steal true love from the hearts of unmarried girls who stray too close to the wood. I believed them a crone's tale, concocted to excuse the fickleness of young maids who transfer their affections lightly from one boy to another.

My hands quiver. Does the presence I feel of Louisa in this Shimmer signify proof that this being of tremulous light has committed such a deed? Has she taken my lover's heart?

"All I know of Shimmers is your thievery," I say. "Have you stolen a heart this night?"

A merry whistle dances through the leaves above me. "We have no need to take what is offered to us freely. We are vessels to protect love, not steal it."

I turn from the light. "I have to time for your play. You have no purpose here."

The Shimmer blocks my way, surrounding me in her haze. "You are wrong. My purpose is to serve your longing and love. I am yours."

Her warmth distracts me, but I manage to speak. "If you are my longing, you would be a warrior to vanquish a Witch."

"If you will it? I am what you wish. I am yours."

"I do."

"Will you pay the price?"

I try to push out of the Shimmer's influence. "No. I do not bargain with evil."

The Shimmer surges away from me as if a brutal wind has erupted from my chest and flung her aside. A blush courses through her body.

"I am not evil. I am for you. I am the love you left at the forest's edge."

What is this torture? The Shimmer wraps an echo of Louisa's love around my aching heart. I would rather melt in the flames of the Witch's oven than dwell on the pain of losing my Louisa for one moment more.

"The price I ask will not harm you," she says. "This is necessary for me to bind with you."

"Stay away. I need my wits."

She grows taller before me. "Wits will not kill a Witch."

"My blade will kill the Witch. It has the power to end all things natural and unnatural."

"Your blade will not last the battle. Do you think you are the first avenger to stalk the child killer through this wood?"

The words drive a spike through my chest. Not the first?

"They all failed?" I ask through a clenched throat.

Her voice rides the breeze. "Every one."

"How do you know such things?"

She flows around the trunk of a tree. "The forest tells its truths to trusted souls."

I rest my head against the ash of a defiled trunk. If the Shimmer speaks truth about the defeated Witch hunters, I cannot succeed alone, even with my blood-fortified blade. I must accept her unnatural aid no matter the bargain. No price is too dear for the hopeless.

"Name your payment."

"Love," says the Shimmer from the branches above my head.

"Love," I choke, shifting my gaze upwards.

"I seek the love you withdrew from Louisa."

Now who is the fool? She held my heart in her silvery fingers. Did she not sense its hollowness? There is no love left in my soul. It flew from the forest with Louisa. It burned in the Witch's kiln with Gretel. This Shimmer's fee costs me nothing.

I return to the path and stand with my arms open wide. "Take what you can find of love within this shattered heart, Shimmer. It is yours."

Like a bolt leaping between clouds, the Shimmer is upon me. She begins at the top of my head and turns in circles around my body. I feel her touch, as light as snowfall against my skin. The deadness in my spirit stirs. I smell the sweet honeysuckle vine that still climbs outside Gretel's bed-chamber window.

The Shimmer reforms before my eyes. Arms wrap around me, pulling me in. I feel the shape of a real woman's body pressing into mine. My own hands move up and down the contours of the Shimmer that is so like Louisa. She is real beneath my fingers. She is flesh. How can this be?

I feel the wanting of a man not a boy as her hands wind through my hair, and she takes my kiss with her shining lips. Her voice fills my head as her lips part further and make mine obey her commands. "I take your shattered heart. It is mine as it should be."

I am here to kill a Witch, not take a woman. I am here to kill a Witch.

With closed eyes I feel Louisa in my arms. We dance under the lover's moon. I take Louisa as my wife. There is no Witch. There is only Louisa and I, spinning to the song of the night's breeze. For a stolen moment I am whole, and I remember joy.

Shivering brings me back to my senses. The Shimmer wafts away from me and I prop my dizzy head in my hands. The bones in my chest knit, fighting the breaths I try to pull in. It is a cruel payment to bless me with my beloved, and then wake me to find her gone from my arms again.

"Do not tempt me with the impossible," I say.

"I am your truth. I am the one you love. Whether or not you believe it is your burden."

I grab my sheath. The knife waits for me.

The Shimmer glows her silver sheen as she hovers above me, framed by the crossed branches in front of the lover's moon.

"You love me, Hansel."

I feel the truth in her words. My desires for Louisa now rest in the Shimmer. "Am I cursed?" I ask, consumed by traitorous feelings.

"You are fortified with the same magic that blesses me. I am your servant against the Witch as long as you call no other Shimmer with your talisman." She sends a silver thread down through the limbs to touch Louisa's button.

"You will help?" I am wary, but hopeful.

"Stay true. Wake no others with your kisses. Touch none but me."

I remember the blaze when I laid my finger on the glowing trunk. "Did I call you with my touch? The fire?"

"Yes. Your kiss gave me the light." She glides down a gnarled trunk like morning fog over the river until she is before me. Her kiss, as light as the tremble of a bird's wing, moves across my cheek. The lips are warm and sweet, Louisa's lips. Oh, pitiless memory.

The lover's moon fills every space between the treetops and shows me the path. The Shimmer's sheen harmonizes with the moonshine.

"Come, love," she whispers as she flutters ahead on the path. Her voice is so like Louisa's that a sickness grows in my gut.

Betrayal turns my feet to stone. I have forsaken Louisa. I have given her to another man with nothing but my will. I have pledged my love to a Shimmer in the woods. It cannot be, yet it is. I am a villain to love, a faithless wretch. Where is good Hansel? What have I become on this quest to kill the Witch?

I wipe the boy's tears from my face. I am no lovesick pup. I am a menace of the wood destined to murder. I pull my knife from its sheath and walk on. I will stay on the path until I confront the beast.

"Slow, Hansel," the Shimmer warns. "Slow steps."

New smells accost me. The woody char of the trees has taken on the character of burning meats.

Can the feast fires reach this deep into the forest?

Suddenly I find myself bent half to the ground retching. I know the scent. It is flesh. My sister's flesh. Innocent childish flesh, a smell so emblazoned in my memory that nothing will shake it free.

The Witch's house is near.

The Shimmer surrounds me. Her silken hands trace the sides of my face in a soothing caress. "You need not do this. Abandon this death and come with me into the wood. We will fly through the boughs of the grandest tree and dance on cloud stacks. I will love you beyond life, beyond fear, beyond sorrow."

Her sweet breath hides the stench that defiles the wood. I feel the pull of her enchantment. She will take me if I falter. Oh, how easy to discard the shards of my shattered life and live in her dream.

No. A surge of heat roils in my blood. "You tempt me with no regard for my purpose." I try to push the Shimmer away. But she circles me like a whirlwind.

"I give you a choice, Hansel. Love or death?"

"There is no choice for me, Shimmer."

"Choice is no illusion. Neither is my love."

"Wrong, Shimmer. Your love is the illusion."

Her face is a mask of sorrow. "My love is the only truth left to you in this wood, in this life. Give over to it and all will be well. I promise. I swear. I vow."

What value is there in the vow of a thief? I wonder how many hearts this Shimmer has claimed.

The path turns ahead. Shards of crystal light break through the leaves above us and throw bright bars across the ground at the curve of the road. This is not the light of the lover's moon. Something waits. My breath catches. These deviant beams tell me that it is here I shall either persevere or fail. If I take the turn, death waits as I face my soul's enemy. If I run to live, then I fail my sister.

There is but one choice. I will not fail Gretel.

Keeping close to the trunk of the mightiest giant at the bend, I peer around and am nearly blinded by the icy blaze blocking my way. Is this barricade an overgrown sugar pane like the ones that Gretel and I feasted on from the Witch's windows? No, it appears as a towering wall of water undulating with light in the way the sun meets the surface of a glassy lake.

I stare, transfixed. It is as if a thousand writhing Shimmers are woven in a tapestry rising to the highest branches in the surrounding trees.

Breath flees my chest as the view becomes clear through the curtain. Beyond the wall, sitting low in the clearing is the candied house of the Witch. I see the hag wobbling about on her crutches in the guise of an old helpless woman. I long to fly through the light shield and slit her desecrated throat. Godless horror.

No. I cannot breach this fantastical wall without drawing her notice. I must find my wits and lay a plan for this killer. She vanishes into her sugar-laden trap.

Wait. Why does she hobble and not stride with her full stature and strength? She is no invalid. That is an appearance to fool....

God save me.

The Shimmer throws herself in front of me. "Look away."

Two children, brother and sister, emerge from the wood. They enter the glade that holds the Witch's house. They are gaunt and move slowly, lost and hungry lambs in the Witch's wood. Here are new victims, a Hansel and Gretel reborn with different names, different lives, but doomed to repeat our tragedy.

A cry escapes my lips. "Do not touch the house!"

They do not hear. They rip at the sweet breads adorning the doorway and lick the candy glass of the windows.

The Witch's voice calls to the damned. "Nibble, nibble, gnaw. Who is nibbling at my little house?"

The children look at one another. The girl covers a giggle with her hand, while the boy answers in the same words I spoke to the Witch all those years ago. "The wind, the wind, the heaven-born wind."

I push past the Shimmer and rush to the unnatural wall. "Flee, children! Your hunger will be your end!"

They do not hear or look my way. It is as if I do not occupy the same world as they.

The Witch prowls from her doorway. She does not look at the children. Her red, aberrant eyes find me instead. She crooks her finger and beckons. She devil! Mockery is the invitation to her death.

I push against the wall, but it will not yield. The children follow her inside. I take my knife from its sheath and pull it back, ready to strike.

The Shimmer's heat surrounds my hand. "No, Hansel. You mustn't touch the barrier with that knife. All will be lost."

A great puff of smoke billows out the Witch's chimney.

"No," I shriek and slash at the wall. The Shimmer blocks my blows. The knife may well have traveled through the waves of smoke rising up to the lover's moon.

"Stay your blade."

A faint whistle starts through the wood, instantly it rises to a cacophony of wails and moans. Death's song fills every leaf, every shard of bark, and every stone along the path. The forest mourns another pair of souls stolen by the killer. Louder and louder the lament grows until my head is battered beyond sense by the dissonant notes. I cannot think. I fall to the ground and drop my head to my knees.

The Shimmer surrounds me in a luminous cocoon. The haunted keening is masked beneath her protection. "My love, would I could spare you from this horror." She hums a counter melody to drown out the sorrow.

"What is this poisonous noise?" I ask.

"It is the soul song of the lost."

I strive for breath. "The children."

"All who have fallen at the Witch's hand."

I lift my head. Gretel. Is my Gretel among the unearthly chorus? "Gretel, Gretel, come to me," I call.

"Gretel, Gretel," cackles a voice beyond the shining wall. The Witch stands before her house, leering with broken teeth. Her presence silences the song of the souls.

Bile rises in my throat. I must look away.

She waves the bone that I used to deceive her all those years ago. "Come, Gretel. Meet your handsome brother. See how he is now a man."

I feel the warmth of the Shimmer tug at my arm. "We must leave. You are discovered. She cannot be taken while she is on her guard."

"No. I will have my vengeance."

The Shimmer begins her twisted dance around my body. Her magic cannot subdue me. My will is focused on the Witch.

I lock my gaze upon the vile one. "Let this enchantment be gone." I raise my knife to the wall. "I will find a way through and end your evil."

"Ask your sister to lower my pretty fence," she says.

At the Witch's words the waving wall stills, and there standing before me is my beloved sister.

"Gretel," I breathe into the night of the lover's moon.

Her blue eyes shine in the night. Her girlish braids fall down upon her shoulders, and her sweet smile peels the scars from my heart.

The Shimmer wraps around my chest like armor. "It is not the truth you see. Gretel is gone. Do not compromise the wall."

"But her soul remains," I say and reach my hand out to touch the vision. "She has come to meet me."

"No, my love. It is the Witch's doing. She plays you. This is a wall built by your village mystic to contain evil."

"Hansel, you were such a clever boy. Shame you have fallen under the trickery of a Shimmer. They are the falsest of friends," says the Witch.

I cannot tear my eyes from Gretel's. She reaches her childish hand to meet mine. We flatten our palms on each side of the cool glassy wall. It is as close to touch as this cursed wood allows us. I long to reach through and grasp her baby fingers. I trust this soul. It is my dearest sister, no foul conjure of a Witch.

Gretel's soft voice drifts over to me. "Free me, brother."

"How, Sister? Tell."

"Pierce me with your blade. Send my soul to the heavens and bring down this wall that keeps you from the Witch. You will not harm me. You will bless me when you see this killer dead."

The Shimmer burns as she encircles my body. "Lies. Do not listen."

Tears flee from my eyes and are trapped in the beginning of the beard that covers my cheeks. "It is my sister, Shimmer. I must obey."

Gretel holds her hands out to her sides, becoming a holy cross under the lover's moon.

"Noooooo!" wails the Shimmer, shaking needles from the trees. She pulls at my knife arm, but her enchantment over me has waned. I will my sister to be at peace. My hatred for the Witch is fierce enough to diminish the Shimmer's influence over me.

"Bless me, Gretel. Go to God." I sink the blade that destroys all things natural and unnatural into my sister's soul. "Go to God."

Gretel vanishes. A thousand cracks emanate from where my knife pierced her soul. They slither out from the gash like a nest of vipers.

I pull my knife back, and the wall shatters into a wave of diamonds that sway back and forth in the forest night. Then they all fall in a mound at my feet.

The Witch's howl sends ice through my veins. "Stupid boy."

She flies at me, her fingers are yellow daggers aimed straight for my chest. I hold my knife in both hands, prepared to plunge it into her black heart. We face each other weapon to weapon, will to will, but when she is no farther than a breath away, the Shimmer lifts me above the trees and out of the Witch's wood.

We keep pace with the insistent night wind as we sail toward the far-away village. I try to twist out of the Shimmer's grasp, but think better of it when I see how far below the wood sits.

"Take me back to the Witch! I will it, Shimmer! Obey me!"

The heat of the Shimmer rises as she tightens her grip on me. "It is too late. You have loosed the Witch. Even now she flies to the village to steal children from their beds."

This cannot be so.

"You lie, Shimmer. The mystic has raised protection between our village and the Witch."

"And you have destroyed it."

"What?"

"The wall, Hansel."

My mind is a muddle of truth and illusion.

"Let me save you, my love," the Shimmer begs. "We will be together as it should be. Let us leave these woods and never return."

"I have no love for you, Shimmer. My love is damned! You've taken poison to your heart. I have but one purpose left in this life and you have robbed me of it. Free me!"

"No. Your love is mine. You promised."

We drop away from the moon toward the treetops. I see the black streak of the Witch below, speeding along the outlawed path.

The Shimmer's fingers rest on my cheek. "Do not withdraw your love."

"It was never yours," I say.

We fall toward the earth.

"Hansel, no. You gave your love where it belonged. Renew your promise. Love for me, love for Louisa. They are not wholly different," says the Shimmer in a voice so quiet I cannot tell if my ears or spirit hear her.

We are close to the village now. Thatched rooftops are silhouetted against a bonfire in the center of town. Newly married lovers dance around the fire; unaware ruin is nearly upon them.

"Fly us to the fire so we can warn them," I say.

"Only your vow grants us speed."

"Shimmer, this is no time for your love games! Danger is at hand!"

"Please, my only love. Keep faith with me."

We leave the wood and cross the fields between the village and the outlawed path. I feel the Shimmer weaken. We fall lower and lower.

"Go back to your wood and enchant another," I cry and jump from her arms onto a soft stack of hay. "I have man's work here."

The Shimmer wanes to nothing more than the wisp of a cloud and settles to the ground. I cannot tell if it is the night wind or the Shimmer that moans, "Hansel."

I leap to my feet and run toward the celebration to sound the alarm. I pray I do not catch sight of Louisa and her newly wedded husband. Nothing must try my will with the Witch on my heels.

"The Witch!" I bellow as I break into the ring of firelight. "The Witch is upon us!"

The mystic sits on a tall, carved chair, overlooking the fire. She stands and holds her knobby hands out toward the wood. Her arms begin to shake with a violence that overtakes her small withered body.

She looks quickly to the crowd. "To arms. Hansel has brought the Witch. Take the children to the church."

Oh, my blackened soul. I have cursed my home, the children, my Louisa. Chaos tangles the village. Shadows and flame from the torches draw macabre faces on my people.

I do not see my Louisa. Pray she does not find my eyes so laden with failure and betrayal.

I run with the men out toward the outlawed path to meet the Witch. We stand, shoulders pressed together, waiting for the filth to show. My eyes fall on the road where I left the Shimmer to be consumed by the night. I shake guilt away to be clear of mind for this final reckoning.

A large limb cracks away from the tree at the edge of the path out of the woods. Muscles of the men on either side of me go taut as we draw closer. Silver light fills the portal to the wood. Legs bend, ready to spring at the figure materializing under the lover's moon. Archers draw their arrows back.

"Wait," I cry, for it is not the vile Witch emerging from the forest. It is the Shimmer.

"Hansel, what do we see?" asks our village leader.

"She is a Shimmer of the wood. She bears us no ill will."

The eyes of the men catch the glint of the Shimmer's weak light. They gaze in silence at the tale turned truth before them.

The Shimmer holds her arms to me. I feel the pull of my promise to her, and I step away from the line. She is formless, merely a glow lost in an outline of silver.

"Come to me, Hansel," sings the Shimmer with the lilt of birdsong. "See me. I beg you."

"Hansel, stay," says our chief.

"All is well, brother," I say. "Perhaps she has word of the Witch."

"Let her leave the forest and come to us," he says.

I look back to the wavering Shimmer. Her light wanes, but she is more human than ever before, her face so like Louisa's.

"See me, my love," she pleads.

"I must go to her," I say. I am drawn toward the Shimmer as I imagine the curve of Louisa's dear lips behind the silver light. No, my love is tucked safely in the village, away from this horror.

The rumble of the villagers grows behind me. I bring malice upon their homes.

Shame colors my cheeks as I near the Shimmer. She gave me love, fellowship, and a song against sorrow. I gave her lies and vacant promises, pretending she was an echo of Louisa.

"Shimmer...." Louisa's eyes flicker from the glow as I speak, and then a shadow surrounds her. Black cloth flaps in the night wind and I see the Witch holding the Shimmer as a shield.

A hideous face slides around the Shimmer's light. "Hail, brave Hansel. Come to save your love?"

The Shimmer fades to blue, the color of despair. I see tiny silver tears falling from eyes I know.

The Witch drags her filthy nails across a tear. "She is yours, is she not?"

I willed this creature to be mine. I accepted her allegiance selfishly. In

161

this dire moment I know I must give her my loyalty or lose my own soul. "Yes, she is mine."

At my words the Shimmer brightens and her silver shine grows.

"My Hansel," she breathes. "You know me."

I feel a swell in my ruined heart, the same glow the Shimmer's touch awakened at our first meeting. The light gives me power to confront my enemy. "Release her, Witch!"

The Witch's brittle laughter fills the air as she moves free from the forest's arch. "I will release her for a dozen of your tasty little ones."

My charge is swift. The boots of the villagers pound behind to join the fight. I curve around the dying light of the Shimmer to bury my knife in the Witch's heart. I misjudge the speed of the dark one. She spins as swiftly as a storm wind and thrusts the Shimmer onto the point of my outstretched knife.

Instead of the vibrant energy of the Shimmer, I feel my blade sink into human flesh.

I release my hold on the weapon, as the light of the lover's moon, free from the branches of the wood, falls not on the Shimmer, but the body of my Louisa.

"No!" I howl, catching, my love in my arms as we fall to the ground.

Louisa clutches my face in her hands. "Forgive me. I could only stay with you in the woods by trusting my love to the vessel of a Shimmer." Her form shifts between Shimmer and human, unable to hold either as life slips away.

My Shimmer was no nameless creature of the night, but my very own Louisa finding passage through the forest protected by the light of a willing spirit. I did not pledge my love to a Shimmer in the wood. I gave it where it belonged, to Louisa.

The villagers and their torches fly forward, crying out Louisa's name.

Louisa, my Shimmer, begins to melt into quicksilver.

The Witch sees her chance, plunging her nails, as strong as any metal blade through skin into my chest. I scream as her hands crash through my bones to snatch my heart, but she does not reach it first. Silver beams soaring from radiant fingers surround my heart. It is no longer flesh, but the same ball of light it became under the Shimmer's loving touch.

Louisa's touch.

The instant the Witch's fingers touch my luminous heart, a streak of lightning shivers up the veins in her arms. Her body erupts into a black flare that forces the advancing men away from her. She becomes a flame that reaches as high as the tops of the forest trees for an instant and then bursts into a thousand ebony drops of rain.

Louisa's love vanquished the Witch. Evil can no longer stay my Gretel's soul from its journey to Heaven.

I gather Louisa's fading form against my shredded chest and nestle her in my arms. I press my lips to her ear. "My love. My only love. I take you to into my heart and marry you under this lover's moon."

Flurries of sparks ignite, swirling around us like fireflies, piercing our bodies. What is this wonder?

I gaze down at Louisa, lying silent in my arms. She shines with her Shimmer light.

But wait, these are not my arms. There is no cloth of a sleeve, or flesh over bone. It is because I am no longer of the earth. I shine with the same silver as my love.

Her eyes open. "My Hansel."

Beyond love's glow I see the villagers dropping to their knees, hands swiping crosses over their chests, as Louisa and I ascend into the night.

We kiss, rising to meet the lover's moon, blessed within the radiance of a Shimmer.

Brownie Points

Wayne Ligon

"ZED, I HAVE a brownie problem," Vickie said, her cell phone on speaker as she worked on new menu designs.

"Nobody has a brownie *problem*, Vic; maybe it's more ghost rats?" came the affable male voice on the other end of the line. Zed Smith was her usual exterminator for the paranormal pests her restaurant attracted.

"Zed. How long have we known each other?"

"Um, five years, I think. What—"

"Do you think I don't know a ghost rat when I don't see one?

"Touché. I can be downtown after I finish the job I'm on. Maybe an hour or so, if that's good for you?"

"Actually, this is at the new house. I'll text you the map link."

"Aha! The famous Casa Martin! You finally got moved in?"

"Finally, yes; here's that link," she said as she hit Send.

He gave an appreciative whistle a moment later. "Oldest residential section of the city. Wow."

"It set me back, but now I have a ten minute commute instead of an hour and a half. I'll meet you there."

"Got it; see you in sixty-ish."

Vickie was curled up in the bay window seat in her home office, reading, when she spotted Zed's pickup pulling up to the curb. A magnetic sign on the door read 'A to Z Exterminating' in big red letters. 'A' had been Albrecht, the father, and 'Z' was Zed, the youngest son. Below, in smaller letters, was 'Paranormal exterminations day or night. Faerie infestations a specialty. No Demons.' She watched Zed hop out in his tan jumpsuit and amble up the driveway. Her house was at the end of a cul-de-sac and sat apart from its neighbors on a steep rise.

She opened the side door off the kitchen for him, and smiled at his admiration once he got into the kitchen proper.

It was her refuge in many ways, something she'd worked towards for a number of years. Large enough to have an island in the center, two separate sinks, a huge gas oven, a large chef's-style refrigerator, double-door walk-in pantry, separate freezer in the adjoining mud room; all of it garnished with marble, blond wood, and brass fittings. A bay window in the breakfast nook, twin to the one in her office, lit the area perfectly.

"So I'm curious: why would brownies be a problem for you?" Zed pulled out a pad to make notes. "Nothing cleans a house better than they do, and I bet you do a ton of work in here."

Vickie appreciated that. Some people assumed an executive chef simply ordered other people around, but he'd seen her work at the restaurant. "They weren't, at first," she said. "The day I moved in, the place was filled with boxes, and I wasn't going to be able to get to them for a week or more. I came home that first night and everything was unpacked. My bed was made. They even put the linens in order the way I like them."

"Yep, nothing does that except for brownies. The problem being...?"

"The kitchen! Half of the dishes I make, they throw out! Last week I spent two hours experimenting with baba ghanoush variants. I went out to pick up some more tahini and when I got back, everything was gone. I almost called the police, except no-one in his right mind would steal five bowls of baba ghanoush. Finally I found the bowls cleaned and put away, right where they should be, but no trace of my spreads."

Zed tapped his pen against the pad, looking thoughtful. "You said 'about half'? What were some of the other things they threw out?"

Vickie puffed out her cheeks with an exaggerated sigh. "Um, sea-salt caramels, a sesame tofu dessert, dark chocolate bacon cupcakes, peanut...what?" she said, as Zed's gentle smile widened.

"So, some fairly exotic stuff?"

"Not *that* exotic, but I need something to perk up the dessert menu."

"Brownies are pretty Old-School faerie-types. They came over on the first merchant ships and you don't usually see them outside of New England. I'm betting this group came West with the earliest immigrants and stayed in the oldest part of the city as things changed."

"So?"

"So their idea of food is red meat and tubers. They probably don't recognize that stuff as *food* at all. They, um, think you're hiding ruined recipes and garbage in the fridge."

Vickie frowned. "Oh, then I *really* want them gone! I *need* them gone.

But I already did the stuff those guys on the Nature Network, um...'Elf Hunters' say not to do: I thanked them out loud, and I told people I had brownies helping me around the house."

Zed shook his head. "Those Elf Hunters guys...those guys are going to get someone torn to pieces one day," he grumbled. "They make people think the only things out there are the cute flower faeries and so people go poking around, looking for places faeries live. If they stumble into a troll lair or run into a raw-hide-and-bloody-bones, the only thing that'll be left of them is their teeth and toenails."

"Harsh."

"That's why a lot of paranormal exterminators who won't hesitate to clear out a nest of ghouls won't touch a faerie situation," Zed explained. "You never quite know what you're dealing with. Faeries live by weird rules that don't make sense to humans, like the thing about not thanking them for a service. No type of faerie creature wants to be put in debt, especially to a human, and thanking them implies they owe you something."

Vickie felt goosebumps on her arms, both at the subject matter and the change in Zed's demeanor. He was normally a smiling, easy-going guy but this had brought out intensity in him she hadn't seen before. "Anything else I should know, just in case?"

Zed nodded. "You never, ever bargain with any sort of faerie unless you're very careful. They hate being called liars, and they also twist any agreement to make sure they come out on top. You are right, though: thanking them should have made the brownies clear out in minutes."

Vickie sighed and leaned back in her chair, arms folded. "Well, that's why you're here," she said with a slight smile. "Okay, then. How do we get these guys to pack up for filthier pastures?"

Zed ran fingers through his shaggy hair and looked around the kitchen. "First things first, just to be sure."

He cleared his throat. "Wow, this kitchen is amazingly clean," he said in a loud, clear voice. He gestured to Vickie. She hesitated, until she realized what he was doing.

"Yes it is. I have a group of brownies living in my walls," she said equally slowly and clearly, like a very poor actress.

"They certainly do a good job."

"Yes, I should thank them. Thank you for all you've done, brownies!"

Zed cocked his head like a terrier listening at a hole.

Silence.

After a few minutes, he shook his head. "Flattery regarding their work always gets their attention. Unless they're all deaf, they had to have heard that. You'd hear a sort of settling sound as they cleared out of the walls, the attic; wherever it is they've made their nest."

"You've done this a lot?" Vickie said.

"Since I took over the business, yeah. When I started with dad, I'd handle the stuff like rat ghosts, poltergeists, gremlins and the like while I was learning the craft magic we use. He handled the faerie creatures."

Vickie was curious about the elder Albrecht; this was the first time Zed had mentioned his father in the two years since he'd been running the business solo.

Zed frowned as he looked around the kitchen. "I...need to get tools out of my truck. This could get weird. I mean, it's already weird, but...."

Vickie walked out with him, enjoying the cool afternoon breeze. She watched Zed casually as he rummaged around in the pickup's cab, but inside she was worried for him. The warding and purging spells he did at her restaurant frequently took a while and increasingly she'd used the time to take a break and talk with him as he worked. She'd gotten used to him radiating the quiet confidence of a person competent in his profession.

For the first time since she'd known him, he looked like someone out of his depth.

Vickie watched Zed wrestle a leather bag from the cab. "The 'could get weird' part. You sounded a little, um, ominous. We're friends, right? Be straight with me?"

He looked a little sheepish. "And here I thought I was being all cool and professional. What we just did should have worked. Unless...they don't want to leave for some reason. In that case, digging them out could get...." He paused and then shrugged. "Weird. The whole unvarnished truth is that I've never heard of this happening, so I'm going to have to improvise. Plan A failed, so...we try Plan B."

Vickie watched Zed put his utility bag on the kitchen table and reach into it until he was shoulder deep. Yet the bag was maybe a foot deep at most. She'd seen him do this a dozen times before, but she never got tired of seeing magic in action.

"Aha!" he said as he found what he needed by touch, and withdrew a large black horseshoe from the small bag. "Cold-worked iron. Every faerie race hates and fears it, because it's pure poison to them. Hang this over a threshold and you're telling them, 'You're not welcome here.'" He fetched a hammer and nail from the bag as well. "Let me hang this over the front door and we'll see what happens."

She found a stepladder for him, and watched from the foyer as he positioned the horseshoe points down and tapped the nail once.

Immediately the lawn sprinklers turned on full force, all oriented towards Zed.

He fell off the stepladder and the jets of water followed him down, soaking him instantly. He scrambled to his feet and sprinted for the front door. Vickie slammed it shut.

He opened his mouth, but Vickie was leaned against the wall, laughing so hard she could only point to the bathroom. He flicked water at her from his dripping sleeves, but that only made her laugh harder.

"I am so charging you double overtime!" he called as he squished down the hallway.

"Do *you* want to mop the foyer?"

"Time-and-a-half?"

Vickie wiped her eyes and walked to the closed bathroom door. "You have clean uniforms in your truck, right?"

"And clean clothes," he called from inside. "They're actually in the satchel; reach in and then back towards your belly button."

"Are you sure your magic bag isn't going to eat me or something?"

"Naw, it likes you," Zed said, and Vickie grinned at the smile she heard in his voice.

"Good to know. The closet over the hamper has extra towels."

"Got it," Zed said.

Vickie was turning away when she heard him try to stifle a sharp intake of breath, not quite a gasp. "Are you okay? You fell pretty hard out there."

A pause. "No, it's cool," came Zed's voice.

Vickie started to open the door, but hesitated and then thought better of it. She eventually found his spare uniforms and prepped packs of jeans-and-T-shirt combos, by sticking her head and shoulders into the wide-mouthed leather satchel and using a flashlight. By the time she got back to the foyer, it was dry and spotless. The brownies had mopped, polished and buffed the entire area until she could see her face in the wood. Vickie shook her head and continued on to the bathroom. Zed's work boots sat just outside the door, dry, clean and polished. She knocked on the door and announced, "Uniform delivery. You're a regular Boy Scout; prepared for everything."

Zed opened the door enough to let her pass the fresh clothing to him. He was clad in a towel, giving her a brief glimpse of a sleek but defined chest and actual abdominals. Vickie had to smile; the jumpsuit she'd always seen him in gave little hint to how well made he was, but he was certainly what her girlfriends would have deemed 'calendar-worthy.' She started to tease him but when he turned, there was something odd about his skin that came and went too fast for her to make it out. It was vaguely disturbing to her on a visceral level.

"Thanks," came his grateful voice after he closed the door. Moments later he opened the door to get his boots. He was wearing the clean jumpsuit, and Vickie was surprised to feel a slight pang of disappointment that he was no longer half naked.

"So much for Plan B," he said.

"Okay, now we're up to 'J'," Vickie said much later, "and so far nothing has fazed the little bastards."

Zed sat at the kitchen table. He was smudged, scratched, wet again, smelled of burning sage, and had dots of strawberry jam in his hair. It was four in the morning and he was finishing off the most recent batch of coffee Vickie had made.

"I don't understand it." He sighed and put his head on the table.

Vickie came over and tried to pick some of the jam out of his hair. "Is there anything else I could do?"

She felt him stiffen, just slightly, as she began to deftly tease clumps of jam from his long hair. Then he relaxed and she looked down at him. *He's blushing like a kid!* She thought, amazed and pleased at the same time.

Vickie watched the young man's blush deepen, and smiled herself. They were both exhausted, but Zed was pushing himself hard. That intense look in his eyes had grown, so she was glad for this break. His damp hair was soft, and she found she liked pulling her fingers through it. She looked down at him and saw his long-lashed eyes were closed, giving him an air of unguarded vulnerability, and she gently brushed his forehead.

"Don't go to sleep on me, now," Vickie said softly, and he laughed.

He sat up, rubbing his eyes. "Thank you. And I'm at a loss. I was sure the strawberry jam would work. You're the mistress of the house. If you offer them hospitality, they *have* to accept it. It's one of the most ancient laws in the world. At least then we could have talked to them and found out why they haven't left." He drained his mug. "Could I ask a favor?"

"If it's for a shower, please, go ahead. Now. We both stink."

Zed shot her a grateful smile. "I'll be quick." He fished another uniform and set of clothes from his satchel before disappearing into the

169

bathroom again.

Vickie yawned and started another pot of coffee, then went upstairs to grab a quick shower herself. When she came back down, the kitchen was spotless once again. She had to smile; in her brief research she'd found there were people that tried all kinds of weird things to attract a brownie clan, and here she was trying to get rid of one.

After a few minutes, Vickie decided to check on Zed. The door was open; he was done with his shower and he stood before the sink, dressed only in his jeans, awkwardly daubing some peroxide on a cut over his eye. She couldn't help admiring his physique, but as she got closer she saw what she'd seen only in passing a few hours before: a good portion of his back and chest were lined with fine white scars.

"I—" she started to say, and Zed yelped in surprise. "Sorry, I thought you could use...." She hesitated but this time decided to simply go ahead. "What happened?" she said quietly.

Zed put his hands on the counter, head bowed. Silence stretched between them until Vickie made the first move to step back. "No, it's okay," came his voice, quiet but calm. "It's been a couple of years now. There was an abandoned warehouse with a goblin problem. The realty company hired Dad to clean them out so they could sell the property and I...messed up. They overpowered me and dragged me down into their tunnels."

Vickie frowned. Everyone had *heard* of goblins just like everyone had *heard* of trolls, but they were—they were *supposed* to be—things that lived in the deep wilderness or in caves, not in or near the cities.

Zed sighed. "They tortured me for several days, until Dad could bargain for my release."

"Oh, no," she said softly. *You never, ever bargain with any sort of faerie unless you're very careful....* "What did he...?"

Zed swallowed. When he spoke, his voice was very steady. "Himself. He exchanged himself for me."

Vickie bowed her head, then she gently turned Zed around and put her arms around him. A second later, he reciprocated, closing his eyes and letting her comfort him.

"Thank you," he said gently.

Vickie held him close, feeling her own heartbeat against his. *I'd assumed Albrecht had retired,* she thought. *I saw him only a few times early on, when he'd come around to spot-check Zed's work...I always thought of Zed as strong; I didn't know how strong. To be tortured, and then to find out....*

"My God, Zed, your poor father," Vickie said after a minute. "I don't...You never said anything. I know it's...."

He smiled a little sadly and disengaged from her, reaching for his t-shirt and putting it on. "It's okay, really. He's still listed as 'Missing' but goblins don't keep captives. They move around too much to haul around a human." Zed stepped into and zipped up his jumpsuit. "Thank you for, um, listening—"

"No, no, I should have asked—"

"I don't normally—"

Vickie quirked a smile as they tried to talk over each other. "Shh. Zed, its fine. We've known each other for—"

"Years, really—"

"I was going to say 'awhile', but—"

They both laughed, and that seemed to break the tension. Vickie smiled and left him to finish cleaning up, but her smile faded and she found herself looking back towards the bathroom.

He's still trying to be strong, but that kind of strength can wind up destroying you.

When he rejoined her in the kitchen, he began to rummage in his satchel once more. "Vickie, I am at the end of my rope. I don't know anything else to try except go straight to Plan Z."

"Paying them off?"

Zed shook his head. "Everything up until now has been soft-ball. It's been about letting them know they're not wanted. But something is keeping them here, and they're not talking. So it's time to pull out the big guns. I really, really don't like doing this."

Finally he found what he was looking for and pulled out what looked like large brass cowbells with long handles.

"I'm guessing those aren't cowbells?" Vickie said.

"Hardly. Handbells from a Welsh church," he said, carefully setting them on the table.

"What could those do?" Vickie said.

"It's not something you hear about on cable, because it's not very PC and raises some uncomfortable questions. But the sound of church bells causes agony in every being from the Faerie Lands I know of. Some types even turn to stone or dead leaves or sea foam if they hear them."

Vickie bit her lip. Annoying as they were, the thought of doing actual harm to the brownies hadn't really crossed her mind. "I don't want to kill them...."

Zed nodded. "I can just call it a lost cause. It's your decision, but I've run out of options." He looked at the handbells and frowned again.

"Vickie...you might want to go elsewhere. Find a friend to stay with. I really don't know what will happen here. I've never tried this."

"No, I—"

"I don't want you hurt," Zed said, and Vickie heard the conviction in his voice.

She put her hand on his as he gripped the bell tighter. "I called you here," she said. "I'm a part of this."

Zed looked at the ground. "I don't want you hurt," he repeated, his voice softer. "Please, Vickie...This touches an old and deep magic. This isn't like the human-made charms and wardings my dad and granddad taught me. I...don't know what might happen."

Vickie shook her head at last. "I appreciate the thought, but you did say things could get weird. At least try it. Maybe they'll vacate before it causes them any permanent harm."

"Here goes Plan Z, then." Zed took both bells by their handles and walked to the island, as close to the center of the kitchen as he could.

He took a deep breath and then slowly rang both bells. Instead of a brassy clang they gave off a grave-deep thundering toll that shook the house and knocked dust from the ceiling. The bells burst into shards but their awful sound continued, as the whole house shifted again, like it was threatening to tear loose from its foundations and slide down the hill. The kitchen windows exploded outwards, and the house was plunged into darkness as the power failed. Zed groaned, and he let the handles drop to the ground. They puffed into dust.

The dim emergency lights from the security system flickered on.

There was the sound of a door opening, somewhere.

"Oh! Oh no. Oh no!" Zed croaked. The house continued to shudder and groan, the ground rolling under their feet like the deck of a ship. Zed bolted for the front door and threw it open as the echoes from the bells faded. "Vickie!"

Vickie pushed past him to see a huge brass-bound door slowly opening on the slope between her porch and the turn-around. Sun-bright light spilled out of it onto the cul-de-sac. Dogs and car alarms sounded off all the way to the main street, and lights were coming on in various houses.

Zed shifted beside her, and she looked over to see his face pale but his jaw set firmly. He swallowed hard.

"Who did you buy your house from?" he asked in a desperate whisper.

"Ah. Um, the...the realtor found it for me. I don't have time to do a lot of house hunting. She said it was perfect."

"Name?"

"Um, Alice something. Alice Blacke, with an 'e'. She was just a voice on the phone, but she was very nice."

"I bet she was. Name of the company?"

Vickie saw he was gripping the door frame so tightly his knuckles were white. "What the hell does—"

"Vickie," he said quietly, in a tone that made her look up at him.

"Um, Good Neighbors. Good Neighbors Realty."

Zed growled. "They're the same people who owned that warehouse. I need my satchel."

Vickie grabbed his arm. "Zed, what the hell is that on my lawn?"

"Vickie—"

"ZED! What the hell is that on my lawn?"

Zed swallowed hard. "It's a direct door into the Faerie Lands. Black Alice sold you a house built on top of a sleeping faerie mound," he said. "And I just woke them up. They are going to kill everyone on this cul-de-sac unless we can shut that door. Let me get my satchel, please. Go and keep anyone from walking over that threshold or they'll be lost forever."

Zed sprinted for his equipment in the kitchen.

Vickie picked up the iron horseshoe from where Zed had dropped it when the sprinklers doused him, and hurried down the steep slope towards the huge impossible door in the side of the hill. She carefully walked around to the front and looked in.

And gasped.

Outside, the world was wrapped in pre-dawn stillness, dark and heavy. Past the door, though, was another world where the sun was shining and a vast misty forest rolled away towards distant snow-capped mountains. The clear pale golden color of the light felt refreshing and right. The wind from the place smelled of pine and loam and wildflowers, and Vickie's gasp brought her a lungful of the freshest, cleanest air she'd ever breathed.

She laid a hand on the edge of the heavy door and took another deep breath. Vaguely she heard Zed calling her name, but he sounded very far away. That was strange. And the horseshoe she was holding...dragged her arm down, as if it was growing heavier by the second. She staggered. Vickie blinked as she came back to herself, the iron weight in her hand unable, *unwilling*, to leave the human world. She frowned and stopped and then slowly looked down to see her foot raised to cross the threshold.

"Vickie, no!" came Zed's voice close to her ear. "I can't lose you!"

The last tendrils of longing she felt for the land beyond the door slipped free, and she pushed back. She had to go back. Back to him.

She fought to take a step back, and her foot slowly moved. She forced herself to take another. Her third step fetched her up against Zed and he gently pulled her a few more steps back, hand on her shoulder.

She glanced back at him, and briefly saw the naked fear on his face. The fear that she would be lost. That changed to a warm smile as she pulled free of the land's influence, and as she fell back against him he gave her a quick fierce hug.

"Close one," he breathed.

"Thank you," Vickie said. She looked past him to see some of her neighbors stumbling outside to see what all the fuss was about, or to shut off their car alarms. Dogs whined and ran away. *Smart dogs*, she thought. She turned her back on the door into the Faerie Lands, and Zed joined her in standing in the light.

"Go back! It's not safe!" Vickie yelled to her neighbors and Zed joined her. "Get back inside! NOW!"

Tentatively, most of the onlookers crept back to their homes. A few stayed on their lawns, though, apparently captivated by the faint scent of pine and wildflowers.

Zed squeezed Vickie's hand. "I think they'll stay put long enough," he said, and Vickie heard a fierce determination in his voice.

Behind them came sounds of movement, and Vickie turned back to the doorway.

Shadows gathered at the edge of the tangled forest and began to spill towards the opening, gradually resolving themselves into hunched malevolent shapes. Most stayed back in the darkness under the trees for now, and Vickie was very glad of that. The ones she could see made her grip the iron weight in her hands hard enough that she couldn't feel her fingers anymore. Dark-furred antlered things with eyes of green fire, things that looked like bundles of thorns, fanged slobbering dwarfs with dripping red caps, and more inched towards the door.

"Zed...I think...." Vickie stammered, and gripped his arm. She felt a cold weight press against her leg and looked down.

Zed was holding a sword in his right hand.

"Go. This isn't your fight, Vickie," Zed said. "They'll want me; I woke them up."

Vickie finally found her voice. "You...you can't be serious! Look at those things! That's not going to do anything to them!"

Zed saw her look, and frowned. "It's steel; not nearly as poisonous to them as iron, but it'll have to do."

Vickie shook her head. "No, no, I mean I'm not letting you do this alone. This is my house. What can we fight them with?"

"I'm not letting you get hurt," he said.

"This is so not the time to get all chivalrous!"

"I have a sword in my hand and monsters threaten my lady. I think it's the *perfect* time to get chivalrous."

"'Your lady,' huh?" Vickie flashed a brief smile at Zed. "Seriously. What can we fight them with?"

"Iron is best, and you have that. St John's Wort. Yarrow. Um, a crowing cock if you have one handy. Flax seed. Red ribbons...."

"Not helping," Vickie said between her teeth.

"You don't happen to have salt, then, do you? I mean a whole lot of it. Not just a shaker you grind or—"

"Yes! I'm a chef, hon, I have pounds of the stuff."

Zed looked relieved. "Bring it. All of it. It'll buy us some time, at least."

Vickie sprinted into the kitchen and threw open the pantry doors. She had a ten pound canister of salt somewhere...aha! On the back shelf! In the dim emergency lighting she thought for a second she saw roaches scattering among the shelves. But roaches didn't make high-pitched yells. The brownies had finally been caught out.

"You little pigs, you're the cause of this!" she snarled as she hefted the salt canister. "Why didn't you just leave?"

"We couldn't," said a soft voice near her head. "Black Alice tricked us, just as she has tricked you."

Vickie turned to see a tiny brownie woman the size of a walnut on the shelf by the jars of anchovy paste. She was brown and wrinkled and pudgy, dressed in old-world skirts and kirtle. The toes of thick black boots peeked out from under the mountain of homespun she wore. A kerchief bound back her iron-grey hair. She had the look of Vickie's formidable grandmother during Spring Cleaning, waging war against dirt and disorder.

"She tricked a promise from me and then used it to bind us to this place for her evil purposes," the brownie woman continued mournfully. "She commanded that we not speak to you. But you've addressed us first, so her command is overthrown."

Vickie shifted the weight in her arms. "Could have shown yourselves a little sooner. I'm sure we could have found a way to help you."

The old brownie's wizened face suddenly grew shrewd. "Is that a promise, dear?"

"No, just a statement," Vickie automatically said, startled at how a sorrowful voice had almost made her swear a faerie promise. Then again.... "But taking down Black Alice would benefit us both, would it not?"

The brownie smiled tightly and leaned on her gnarled cane. "Aye, it would. I tell you this for free: I see you've a load of salt with you, there. That will not stop them. They will have to count it, each and every grain, but they will and well before dawn, too."

"That's only forty minutes from now. The door will close then?"

"Yes, but time runs strangely in the Faerie Lands, and part of it lies open on your pasture out there. There will be time enough. Then Black Alice will finally be able to walk freely in your world."

"Black Alice, that is, my realtor, knew I'd know an exterminator who really knew his business, so all she had to do was hold you here until Zed used the church bells. Is that about right?"

"Feh, your speech is strange but that be her plan, alright. She seeks a holding in your world, the better to work her wickedness. I suspect she will take your skin so she can walk unseen as one of you."

"Fantastic. You like it here?"

The nut-brown little faerie woman smiled, showing huge cheeks that almost swallowed her beady eyes. "Oh, yes. You are so messy! So many things to do!"

Vickie spotted a bottle next to the salt. A plan came to mind. She took a deep breath. *I have to save Zed's life. But how?* She felt sick with fear at the thought of Zed dying. Yesterday, he'd been a friend. Now, though? *He's willing to risk everything for me, so can I do any less? If this is going to work… I have to make a deal with her.*

"You can bake, right?" she asked the brownie woman.

"Only the best, but we've not time for tea now."

Vickie remembered the way Zed had flattered them earlier. "Surely it's no problem for you to make a half-dozen walnut muffins in, oh, ten minutes, right?"

The brownie woman snapped her fingers. "Too easy! We could do it in half the time! And what do we get?"

"A bowl of milk, every night, and a saucer of strawberry jam every new moon."

"A quart jar."

"A pint jar. And you clean the way I tell you to."

"Done and done."

Vickie grabbed the bottle she'd seen a moment before and set it near the brownie woman. "This seasoning will go well with them. Use all of it," she said, and the old matriarch's face split with a grin.

Zed was standing in the doorway, sword held at ready, when she ran back with the salt.

"Did you have to go buy it?" he asked.

"Don't start with me," Vickie said as she tore the top off the canister and laid down a thick line of salt on the threshold. "Will this buy us ten minutes?"

Zed nodded. "At least, yes."

Some of the dark creatures were within feet of the door, and they drew back from the mounds of white. They also eyed the horseshoe in Vickie's hand and took another step back, unwilling to risk the touch of iron. Vickie gagged on the smells coming off them.

Zed narrowed his eyes. "I think this is where things get interesting."

Vickie looked up. The creatures were parting, and a woman in a charcoal business suit was walking unhurriedly towards the doorway.

"Ms. Blacke?" Vickie said.

The woman could have been a corporate executive: pale skin, gleaming nails, razor-cut black hair that didn't touch her neck. But when she smiled she showed long, narrow, needle-sharp teeth stained black.

No wonder she needs my shape, Vickie thought.

"Hello, Vickie," the creature said.

"Liar. You are not Alice Blacke but Black Alice," Zed said. "Go back under the hill and bother these good folk no more."

Black Alice threw back her head and laughed. "Ah, boy, find another to match wits with. I have told no falsehood; I did not acknowledge her greeting, merely gave one of my own. You cannot name me liar, seventh son," she said, smiling her terrible smile. "You have woken the hill, and must now pay our price. Not even her iron trinket will stop me." Black Alice stared past the pair at the groups of neighbors that had edged close enough to see. "We will claim all of *them* as our payment, and we will use their skins to walk in the daytime."

As she spoke, a multitude of tiny leaf and grass fairies, no bigger than ants, swarmed suddenly at the line of salt. Vickie had no doubt they were counting each grain as they removed it, and they made excellent time.

Zed chanced a look at Vickie, and Vickie saw he was sweating but also wore a fierce grin, the kind she imagined his ancestors wore into battle. He turned back to Black Alice. "You have no claims here. You have duped this woman and myself. Falsehood removes any obligations."

Black Alice snapped her fingers in a dismissive gesture. "You banter to waste time. I shall mount you, drain your manhood, and then give you to the red-caps as a toy. The child of a mage's seed has many uses."

Zed swallowed. "Then I off—"

Oh, shit! Vickie thought. *He's going to offer himself up so we can all go free, like his father did!*

Vickie glanced at her watch, then grabbed the front of Zed's jumpsuit and jerked him down into a fierce kiss. She splayed one hand on the back of his head, twining her fingers in his hair. She held the kiss for three pounding heartbeats and then slid her lips away from his, feeling the rasp of his stubble before she jerked him down a bit more to nuzzle at his ear.

"You are *not* throwing yourself away, do you hear me? You don't...you don't have to be your father," Vickie whispered, urgent. "You need to live!" Then she added, "Live for *me*."

"They'll kill you otherwise. She wants to *wear your skin*, Vickie!" he responded softly, his lips at her ear. "I have to. Your life, the lives of all these people...I can't have that on my conscience."

"Screw your conscience, Sir Galahad." She tightened her fingers in his hair until she heard him complain. "You are not dying today. You just need to keep them *busy*."

"What...?" Zed grunted.

"They love deals so much, offer her something she can't refuse: a chance to screw you over. I got this. Plan Z-2. Eight minutes. Trust me?" she whispered.

"I do," Zed murmured back. "With my life." He pulled back and met her eyes, removed her hand and squeezed it gently. "I do," he mouthed. Then he turned to face Black Alice once more.

"I offer one-on-one combat. Send forth your champion, unseelie wight. If I slay him, you and all under the hill go back and slumber once more. If your champion slays me, then...then ourselves and all behind us belong to you."

Black Alice struck her fingernails together, and green sparks curled away from them. "Accepted, and answered," she said in a bored tone of voice. "I suppose I can still mount you...on my wall."

She gestured and the creatures parted. Vickie bit her tongue, trying not to scream as Alice's champion shambled forward. It was easily ten feet tall, with a huge belly and fists the size of watermelons. In one hand, it held a fire-hardened oaken spear. Its face was dog-like, with a long snout where the lower jaw shot out a good foot or more past the upper one, revealing fangs like ragged thorns and a lolling black tongue. Yellow drool ran from its lips to spatter sizzling on the grass. The tiny faeries splashed by the stuff blackened and died instantly.

Zed squared his shoulders. "An ogre. Just...great!" he muttered. He leaned his sword against the doorframe and took off his shirt, quickly pulling it inside out before putting it on backwards. He let his jumpsuit fall away and stepped out of it.

"What—?" Vickie started, but then remembered some bit of lore from the cable shows: fairies loved order, so doing something pointedly nonsensical like wearing your clothing backwards could confuse them.

"Gonna need every advantage I can get," Zed said, noticing Vickie's look. "Fortunately, ogres are stupid as logs. Still...."

Vickie clutched his free hand briefly, for luck, for strength, and then

Zed stepped over the swiftly-dwindling line of salt. The other creatures shuffled back to give the combatants plenty of room.

Vickie clutched the horseshoe like a talisman, hoping Zed could run out the clock and not die in the process. She watched him as he slashed the blade back and forth, limbering up; the lesser creatures quailed back from the sight of steel, but she noticed Black Alice only looked at the line of salt. She checked her watch. Less than five minutes.

Zed spun his sword in hand and then turned his back on the ogre. He walked backwards toward it, head bowed.

The ogre narrowed its piggy eyes and spat on the ground, then took a tentative step forward. It rattled the spear and bellowed, but didn't charge Zed's defenseless back.

Vickie felt her nails bite into the palms of her hands, until she realized the ogre simply couldn't see Zed. With his shirt inside-out and walking so he could see his own footprints, he was effectively invisible to the thing.

She chanced another look at Black Alice, who was standing there smug and smiling. *I was right; she couldn't resist the chance to show how clever she is,* Vickie thought. *Where's the trap?*

Zed advanced, his sword held to thrust behind him into the monster beyond. He obviously planned to sheathe his sword right in its gut. As he got within roughly arm's reach, though, already pulling the sword back for the killing blow, the ogre's nostrils suddenly flared. It sniffed then, crab-walked sideways and drove the spear two feet into the ground, inches from where Zed had just stepped.

Zed yelped and jumped backwards, his sword slashing through the ogre's knee instead of its massive belly. The ogre's flesh bubbled and steamed at the touch of steel, and it squealed in sudden pain. Zed sprang forward before the spear could come up and strike. Even so the point drove past his side, drawing a deep bloody line and ripping the shirt. The ogre snuffled and brought the spear point close to its bulbous nose, its huge nostrils flaring again as it got Zed's blood-scent.

Vickie groaned. This was why Black Alice wasn't afraid of losing. The thing hunted by scent as well as sight.

The ogre rumbled its defiance, black blood streaming down one leg. It jabbed twice more at Zed, missing him, and then slashing directly across his back. Zed cried out and went down in the grass. He rolled away just in time to keep the spear out of his belly, though it cost him another flap of his shirt. He jumped up and blocked the spear, then slashed the ogre on the bottom lip, the steel blade drawing a sizzling wound.

"Graphaaagh!" the ogre spat.

Zed leapt back but the steaming poisonous spittle still splashed him. He ripped open his shirt and tossed the sizzling fabric to one side, where it disintegrated almost at once, then quickly wiped the remaining droplets from his skin. Zed stood there, barely breathing hard, sweat gleaming on his smooth pecs, and then ran forward.

The ogre could see him now, though, and it swatted his blade aside. The other clawed hand caught his leg and jerked him eight feet off the ground. Zed slashed and caught the monster's protruding jaw again, this time shattering several of its teeth. It screamed and dropped him. Vickie cried out in sympathy as she watched him almost right himself, then land so that he rolled over one ankle, the pop audible from the doorway.

Zed limped backwards, and the ogre lumbered after him, laughing.

Vickie felt a touch at her foot, looked down and saw a tray bearing a plate of fresh muffins, a steaming carafe of breakfast tea, and two cups.

Vickie picked up the tray and set aside her horseshoe.

"Stop!" she called in a loud, clear voice. "I am mistress in this place, and I say...it's time for tea."

The ogre stopped in confusion. Zed goggled at her.

Black Alice turned a dark awful gaze on her, and Vickie smiled back. "I invoke my right as host and mistress of this house and land. Break bread with me." She held up the tray. "Or you can break the sacred bond, and retreat back to your woods. Your choice."

Black Alice's expression turned to a cold smile. "You are a quick study, but this buys you mere moments. My champion will destroy the boy in another few heartbeats, and you will be mine. Desperation does not become you, dear."

"If we're going to play by the rules, we're going to play by all of them. Your walnut muffin, and tea," she said, pouring a small cup for herself and the faerie woman. She broke one of the muffins in half, offered one half to Black Alice, and took a big bite from the other.

"Indeed," Black Alice said. She picked up the muffin half and bolted it down, then drained the small teacup. "Propriety has been observed, hostess. We can get on with the bloody business. At least you have bought your champion time to catch his brea—"

"What was that, Alice?" Vickie said, putting down her muffin.

Black Alice grew pale and clawed at her throat as a flood of sickly white foam poured from her mouth. Her eyes blazed with an unholy fire that began to die even as it was kindled. Beyond her, dark clouds formed over the forest. The trees twisted as if they, too, were in agony.

Zed glared at the ogre as he backed, limping, to the doorway. Black Alice silently writhed on the ground in agony and reached claw-like fingers for the sky, her chest and stomach heaving as great gouts of muck and foam poured from her mouth. With a final awful gurgle, she died. The shadowy beasts broke for the tree line, the ogre the last to go. Zed sent a gesture after him, then helped Vickie close the formerly-immovable door. Once shut, the door vanished and it was just a steeply-sloping lawn again.

Vickie stumbled against Zed and they fell into the dew-spangled grass. "Are you okay?" were the last words he said before he fell unconscious.

The next evening, Vickie sat by the guest bed and watched Zed sleep. Idly she traced a curling white scar on his upper arm. What they did to him... and he'd been willing to go back to that, for her. She brushed hair out of his eyes, and then laid her hand on his forehead to check his temperature.

She smiled as Zed opened his eyes and looked about, confused. He was obviously still hazy from the meds he'd been given at the ER. She reached to stop him from trying to sit up. "Whoa, you're not getting on your feet for a while," she said.

"You're still here," he smiled, "I mean, you never left; I...."

Vickie put fingertips over his lips for a second. "Shh, you needed your rest. Someone had to keep you from pulling your stitches. I looked inside your satchel but didn't see any bottles labeled 'drink in case of injury,'" she said, "So I left it alone. Is there anything in there that can help you?"

Zed moved a bit, now careful of the stitches down his side. "You're OK. That's helping," he said with a smile.

"Flat on your back and you're going with the charm?"

Zed blushed. "Hey, you saved my life. It doesn't get more charming than that."

"You saved mine, so we're even."

"Oh, no, I seem to remember you doing...more," he smiled.

"Oh, there'll be 'more'," Vickie said.

Zed raised an eyebrow. "I'd like that, a lot. How much 'more' are we talking about?"

Vickie bent and brushed his lips with hers, then turned that into a gentle kiss. She pulled back, and smiled.

"As it happens, I know a fantastic restaurant where we can work that out once you're on your feet. I have an in with the owner." Vickie said as she adjusted one of his bandages.

"Ouch. How are your, um, friends?"

"Things are fine, now, once I could talk to them. I don't think there will be any problems from here on out. I won't be needing an exterminator after all."

"You killed a high-court faerie; I don't think you needed one to begin with." Zed winced as he shifted. "What did you *do* to her?"

"You keep squirming like that and I'll sit on you. I just had to do a little magic of my own is all. Actually my, ah, staff helped me. I had them add this to the muffins and tea."

Vickie smiled and held up an empty super-saver-sized bottle that simply read 'Iron Supplement.'

Chindi Moon

Kevin Hosey

A DEVIL FOLLOWED LOGAN Harris through the desert into the encroaching darkness.

Logan spotted it from the corner of his eye as he kept his attention focused on the dry, cracked dirt road ahead. The funnel of dust particles was easy to see under the light of the rising half moon. Like a miniature tornado, it forged ahead, dauntless in its trajectory, as if pacing Logan's pickup truck.

He suddenly remembered what it was called. Dust devil.

Odd thing though. He'd read once that they only appear during calm days when the sun was high; something to do with the rise in warm temperature. But the sun had vanished and the wind had kicked up. Yet the persistent whirling dervish showed no signs of dying off.

Above the desert, a sparse layer of clouds smeared across the moon, creating the illusion of a vapor trail as if the moon also seemed to follow Logan. A shiver gripped him. The moon reminded him of his night patrols as a medic in Viet Nam.

Logan had watched too many of his fellow soldiers die in that damn useless war as he tried desperately to save them. Four months after leaving the Army and the blood-soaked Vietnamese jungles, the look in their fear-stricken eyes as their lives slipped away still haunted him.

The desert floor dropped away as the road climbed. Logan had mountainside to his left and a deepening cliff to his right. The mountain cast a moon shadow that painted the road black, so he flicked on his high beams—and cried out in shock.

Someone was standing in his path!

Instinctively, Logan jerked the steering wheel to the right. "SHIT!" he cried when he realized he'd veered toward the cliff. He slammed the brakes, but it was too late. Momentum carried the front wheels over the edge toward the darkness below.

Then the truck jolted to a stop, slamming Logan's forehead against the steering wheel. Dazed, he opened his eyes. Vertigo sucked his breath away when he stared into the black chasm below. The front of the truck was teetering over the edge of the cliff. It seemed stable, though no telling how long that would last.

Military training kicking in, Logan moved quickly, but carefully, into the back seat. He didn't want to risk opening the door and throwing the truck off balance, so he squeezed through the open back window into the truck bed. But the vehicle abruptly tilted forward, throwing him against the cab.

Just as he was about to chance leaping off the side, he recoiled when something hit his arm. At first, he thought it was a snake, but then realized it was a lasso. To his surprise, he spotted a woman on horseback a few yards away. She pointed urgently at the rope. As soon as Logan grabbed it, she pulled the reins and her horse walked backward. The rope tightened, and dragged Logan off the back of the truck where he landed with less than dignified grace on the ground.

Breath pumping in his chest, he expected his vehicle to slide off the cliff. It didn't. With his weight no longer throwing it off balance, it seemed satisfied to stay put.

Heart still pounding, Logan turned to discover the woman had dismounted and was offering her hand. The moment he touched it, a pleasant jolt shuddered through him as she helped him up.

Static electricity, he figured.

"Are you all right?" the woman asked.

Logan nodded—and then his breath caught. He was stunned by her beauty. Her slender, elegant Native American features were framed by hair so black it was almost blue, and her dark eyes glistened in the moonlight.

"Yes...*thank you,*" Logan said. "Ms...?"

She seemed surprised for a moment. Then she smiled. "Sialei."

"Sialei," he repeated softly. "That means 'little blue bird,' right?"

Her smile widened. "How did you know?"

How *did* he know? "Um...lucky guess?"

"You always that lucky?"

He glanced at his truck. "Depends on your point of view."

Logan peered over the cliff. He couldn't see the base, but the fall would have undoubtedly killed him. Kneeling, he saw that the truck had stopped because its back axle had wedged on a good-sized rock.

Maybe he *was* lucky after all.

When Logan stood, Sialei had remounted her horse. "Climb on," she said. "I'll give you a ride to the rez."

"The what?"

"The reservation. That's where you're going, right?"

"What about—?"

"Your truck looks secure," Sialei said, as if anticipating his question...or reading his thoughts.

With a firm grip, Sialei helped Logan mount the saddle. Settling behind her, he caught a whiff of a wonderful scent. It drew him toward her, but he resisted the powerful urge to nestle his face in her long, silky hair.

"Ready?" she asked.

Before Logan could reply, Sialei nudged her horse into a confident trot and Logan wrapped his arms around her. Again, her scent enchanted him. It seemed to calm his nerves. He'd been shaken up by the accident, and he banged his shoulder when he fell against the truck cab, but suddenly his anxiety and pain evaporated like frost on a warm day.

"So," she said, breaking him out of his trance, "how did you almost drive off that ridge?"

"I swerved to miss someone on the road. I think it was an old man."

"That may have been *Análi*. He takes long walks out here."

"You know him?" Logan asked.

"My entire life. *Análi* is Navajo for 'grandfather.'"

"He always walk in the middle of the road? That's pretty dangerous."

"Yes he does, and no it's not. This isn't Houston."

"I could have hit him."

"I doubt it. Even at eighty-nine, he's pretty spry."

"Wait, how do you know I'm from Houston?"

Sialei glanced back and smiled. "Lucky guess."

She nudged the horse and it broke into a faster gait. This time, Logan did nestle his face against her hair as he held her tighter. Thankfully, she didn't seem to mind.

Groaning, Logan stepped out of Sialei's shower. Stretching his sore muscles, he grabbed a towel, dried off, and studied his face in the mirror. A purple welt marred his forehead below his short-cropped brown hair.

Could have been worse, he thought. *I could be dead.*

During the ride to her house, Sialei had admitted she knew Logan was from Houston because she was expecting him. She'd also offered to let him use her shower to clean up because the one at the Navajo medical clinic where he'd be living and working was out of order.

He retrieved his neck chain and medallion from the back of the sink and slipped it on. Wrapping the towel around his waist, he walked into Sialei's bedroom. On the patterned blanket of her bed was a clean shirt and faded jeans she had leant him since his luggage was still in his truck. As he picked up the shirt, he stared at the bed. *Her* bed. Thoughts of her lean, toned body and beautiful face beckoning him to join her made Logan pause. He felt a sudden carnal urge, but shook it off.

Once dressed, he found Sialei in her kitchen.

"Clothes fit all right?" she asked. "My neighbor lent those to me."

"Perfect." The fact that the clothes didn't belong to a boyfriend or husband relieved Logan for some reason. "Thanks for the shower. I needed it."

A sudden image of her showering flashed through his head. He could picture her naked body as soapy water cascaded along her tan skin—

He blinked it away. That was the second sexual thought he'd had of her. While he possessed a normal male libido, he didn't have the habit of imagining women he'd just met in the nude; not even women as beautiful as Sialei.

"How are you feeling?" she asked.

"Fine," he said quickly, just to be polite. Then he realized he *did* feel fine. His aches and pains were gone. Odd. He could barely move a few minutes ago.

She invited him to sit at the table where she served sandwiches.

"Thank you again for rescuing me," he told her as they ate.

"I couldn't let our new doctor plummet off a cliff, could I?"

"Ah. So *that's* why you saved me?"

"Seemed like a good reason." Then she grinned. "And you do realize that *Diné* custom says you now owe me your life."

"*Diné?*"

"The traditional term for Navajo."

"Actually, I think that's a Chinese custom, and it says *you* are responsible for *my* life."

"They borrowed it from us," she said, grinning wider.

"Well, then I'll definitely do anything I can to return the favor."

"You're here to help my people. That's a start. I called James and told him you arrived."

"James Zah? The Indian Health Service put me in touch with him before I left Houston."

"Yes. He's community services manager for our Chapter."

Logan learned through the IHS, the federal agency that provides health care to the Navajo Nation, that the huge reservation was divided into Chapters, similar to townships, in New Mexico, Arizona and Utah. Sialei's Chapter was one of the smaller ones in Arizona. It was also too far from the larger medical facilities established by IHS, so a satellite clinic was set up over ten years ago.

"You'll like James," Sialei said. "He said he'll send someone for your truck in the morning."

"Great. So what do *you* do, besides rescuing people, I mean?"

"I teach *Diné* culture at our school. But it's summer, so I'll be helping at the clinic while the regular nurse is on maternity leave. That's how I knew you were coming."

Logan smiled at the prospect of Sialei working with him. He'd just met her, but already he enjoyed having her around.

"Something I've been wondering about," she said. "Why did you decide to work here, so far away from the city?"

When Logan opened his mouth to answer, he suddenly yawned. "*Whoa*. Sorry. It's been a long day."

"No worries. Finish your food and I'll drive you to the clinic so you can rest. It's going to have a busy day tomorrow."

As they drove the short distance to the clinic, Logan felt as if they were falling into a bottomless well. Except for scattered lights from what he assumed were distant buildings, the night was pitch black outside. It was a nice change from the dense sea of lights in Houston.

"Here it is," Sialei said as they pulled up to a small one-story brick building connected to a general store and other shops. "The best medical facility within an 80-mile radius. Well, the *only* one."

A tiny bell over the doorway chimed when they entered. Sialei flipped a wall switch and the fluorescent lights flickered on. She gave Logan the grand tour. Besides the reception area, which included six folding chairs and an office desk, there was an examination room, a recovery room with three hospital beds, and a small office.

"I'm sure you're used to bigger and more modern," Sialei said.

Logan's mind flashed back to suturing a screaming solder's severed artery as bullets ricocheted around them. "You'd be surprised. This is great."

Finally, Sialei led him to his living area in back. It was about the size of a small, though comfortable, apartment with a kitchen and one bedroom.

When Sialei stood next to him, Logan caught a hint of her intoxicating scent again. A sense of well being spread through him.

"Do you mind if I ask what perfume you're wearing?"

She looked puzzled. "I don't wear perfume."

"Oh…." There was an awkward pause as he felt himself drawn into her deep brown eyes.

After meeting his gaze head-on a moment, Sialei raised an inquisitive eyebrow. "Yes?"

"*Oh…um…thank you for the tour*," he said quickly.

"My pleasure."

When Logan walked her to the entrance to say goodbye, he caught himself when he almost leaned in to kiss her.

Why the hell did I do that? he thought.

The moment she left, he was suddenly overcome with soreness and fatigue. After swallowing a handful of aspirin, he stripped off his clothes and collapsed on the bed. The worn springs twanged like a bad country song, but, thankfully, they didn't snap loose.

The moment Logan's body went limp, he fell hard asleep—

—and into the grip of a horrifying nightmare.

When the sun rose the next morning, Logan was already awake. Remnant images of the nightmare that roused him during the night still unsettled him. He had tried to fall back to sleep, but never could. Maybe his mind was protecting him from the horrors that awaited him there.

Exhausted, he dressed and ate breakfast with lots of coffee. Afterward, he familiarized himself with the clinic. As he did, his thoughts shifted back to his nightmare…or rather, night*mares*. He'd been averaging one every few nights since returning from Nam; all induced by memories of the carnage of combat.

Usually they consisted of a rotting jungle filled with the blood-covered bodies and terrified screams of his fellow soldiers. He sought solace with the military psychiatrists, but they simply called it "post-traumatic stress" and prescribed a variety of medications. None helped.

Strangely, the nightmares began to increase about a month before he learned of the Navajo clinic opening. They also began to change. The endless jungle morphed into a barren desert landscape that burned like a sea of flames. Logan could still see soldiers writhing in agony, only now something loomed over them; something dark and demonic. It was a malformed shape, never quite in focus. Above it, a red moon hung like a bloody stain on the night sky. For some reason, that new presence and the moon terrified Logan more than the nightmares normally did.

He had no idea why that evil specter or the burning desert intruded upon his dreams. But when a recruitment agency called about the Navajo clinic in the Arizona desert, Logan was beset by a startling sense of déjà vu. It also set off warning bells. But at the same time, he felt an overwhelming compulsion to accept the offer, as if he just *had* to be here.

So he came to Arizona; if for no other reason than to discover if there was a connection between the desert and his nightmares, or if it was all just one big freakish coincidence.

The bell chiming over the front door pulled Logan out of his thoughts. "Anyone here?" a pleasant male voice called out.

Logan followed the voice to the waiting room where he found a middle-aged Navajo man in jeans and button shirt.

"Dr. Harris?" the man asked, smiling as he shook Logan's hand. "James Zah. Welcome to the Navajo Nation."

"Call me Logan. It's a pleasure to meet you in person."

"Same here. Sorry about your accident. Are you all right?"

"Fine, thank you. Not so sure about my truck though."

"A tow truck picked it up earlier and a mechanic is looking it over. He'll drop it off after lunch. I'll also have someone fix your shower today."

"Wow. You're spoiling me."

James smiled. "I'm on the way to a meeting, but I just wanted to stop by to say hello. Is there anything else you need?"

"Actually, yes." Logan handed James a sheet of paper. "These are equipment and supplies we could use."

James read the list. "Unfortunately, this is a bit over our budget. We're funded by the Indian Health Service, and there's only so much money to go around. I'm sorry."

"Believe me, I understand." Logan had grown accustomed to working with low supplies in Nam.

"Hey, would you like to come to my place for dinner tomorrow night?" James asked. "You can meet my family."

"Sounds wonderful. What time?"

"Seven. I'll call you later with directions. Other than supplies, are you settling in all right?"

"Thanks to Sialei. She's a lifesaver, in more ways than one. She's been *very* helpful getting me acclimated."

James looked surprised. "Really?"

Logan noticed his reaction. "Yes. Why?"

"Because she doesn't—" Two adults entering the clinic with their children distracted James. "Looks like your first patients are here, so I'll get out of your way. Welcome again, Logan."

After James left, Logan turned to his new arrivals. Smiling, he introduced himself and jumped into his first day.

Sialei arrived soon after James left. Acting as receptionist and nurse, she did an excellent job of keeping the constant stream of patients organized while Logan met with them. He'd have been overwhelmed without her.

During the examinations, Logan noted that many of his younger and older patients were exhibiting flu-like symptoms, mainly weakness and fever. Some also experienced feelings of suffocation, as well as recurring nightmares. That was odd, but easily explained. Congestion would account for the difficulty breathing, and high fevers often caused nightmares.

With the limited supply of medicines on hand, he hoped they weren't facing a significant outbreak.

Just after noon, they took a break for lunch. Sialei suggested they eat outside on a bench to enjoy the fresh air.

As they ate sandwiches and coffee, Sialei pointed at the endless desert around them. "Beautiful, isn't it?"

Logan cast a furtive glance at her, and said, "Very beautiful." But he did agree that the magnificent panorama *was* incredible. It definitely deserved the name "Painted Desert." The ground was awash with vibrant shades of lavender, orange, pink and gray that stretched to hills and buttes in the distance. And scattered across the geological canvas, tall cacti resembling warped pitchforks touched the bright azure sky.

It *was* beautiful. Best of all, it was the total opposite of the jungles of Viet Nam. Yet, at the same time, the view and the scorching dry heat prompted disturbing memories of the hellish desert in his nightmares.

"There's so much open space here," said Sialei. "I can't imagine living in a city like Houston. Which reminds me, you never told me why you decided to work here."

"I wanted to help people."

"I see," she said in a tone hinting she suspected he wasn't telling the whole story.

She was *very* perceptive, Logan realized. But how can he explain his real reasons for coming when he wasn't even sure himself? "So have you lived here all your life?"

"Born and raised. Never saw any reason to leave."

"Big world out there. Lot's to see."

Sialei shook her head. "Not for me. This is my home. I love this land and our people. I've also spent my life doing whatever I can to preserve a culture that is slowly being eroded by the outside world, and I don't plan on stopping now. My parents felt the same way. So do many others. In fact, you're the first non-*Diné* I've ever known."

"*Seriously?* That seems almost impossible."

"Not really. Our Chapter is small and secluded. Tourists and other non-Navajos rarely visit us, and I've never had reason to interact with them. That's why, when I met you, I was so glad to discover you spea—"

A sudden breeze blew the napkin off Logan's lap. Sialei caught it and handed it back to him. As she did, their fingers touched and a warm, pleasant sensation spread through Logan.

"So, what about your parents?" he said. "Where are they?"

"They died in an accident when I was eight."

"Oh…I'm sorry."

"*Análí* took me in and raised me. I owe everything to him." Then she asked, "No girlfriend or wife, I take it?"

Her sudden shift in subject matter caught Logan off guard. "What?"

"No one to keep you tied to Houston?"

"Oh. No. With medical school and the military, I never had time for a serious relationship. How about you?"

"Wife or girlfriend?"

He chuckled. "Anyone serious?"

"Not so far."

Before Logan could catch himself, the word "good" slipped out. When Sialei's eyebrow popped up, he quickly added, "It's uh, *good* that you're helping me today. I appreciate it."

She nodded, but he could tell by her amused expression that she didn't buy his reply.

When the second round of patients began arriving, Logan and Sialei went back to work. Logan could tell by the way that she interacted with each person that she really cared for them. Beauty, intelligence *and* compassion. Logan found it hard to believe she wasn't in a committed relationship. He also found it interesting that all the patients spoke to her in Navajo, yet she replied in English.

At the end of the day, Logan walked Sialei outside to her car and thanked her for all her help.

"You're welcome." She grinned. "You'd probably have been totally lost without me."

"Or fallen of a cliff."

Sialei laughed and Logan's heart skipped a beat. It was soft and lyrical. Once again, he longed to kiss her. The urge was almost overwhelming. Logan couldn't explain why he was so taken with her after just one day. But the last thing he wanted to do was scare her away or offend her. Sighing, he told Sialei good night and she drove away.

Logan cried out as the demonic presence reached for him. Then he realized it wasn't coming for him, it was after someone else. A woman. Flames and the red moon cast the barren desert in a bloody glow, yet her face was still hidden in shadows. He didn't know who she was, but he felt she was important to him. The demon's massive hand tore into her, and she screamed Logan's name. Desperately, Logan tried to save her, but he couldn't move. He felt powerless against the malevolent phantom. And then it lifted the woman to its mouth—and began to devour her.

Bolting upright in bed, heart pounding, Logan fought to control his rapid breathing. It had been another damn nightma—

He froze. Someone else was in the room.

In a single move, Logan leaped out of bed and flipped on a lamp, ready to defend himself. But when he saw the intruder, he just blinked. Standing in the doorway was an ancient-looking Navajo man holding a cup of steaming coffee.

"Who the *hell* are you?" asked Logan. "And why are you in my house?"

"Many reasons."

"Are you a patient? Clinic hours are….Wait." Logan suddenly recognized the stranger, even though he'd only seen him for a split second. "You're the one I almost hit on the cliff road. Sialei's grandfather."

The old man nodded. "My name is Frank."

Irritation mounting, Logan asked, "Why were you just standing there in the dark?"

"I didn't want to disturb you."

Logan pulled on his clothes. "This is the second time you've popped up out of nowhere. The first time almost got me killed."

"You were in no danger." The old man pointed a boney finger at Logan's chest.

Logan followed it to the medallion around his neck. "What are you talking abou—?"

"Tell me about your nightmares."

Logan eyed him warily. "How did you—?"

"They have haunted you for some time."

"Look, you can't just—"

Frank suddenly derailed Logan's train of thought with a very loud slurp from his cup.

"Where did you get the coffee?" Logan asked.

"I made it. Would you like some?"

Logan was about to continue his lecture on home invasion, but figured why bother? Instead, he said, "Sure." Maybe if he humored Frank, the old man would leave. Besides, he didn't want to upset Sialei by rushing her *análi* out the door.

Two hours later, Logan was still sitting at his kitchen table listening to Frank narrate intricate tales of the *Diné* and their history. At first, Logan listened to be polite, but then he became captivated by the rich details and colorful descriptions. Frank was a born storyteller. And at 89, he had a hell of a lot of stories to tell.

When the old man paused to sip coffee, Logan said, "I'd love to hear more stories, but it's almost five. I need to get some sleep. Can we continue this another time?"

Frank nodded. He sat his cup down and they walked outside. Logan expected to find a vehicle, but there were none in sight. "How did you get here, Frank?"

"I walked."

"You need a ride home?"

Frank turned to Logan. "Tell me, do you speak Navajo?"

"No, sir, I don't."

A sliver of a smile creased the old man's lips. "It is good you are here…for Sialei."

Logan had no idea what he meant by that. "She's a terrific woman."

"Did you know our previous doctor died?"

"No, I didn't." Logan had never asked the recruitment agency about his predecessor. "How?"

"Ghost sickness."

"I'm not familiar with that."

"It is affecting my people. The illness."

"You mean the flu virus?" Logan guessed.

Frank shook his head and pointed up. Logan looked up at an unfinished moon. Sitting behind clouds, it cast a sickly, muffled red glow as if swimming under a sheet of ice. The sight of it startled him. It resembled the moon in his nightmares.

"*Chindi*," Frank said. "Be prepared."

"Prepared for what?" Logan turned toward the old man, but Frank was already several yards down the road. "Sialei was right. He *is* spry for his age."

After one more anxious glance upward, Logan ducked inside the clinic and away from the light of the bloody moon.

When Sialei entered the clinic the next morning, Logan had just finished showering. The first patient wasn't due for an hour, so he offered to make her breakfast.

While enjoying omelets and home fries, she told him about the Navajo culture and growing up on the reservation. He told her about his Texas upbringing, medical school and his stint in the Army, though he left out the more harrowing aspects of that period in his life.

Logan really enjoyed her company. She was so different from any woman he'd ever met. Not just her intelligence and confidence, but also her classic, natural beauty. She didn't wear makeup, yet she was gorgeous. She possessed a refreshing lack of vanity, unlike some of the women he'd dated in Houston.

Most of all, he loved the way he felt at ease around her, as if he didn't have a care in the world. He even noticed that his aches and pains, which still persisted after the accident, seemed to vanish when she was around. It was obviously psychosomatic, but the pain was still gone nonetheless.

"By the way," he said, "your grandfather paid me a visit last night."

Sialei looked surprised. "He *did*?"

"We had a nice long talk. Actually, he talked and I listened."

"Did he tell you his stories?" She smiled. "I love listening to them."

"So did I. Just out of curiosity, does Frank normally visit unannounced in the middle of the night?"

"No. He must *really* like you. He's a good judge of character. *And* I may have mentioned you."

That piqued Logan's interest. "Good things?"

Sialei merely grinned coyly. Logan wanted to continue that line of conversation, but the front door bell signaled the arrival of patients. He and Sialei set their dishes in the sink and went to meet them.

At the end of another long day, Logan had just enough time to freshen up before driving to James's house for dinner. On the way, he spotted a very tall swirling dust plume a few yards from the road. Another dust devil. Then he blinked, and it was gone.

Using James's directions, Logan found the house easily. James welcomed him in and introduced his wife Johona.

Smiling, she said, "Call me Jo. Unfortunately, our daughter, Lina, isn't feeling well, so I put her in bed."

"I can look at her if you'd like," Logan offered.

"Thank you, but she probably just needs rest. Dinner is ready. Hope you like spaghetti."

After a very enjoyable dinner and conversation, Jo excused herself to check on Lina. Beers in hand, Logan and James sat in the den under a deer head mounted on the wood panel wall.

"Sorry your daughter isn't feeling well," Logan said. "Bring her by the clinic if she gets worse. I think you may have a flu outbreak."

"Anything we should be concerned with?"

"Hopefully not. But I'll let you know if anything changes." Sipping his beer, Logan said, " I didn't get a chance to say it yesterday, but thank you again for hiring me."

"We owe you *our* thanks. It wasn't easy finding a physician willing to move to the middle of nowhere. So what do you think of it so far?"

"It's wonderful. And the people I've met so far are all terrific. Speaking of, Sialei's grandfather visited me last night."

A grin spread across James's face. "You met her *análi*, eh?"

"Yes. We had a wonderful conversation. He also mentioned that your previous doctor died. Is that true?"

James's jubilant expression faltered. "Charles Yahzee. One of our own. He was murdered."

"I'm sorry. What happened?"

"A drifter broke into the clinic one night to steal drugs. He shot and killed Charles."

"Jesus," Logan whispered.

"A rez deputy caught the bastard an hour later and shot him during a gun battle." James took a swig of beer. "Charles was a good friend. His death was a tragedy and a damn waste. To make matters worse, his own parents wouldn't even claim his body."

"Why not?"

"They're old school superstitious. They were afraid Charles's murder had released a *chindi*."

"Frank mentioned that. What is it?"

"According to *Diné* lore, a *chindi* is the embodiment of everything that is mentally or spiritually bad about a person. It's released when someone dies a violent or otherwise abnormal death."

"An evil spirit?"

"Yeah." James said. Then he smiled. "Though it makes you wonder how dangerous it can be when one of the telltale signs of its presence is the appearance of dust devils."

"Well, that's creepy. I've been seeing those lately. Big ones."

"It's the desert. Comes with the territory. Also, when the *chindi* is near, it spreads the ghost sickness."

"Frank said that too. He suggested this ghost sickness is the cause of the virus outbreak."

James chuckled. "I love Frank, but I think his age may finally be catching up to him."

"What is ghost sickness?"

"Weakness, fatigue, suffocation. People affected also suffer from nightmares and feelings of terror."

A chill tickled Logan's chest. The parallel between the ghost sickness and the symptoms affecting his patients was pretty damn weird. He wasn't convinced ghosts existed, but he'd seen enough strange stuff in Nam to at least keep an open mind.

"So how do you know so much about the subject?" he asked.

"Frank used to tell Sialei and me stories about it when we were kids." James grinned. "Scared the shit out of me. He's just always seemed obsessed with them."

"Frank also told me to 'be prepared'," Logan said. "Any idea what he meant by—?"

A high-pitched shriek pulled both men from their chairs.

"That's Lina!" James cried, eyes wide with concern.

Logan followed James into his daughter's bedroom. Inside, a frantic Jo was trying to hold Lina down on the bed. The little girl's eyes were closed, but she was thrashing wildly and screaming in horror.

"What the hell happened?" James yelled.

"I don't know!" Jo cried. "She suddenly started screaming. I can barely hold her down."

Suddenly, Lina collapsed and began shaking violently. Her shrill shrieks were replaced by rapid-fire mumbles and gibberish.

Eyes pleading, Jo looked at Logan. "What's *wrong* with her?"

Logan felt the girl's forehead. It was burning up. He pushed back one of her eyelids and saw that her pupil had rolled back into her head. "I need to get my medical bag at the clinic."

"Shouldn't we take her to the clinic?" James asked.

"No time," Logan said. "Her fever is too high. Get her into a tub of cold water right *now.*

Logan hurried to his truck. As he climbed in, he spotted someone across the road. It was Frank standing with two young Navajo men. Frank glanced at Logan, and then looked up. Logan followed his gaze to the same sickly red moon he'd seen the night before.

Ignoring it, Logan started the truck and rushed to the clinic. When he returned with his bag about fifteen minutes later, he charged through the front door and into Lina's bedroom. There, he found Frank and his two companions standing by James. On the bed, Jo cradled her daughter in her arms. Tears soaked Jo's cheeks, and for a second Logan feared that Lina had passed away. But then he saw her chest rising as she took in a slow breath.

"What's going on?" Logan asked.

Frank walked up to him. Logan noticed he was trembling, as if exhausted. The old man nodded, and then simply left the room followed by his companions.

Visibly shaken, James said, "Can you check my daughter, please?"

Logan examined the girl, but her temperature was now normal. "She seems fine." He didn't want to alarm her parents, but there was no way Lina should have recovered as quickly as she did; at least, not without medical help. "But let's take her to the clinic, just to be safe."

Jo gripped her husband's arm and shook her head. He nodded and said, "We want her to stay here, Logan. Okay?"

Logan was about to object, but something in James's haunted expression stopped him. "Fine. Keep her warm and make sure she gets plenty of liquids. Call me immediately if anything changes."

James walked him to the door. When Logan stepped outside, all James said was, "Listen to Frank." Then he closed the door, leaving Logan to wonder what the hell had just happened.

In between patients the following morning, questions kept pricking at Logan's brain. How did James's daughter recover so quickly? Why were her so shaken up by her recovery? What did Sialei's grandfather have to do with it? Also, James had said to "listen to Frank." About what?

He decided he would look in on Lina after work. While he was there, he'd also press James for more information.

Logan glanced at his watch and wondered what was keeping Sialei. When she hadn't arrived earlier, he just figured she had been delayed. But it was now noon and she still hadn't shown up. She wasn't officially working for him, so she could arrive any time she wished. He just missed having her around. He called her home, but there was no answer.

After his last patient left that afternoon, Sialei still hadn't appeared. After another unanswered call, Logan decided to swing by her place on the way to see Lina. Then he heard the front bell chime.

"Logan?"

"Sialei?" he called as he hurried to the reception area. "I was beginning to get worri—"

He almost dropped his keys when he saw her. The left side of her face was caked with splotches of dried blood, and her shirt was torn open in front. She was holding it closed with her right hand.

"What the hell happened?" he said as he rushed to her.

"Fell off my damn horse," she said.

"Jesus. You okay? Anything broken?"

"No. I scraped my face and chest, and banged up my left shoulder. Hurts like hell…." She looked surprised as she gingerly moved her left arm. "Strange. Now it feels fine."

"Let's go take a look."

Logan led her to the exam room and sat her on the cushioned table. After confirming her injured arm wasn't broken, he focused on the blood on her face. Thankfully, it wasn't as bad as he first feared. "Just superficial cuts; nothing serious. Remove your shirt so I can get a better look at you."

She chuckled. "Right. I've heard *that* before."

"What…? Oh, no, no. So I can—"

"Relax, Doc." Her smiled widened. "I know what you mean."

He turned away and grabbed a cloth exam gown from a cabinet drawer. "Here, change into—"

The words log-jammed in his throat when he saw she was now topless, her right arm covering her breasts. The torn shirt and her bra lay on the table next to her.

Averting his eyes, he said, "I was going to have you change into this gown *after* I left the room."

"That's okay. I'm not shy."

"Well, I'm a fairly shy guy. How about doing it for me?"

She took the gown. "How's this?"

Facing her, Logan saw she was holding the gown against her chest. "That'll work," he said, though, deep inside, he felt an unexpected pang of regret that she was now covered.

He examined the abrasions along her side, stomach and left breast. Luckily, they weren't very deep either. Donning latex gloves, he began gently cleaning them as he tried not to be distracted by her wonderful scent. "Normally, I have a nurse in the room when I examine female patients."

"Technically, I *am* your nurse," she said with a wry smile. "So I think that counts."

"How did you fall?"

"Dust devil came out of nowhere. A big one. Spooked my horse and I fell off. My foot caught in the stirrup and I was dragged a few yards."

"I'm so sorry."

"Then my horse rain off and it took a couple of hours to find him."

Logan peeled off his gloves once he had cleaned her wounds. "Well, except for scrapes and bruises, you seem to be fine. You're sure you're in no pain?"

"It all vanished the moment I walked in the clinic. You must be a *damn* good doctor."

"Well, when the new equipment arrives, I want to x-ray your arm and head just to be sure."

"What new equipment?"

"I called a senator I know in Washington this morning. I saved his son's life in Viet Nam, and he told me to call him if I ever needed a favor. A medical company in his district is donating supplies and equipment."

"Logan, that's wonderful!"

She leaned over and hugged him tight. As she did, her scent overwhelmed him. When she pulled away, she paused as her hypnotic eyes held his a moment, and then she kissed him. A pleasant feeling of electricity, similar to when he first touched her hand, tingled his lips. It spread into his face, and then downward into his entire body.

Her kiss wasn't a friendly peck of gratitude either. It was a lingering, passionate invitation for something more.

Logan felt Sialei's gown fall away, and they melted into each other's arms. Somewhere in a deep recess of his mind, the place where rational thought was exiled the moment Sialei's lips touched his, Logan felt he was violating his medical ethics.

But at that point, he didn't give a damn.

As soon as they entered his bedroom, tore off their clothes and tumbled onto his bed, he explored every inch of her lithe, tan body with a desire and hunger he hadn't felt in years; first with his fingers, and then with the tip of his tongue. As a physician and as a single man, Logan had seen several nude women in his adult life. But with Sialei, it was as if he had discovered the female form for the first time.

When they made love, her scent was an aphrodisiac enflaming his sexual and emotional desire. He couldn't get enough of her. Throughout the afternoon and well into the evening, they made love three times, yet he still wasn't satisfied. And each time, Sialei's enthusiasm grew more energetic.

After the third round of sexual intensity, they collapsed and held each other in the darkness.

After catching her breath, Sialei whispered, "So, doctor, you always sleep with your patients?"

Logan swallowed wrong and began coughing. When he caught his breath, he saw that Sialei wore a huge, mischievous grin. "Lady, you have one wicked sense of humor."

Sialei laughed. Then she lightly touched the scars on his chest. "What happened here?"

"Souvenir from Viet Nam."

"You were *shot?*"

He shrugged. "They didn't have a gift shop." When he noticed she was genuinely alarmed, he added, "I'm *much* better now."

She held up the small wood medallion on his neck chain. "Beautiful. Where did you get it?"

Logan looked at the swirling primitive design depicting an eagle gripping a snake in its talons. "My mother. It was handed down from her side of the family."

"It's similar to designs in an old book *Análi* showed me long ago."

"Really? I just think it looks cool. It's also my good luck charm."

After nestling a few moments, Sialei said, "So, why are you *really* here? And not just the 'helping people' part.' "

Logan sighed. "To be honest…I don't have a clue."

"*What?*"

"Well, I'm not quite sure why I came *here*, but I know why I left Houston. After Nam, I couldn't handle the stress of a large city. Also, the only job I could find was in an emergency ward. But the constant blood and suffering reminded me too much of combat."

She kissed him lightly. "I'm sorry."

"I called a recruitment agency to find something *anywhere* away from a metropolitan area. I received a few offers, but none seemed right." He pressed closer to her. "Then they told me the IHS was interested. When I heard about this clinic, I felt an…overwhelming compulsion to accept. It just seemed like…*this* is the place I needed to be."

Sialei sat up suddenly. "And you have no idea why?"

"Well, I didn't…until…well, until the day you saved me. I think I'm here…because of *you*." He feared she'd laugh at that. Instead, Sialei watched him silently, as if waiting for him to continue. "And I *knew* it the moment I first touched your hand. I realize it sounds crazy, but I just…I love you, Sialei…more than any one I've ever—"

She suddenly cut him off with a kiss so deep and passionate that it shook Logan to his soul.

"I love you, too, Logan," she said. "So damn much. I felt the same thing when we touched. It was some kind of…*spark*. Ever since, I've only thought about you. I only want to *be* with you. And that feeling keeps growing stronger, as if—"

"We're meant to be together," Logan finished. It sounded cheesy, but it was the truth.

"*Yes!*" she said. "It *does* seem crazy…but I don't care."

When Sialei kissed him again, his body reacted instantly. He heartily rolled on top of her and into their fourth round. Afterward, exhausted and spent, they finally fell asleep in each other's arms.

Sialei screamed as a wall of fire circled her. Higher and higher, the flames rose toward a monstrous full moon dripping with red blood. Logan reached for her. But something stopped him; something dark and primordial. The demonic presence. Sialei cried out Logan's name as the fire engulfed her. All he could do was watch helplessly as she shrieked in torment while the flames began to melt her flesh.

Logan jerked awake. Coated in sweat, he searched his tiny bedroom in a panic. But it was empty. No flames. No screams.

Then he realized that Sialei was gone, too. He smelled her scent on the pillow reminding him that her presence hadn't been a dream, as well. Burying his face in the pillow, he inhaled deeply like a drowning man breaking the surface of the ocean.

The anxiety of the nightmare quickly evaporated. But not the memories. The woman he saw in his nightmare the night before last must have been Sialei.

But why would he be dreaming about her suffering then, and especialy now, after the pure happiness they'd just discovered with each other?

It was just one more infuriating layer on top of the damn mystery that brought him to Arizona. There had to be a logical explanation for it, but he'd be damned if he could figure it out.

Joyful humming and the smell of bacon drifted from the kitchen. Pulling on gym shorts, Logan found Sialei making breakfast. She was wearing one of his medical school t-shirts. When she bent over to get butter out of the fridge, he noted she was naked underneath. Suddenly he wasn't hungry anymore. At least, not for food.

She smiled when he led her back to bed. But just as they embraced, the door bell chimed in the clinic.

"Sounds like your first patient is here," Sialei whispered.

Groaning, he said, "Can we continue this later? Please say yes."

In reply, she slid her fingers between his legs. His body reacted instantly, but he forced himself to pull away. Duty called. *Damn it.*

Smiling, she said, "Take a cold shower. I'll stall them."

He watched her cute, firm bottom as she slipped on her jeans. After tucking in her shirt, she kissed him and hurried off.

Ten minutes later, Logan entered the clinic and noticed that Sialei now looked very pale. "Are you all right?" he asked.

"Yeah, I just…suddenly I don't feel well."

She suddenly stumbled and Logan caught her. He feared her fall off the horse might have hurt her worse than he thought. "Sialei, let me make sure you're—"

"*Damn it!*" she screamed as she slapped his hand away and glared at him with pure hatred. "I said I'm *fine!*"

Shocked, Logan held up his hands. "Okay, sorry. I just—"

Sialei brushed past him and out the front door.

Ignoring the startled look from the waiting patient, Logan watched Sialei through the window as she drove away. A range of confused emotions surged through him. But he wasn't sure which concerned him more: that she might be suffering from an injury, or that he might have just fallen in love with an unstable woman.

Sialei never returned. She never answered her phone either. So when the sun sank behind a distant butte, Logan drove to her home to check on her. No one was there.

He began to worry that Sialei had suffered a concussion from the fall off her horse. What if she was lying unconscious somewhere—or worse?

Not knowing where else to search, Logan drove to James's house to look in on Lina. Thankfully, the little girl still appeared perfectly healthy. Logan wanted to ask James about what happened the night she was sick, but at that moment he was more concerned with Sialei. But James hadn't seen her either.

Returning to the clinic, Logan was about to call Sialei's house again when the front bell chimed. But instead of Sialei, he found one of the men he'd seen with Frank at James's house.

"Doctor Harris," the man said. "Frank needs you."

"Is it Sialei?" Logan asked, anxiously.

"Yes. Come with me. *Now*, please."

Logan grabbed his medical bag. As soon as he settled into the man's battered truck, it shot onto the road. When Logan asked where they were going, the man ignored him. Logan grew irritated, but he had no choice but to trust him.

To the east, Logan spotted the full moon. It was once again bathed in red; deeper than Logan had seen so far.

The driver suddenly veered onto a rough dirt road and increased speed. Ten minutes later, the truck skidded to a stop in front of a very old building with a sagging pointed roof, and walls constructed of decaying logs. Logan remembered from the research he did before coming to Arizona that it was called a hogan. Lights shone through the tattered curtains.

When the driver climbed out of the truck, Logan followed him across the dead grass.

Then they both froze when a piercing guttural scream erupted from inside the building. It was deep with an almost inhuman quality. Yet Logan knew it was Sialei.

Shoving the driver aside, Logan entered the hogan—and froze as a boiling anger swept over him.

Inside, large flickering candles circled the main room. And in the center, Frank's second companion and another Navajo man were pinning Sialei down on an old bed with frayed, dusty sheets. She thrashed and screamed as she struggled to break loose. Her blouse had ripped open, and her arms and face were covered in bruises.

"What the *hell* are you doing?" Logan yelled as he rushed toward them.

But when he reached the bed, Sialei tore an arm free and lunged at Logan like a wild animal. Her nails dug into his arm. Before he could react, his mind was assaulted by the horrifying image of a demonic creature swallowed in flames. Fear gripped Logan's heart when he recognized it.

It was the thing from his nightmares.

Then, somewhere amidst the hellish chaos, he heard Sialei's voice crying out frantically, *"Logan! Help me!"*

He gasped when he suddenly found himself back in the cabin. He had pulled his arm away from Sialei's grip and stumbled back against the wall.

In all the years he'd spent in combat, he'd never been as terrified as he was at that moment. He had no damn idea what had just happened. But somehow, he knew it was all real and that Sielai was in mortal danger. Not just for her life, but her very soul.

"Jesus!" Logan jumped when someone touched his arm. It was Frank.

"Come with me," he said.

Trembling, Logan paused to watch as the three Navajo men secured Sialei's wrists to the bed with straps. Her face was contorted in feral rage. It killed Logan to see her that way, but he didn't know what to do. Whatever was threatening her was far beyond his medical *and* military training.

Outside, Logan ignored the blood on his injured arm as he gripped the old man' arms. "Frank, what the hell—?"

"Sialei needs your help."

"Anything! But what can I do against…What was that damn thing I just saw?"

"The *chindi*. The creature from your nightmares. It possesses Sialei. We must help her, but I can not do it alone. You and Sialei share a bond. It is why you were drawn to the reservation."

"What are you talki—?"

"The *chindi* is growing stronger. Your bond with Sialei will help fight it. But you must be prepared. Logan…do you trust me?"

A million questions tore through Logan's mind. But Frank's urgency, and the anguish of hearing Sialei's cries of anger and pain, kept them locked inside. "Yes. What do I need to—?"

Frank touched Logan's medallion—and the pitch-black night flashed to pure white.

Then…nothing. No sight. No sound. For a moment, Logan thought he had died.

"Logan!!" Sialai's voice screamed as a wall of flames suddenly erupted around him.

He was back in the hellish world he had seen when Sialei touched him. The world of his nightmares. The domain of the *chindi*.

Logan felt that he should be terrified, yet he wasn't. The fear was still there, only it was suppressed. When Frank touched his medallion, it had filled Logan with an incredible sense of serenity and confidence. He felt...*prepared* to confront whatever force threatened Sialei.

Then he heard chanting. It was Frank. Whatever he was saying seemed to fill Logan with strength.

Keep it up, Análi, Logan thought.

The flames rose higher, and Sialei screamed his name again. Logan knew the flames weren't real, but he could still feel the blistering heat.

"Sialei!!" he cried out.

She is mine. Several voices in unison suddenly assailed Logan from every possible direction.

The *chindi.*

"Why her?" Logan screamed.

Her soul is rare. It is pure, which makes it more powerful. It belongs to me, just as her mother's soul should have.

The wall of flames directly in front of Logan began to wane. Behind it, he saw Sialei writhing in pain. He sensed that the *chindi* wanted him to suffer as he watched her torment. Logan reached for her, but the Stygian flames burst upward, throwing him back.

"You're not going to stop me that easy, you son of bitch!" he yelled.

Drawing on the strength Frank's chant gave him and his undying love for Sialei, Logan leaped into the inferno. His skin sizzled and burned away as if he'd plunged into a pool of lit gasoline. He heard a scream, and realized it was his own.

The pain was excruciating. He couldn't feel his legs. Stumbling, he dropped to his knees and began to crawl. Inch by inch, he moved toward Sialei with Herculean effort.

Then his eyes burst. Blind, he still forged ahead, unwilling to surrender or fail her.

Finally, Logan's fingertips brushed against something solid. He tried to call Sialei's name, but his vocal cords were gone. Then something gripped his hand, and an incredible jolt of intense energy exploded through him.

It was Sialei. Her touch...no, *their* touch, filled him with power. It filled them both with power.

All his pain was gone, just as it had vanished whenever they were together. The bond Frank mentioned. Whatever it was, natural or supernatural, it drew them together. It made them whole. It was the reason for their unbridled passion, and why nothing could ever harm or defeat them as long as they stood together.

Logan felt Sialei pull him out of the flames and into her arms. He held her tight, vowing never to let go. Around them, the *chindi*'s voices cried out in primal rage. The cacophonic assault rose in volume until the hellish world around Logan and Sialei finally ruptured and shattered.

And then darkness consumed them.

Logan awoke in his own bed, his mind adrift in a haze. Had he been asleep? Was he dreaming?

The bed springs creaked in defiance as he draped his legs over the side. The tile floor was cold. It felt good.

Then he noticed the fresh bandage on his arm. He remembered murky images of something horrifying and ungodly. He couldn't bring them into focus, so he stopped trying.

But something nagged at him. Something was missing.

Something important.

"Sialei...." he whispered.

"She is asleep."

Logan looked up to find Frank standing in the doorway holding a cup of coffee.

"Is she all right?" Logan asked.

The old man nodded. "You saved her. Actually, you saved each other."

At that, some of Logan's memories came into focus. "It...it was all real? The *chindi*? The burning desert?"

Frank simply sipped his coffee and walked away. So Logan followed.

"Do not dwell on it, " the old man said as they walked to the recovery room. "It is too much to handle...for now."

Logan smiled when he saw Sialei sleeping in one of the beds. After a brief examination, he released an anxious breath. She seemed unharmed. Physically, anyway.

"Like you, she will not remember all of what happened," said Frank said. "It is better that way."

"How did we get here?"

"We brought you two here from the hogan. It is where I fought the demon for the soul of her mother."

Logan brushed a stray hair from Sialei's forehead. "Where did the damn thing come from?"

"The *chindi* followed my people from the First World. It feeds on torment and despair. My family has fought it since long before I was born."

"Why did it want Sialei?"

Her soul is rare. It is pure.... The *chindi*'s words pierced the veil of Logan's misty memories. When he turned to Frank to confirm, the old man just nodded. Frank was either incredibly intuitive, or he *could* read minds.

"It attacked my daughter twenty years ago," Frank said. "Sialei's father tried to help, but he did not survive. I drove the *chindi* away, but Sialei's mother never recovered. She died soon after."

"I'm sorry. You never told Sialei how her parents died?"

"I saw no need to burden her."

"So how did that…*thing* come back? Wait, James said the *chindi* appears when someone dies a violent death. Was it Charles Yahzee?"

"No. He was an honorable man. It was the death of the drifter who murdered him that gave the *chindi* access to our world. Then it waited, and as it grew stronger, the ghost sickness spread."

"And James's daughter?"

"The demon wanted Sialei, but it possessed Lina first, knowing I would fight it. It did so to weaken me. That is why I needed your help to protect my granddaughter."

"Our bond, right?"

Frank nodded. "Every generation, two *Diné* have a…*special* connection. Even across a great distance, it will call to them, though they may not know it. Did Sialei tell you *she* was the one who chose you from the physician names they considered?"

"No, she didn't."

"She said she felt you belonged here. Did you feel the same?"

"Yes. I still do. But…I'm not *Diné*."

Frank pointed at the medallion around Logan's neck. "That talisman helps ward off evil spirits. It belonged to your great, great, great grandmother. She was *Diné*. Our blood runs through you."

"She was? How do you—? Never mind. I'll take your word for it. So the spark I felt when I first held Sialei's hand, her scent and feeling of peace I feel when we're together, the fact that any pain we felt vanished, that was all part of our bond?"

Frank nodded. "It also gave you strength to survive the ordeal." Then his face seemed to age. "But at a cost."

Logan didn't like the sound of that. "What kind of cost?"

Frank paused when Sialei woke and said Logan's name. Then she spoke, but the words were in her native language.

"I don't understand," Logan told her. "Are you all right?"

When she answered in Navajo again, Logan feared she might have suffered mental trauma.

"What's wrong?" he asked Frank. "Why isn't she speaking English?"

"Because she does not know how. She never did."

"*What?* That's ridiculous. We've been talking since I arrived."

"No." Frank walked to the bed. "She only speaks the language of the *Diné*. The night she met you, she told me you spoke with each other. But then you told me you do not speak our language, so I knew you were bonded. You understood each other with your hearts, not your voices."

Stunned, Logan stared at Sialei. "My God....But...why can't I understand her now?"

Frank looked dejected. "The effort and energy it took to rescue Sialei severed your bond. I am very sorry."

Logan looked at Sialei, who smiled and squeezed his hand. That *something important* he felt was missing when he woke, it must have been the bond they shared. The one thing that drew them together, that saved them from the *chindi*, was now gone. He gripped her hand tighter, afraid that she might somehow slip away too. And that was something he'd never let happen. "What does that mean for us?"

"Do you love her?" Frank asked.

Gazing into Sialei's eyes, Logan said, "Yes, of course."

"Then you will both be fine."

"Does she know?"

"She woke briefly earlier. I told her then. I'll leave you two alone."

"Frank. Thank you....for everything."

A hint of a smile cracked the old man's stern facade. "Call me *Análi*."

When Frank walked out, Logan leaned down and kissed Sialei softly. There was no spark or even the wonderful scent, but the kiss still sent a rush of exhilaration through him. The bond **might** have brought them together, but it was love that would *keep* them together.

She caressed his cheek, and whispered something in his ear. Logan didn't understand the words, but he understood the meaning. He had no doubt she felt the same way he did.

Of course, if they were going to have any life together, he'd need to learn the language of the *Diné*. He could always ask her to learn English too. But, no. It was her life, her people, her culture. He would adapt to them, not ask her to adapt to his.

He also swore that he would never leave her side, no matter what force—natural or supernatural—tried to separate them.

About the Contributors

Alicia Wright Brewster ("Angel's Touch") is a lover of all things paranormal, both fantasy and science fiction. By day, she is a patent attorney. By night, she is various other things, including an author, an electronics junkie, and a secret superhero. Find her on her website at aliciawb.com.

Timothy Buller ("Dancing with the Rain") is a father and husband who is inspired by writers like Gene Wolfe, Ray Bradbury, and H.G. Wells. An ordained minister that hails from the St. Louis area, he hopes you enjoy his work as much as he enjoyed writing it.

Nicole Dethmers ("Bump In The Night") writes stories for children and adults. She loves stories most when they make her laugh. Currently, she is pursuing an MFA from Hollins University. Her home is in Michigan with her husband and a small furry menagerie. You can also read her story "A Touch of Sand" in the first volume of Paramourtal.

Kevin Hosey ("Chindi Moon") is an author and co-editor of this book. See his stories in *Star Trek Strange New Worlds*, *Hint Fiction*, *Beyond Centauri* and 365Tomorrows.com, among others. He also wrote for and co-edited *Paramourtal* and *Gods of Justice* for Cliffhanger Books. "Cure" (*Hint Fiction*) was the subject of a sculpture and two films. Visit him at kevinhosey.net.

Tari Kudrick ("The Fourth Wish") is the chief editor of the fiction magazine *OnThePremises.com*. He has sold fiction to *ChiZine*, *Anotherealm*, *The Town Drunk*, and others. If you like this story, you might want to read the first "Candace and Skragg" story at towndrunkmag.com.

Wayne Ligon ("Brownie Points") has worked as a systems analyst for public service most of his adult life, eschewing the typical laundry list of weird jobs authors seem to accumulate. He lives in Montgomery, Alabama with far too many comics.

Julie Luton ("A Single Touch") is a former copywriter with several award-winning advertising campaigns. She graduated from real-life fiction (advertising) to the more usual kind of fiction (writing short stories and novels). She currently lives in Texas with her husband, two children, and a badly misnamed dog, Harmony. Read her blog at txsunshine.wordpress.com.

Nicky Peacock ("Split Apart") is an English author living in the UK where she runs a local writers' group. She has had a vast collection of paranormal stories published in the UK and the USA. For further information, go to nickypeacockauthor.wordpress.com.

Leslie Rose ("The Shimmer in the Woods") was on the design faculty of the theatre department at UCLA for many years. Now she is a member of the SCBWI and loves writing for teens. Her *Yes, This Will Be On the Test* blog celebrates both writing and the crazy world of teaching fifth grade. Visit her at lesliesullirose.blogspot.com.

Cheryl Rydbom ("Lending Luck") lives in Huntsville, Alabama, and like much of the city's population is an engineer. Until her twins came along, writing aspirations were just wistful longings. Now they are self-defense against toddler tempers. Her most recent publication was as *Redstone Science Fiction's Identity Crisis* contest winner. Follow her on Twitter @Chy32.

EDITORS

K. Stoddard Hayes is an editor and entertainment writer who has written hundreds of articles, interviews and essays about screen fantasy and science fiction, including *Xena: Warrior Princess, The Complete Illustrated Companion*. She also had a story in *Paramourtal*, and she wrote for and co-edited *Gods of Justice*. Read her blog at worldbuildingrules.wordpress.com.

Kevin Hosey (see previous page).

ILLUSTRATOR

Mark Offutt is a professional illustrator based in El Paso, Texas. His work has appeared in various magazines, including *Discovering Archeology* and *Southwest New Mexico*, and Cliffhanger Book's *Gods of Justice*. His art has also embellished children's books and promotional work.

Thank you for reading

volume two

Paramourtal™

For information on other
exciting anthologies, please visit:

cliffhanger
BOOKS.COM
The Edge of Gripping New Fiction